$\mathcal{M}$arried

to the

$\mathcal{M}$arquess

Also by

Rebecca Connolly

An Arrangement of Sorts

Coming Soon

Secrets of a Spinster

Also from

Phase Publishing

by
Lady Jane Davis
The Original Pink Collar Workers

by
Christopher Bailey
Without Chance

Married
to the
Marquess

Rebecca Connolly

Phase Publishing, LLC
Seattle

Cover art by Tugboat Design
http://www.tugboatdesign.net

Phase Publishing, LLC first paperback edition
December 2015

ISBN 978-1-943048-04-5
Library of Congress Control Number: 2015957576
Cataloging-in-Publication Data on file.

Acknowledgements

To Lori, for being one of my very first fans, for introducing music into my life, for our shared love of all things British and all things hot chocolate, and for your unfailing friendship and guidance all these years. For everything you are and everything you have ever been. Thanks, Mama R!

And to Bewleys, Galaxy, and Cadbury, for being the most incredible hot chocolate on the other side of the sea and changing my life. We'll always have the memories. And international shipping. Cheers!

Thanks go out to Chris Bailey and the gang at Phase Publishing for making me look better than I am and keeping the dream going. Deborah Bradseth with Tugboat Design for yet another stellar cover that defies my imagination. Whitney Hinckley for your mad editing skills and actually enjoying the stuff I send. Ashley, Hannah, and Jordan for your excitement, keeping me sane, and loving me when I'm not. And for saying it's okay to have more cheesecake.

Thanks to my family for being with me on this journey and being fans, too. Love you!

And thanks, of course, to my Musketeers. You can bill me for the therapy sessions at any time. I'll send chocolate.

Chapter One
Hampshire, 1818

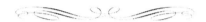

*I*nvariably, when one feels that one's life cannot possibly get any bleaker, it does. Or, conversely, when one feels that one's life is perfectly situated, something rather disastrous occurs to change that opinion rather quickly.

Derek Chambers, Marquess of Whitlock, had been quite simply minding his own business one fine summer's day when he was approached by his father and mother, the Duke and Duchess of Ashcombe, and informed that he was to be married in a week to the Honorable Katherine Bishop, daughter of the Viscount Dartwell. It was not such a shocking surprise, as he had known of his impending marriage from childhood when it had been arranged for him.

It was a still rather dreadful prospect, despite his knowledge. His long-standing relationship and interaction with Katherine had done nothing to endear her to him by any stretch of even the most imaginative of imaginations. Poisonous reptiles have that effect on people.

But he knew his duty to his family and their long heritage of well-made matches as far as standing, titles, and fortune went. It was quite simply the way things were done.

So he had married Katherine, and for the last several years; he was never able to remember just how many as each year seemed a lifetime; they had lived blissfully apart, and only came together when forced. Aside from the occasional correspondence and the unfortunate meetings in London, which oftentimes felt like penance for a multitude of sins he had yet to commit, Derek could almost forget that he was even married at all.

It was quite a wonderful arrangement of his otherwise rather depressing life.

Being in such an arrangement also allowed him ample opportunity to spend as much time as he wished with his friends. At the moment, he was preparing for what was destined to be one of the greatest naps ever taken in the front drawing room of his friend Nathan's estate, Beverton House. Nathan, the Earl of Beverton, and his new bride Moira were still on their honeymoon trip, and had entrusted the house and repairs to the watchful eyes of Colin Gerrard and himself. Their other compatriots, the ever charming Geoffrey Harris and the less than graceful Duncan Bray, were also around somewhere at present, as each had a strong aversion to being in London without the appropriate company.

They had worked very hard this morning assisting the remaining tenants with their repairs, and Derek, for one, was absolutely exhausted. As fit as he thought himself, Nathan's tenants were able to outwork him easily. Such strenuous physical labor was not something Derek was accustomed to, though he didn't object to it. His father would have been furious and appalled had he knowledge of it. If he were to be perfectly honest with himself, Derek would have to admit that was part of the attraction.

"D'you know, I think that Nate's going to stay away forever and leave all of this mess to us to take care of," Colin announced from his position on the sofa in the corner.

Derek grinned and opened one eye to look at his friend. "What, you think he is intentionally prolonging this honeymoon trip purely to avoid all the work here for him to do?"

"Exactly," Colin said, pointing a finger and giving him a calculating look.

A disbelieving snort escaped Derek as he settled himself deeper into his chair and adjusted his feet on the ottoman before him. "I doubt that very highly."

"Why? It's not as though he's made an effort to be here with all of this work."

Derek leveled a knowing look at him. "Have you seen the way those two look at each other? They're taking their time, all right, but not to avoid work here."

Colin snickered and shook his head. "Point taken, but you forget he was gone for two weeks before Moira ever came storming back."

"Yes, but he was *with* Moira most of that time," Derek pointed out, gesturing with his hands slightly. "You can hardly blame him. Would *you* want to spend time with us when you could spend time with her?"

"I still think he's avoiding work," Colin muttered as he shifted his position grumpily.

"Oh, come off it. You're not still upset that Moira called you a frog, are you?"

"A toad!" Colin cried, waving a finger in protest. "A toad, Derek, not a frog."

"And the difference there is…?"

Colin sniffed in a rather indignant manner. "Well, if you don't know, then I am not going to tell you." He sighed moodily and folded his arms. "I fail to see why any of us have to bother with wives anyway."

"Are you truly complaining because Nathan got himself a wife, and now he is slightly less available than before?" Derek asked in disbelief. "I've never seen him happier than he is now, and you must admit that Moira has done that for him."

"You've got a wife, and it's hardly done any wonders for you."

Derek glowered. "What I've got is a bad case of some horrible growth that no physician can remove. *That* is not a wife."

Colin laughed out loud. "Oh, come on, Derek. You have got to admit that Katherine is pretty enough."

"For what? Beauty is in the eye of the beholder, and woe unto any man that beholdeth that tyrannical hag, for they will not only turn to stone, but a gargoyle to boot."

Colin was laughing too hard to make any further comment, and Derek found himself smiling a touch to himself. Katherine had but two purposes in life; producing the heir to the dukedom, and driving

Derek's sanity to its breaking point and beyond. He shuddered at the very thought of the first, and the second... well, he shuddered a bit at that, too. He rather liked his sanity as it was.

To be perfectly fair and honest, Katherine was the perfect marchioness, and would be the perfect duchess one day. She knew every single detail of the estates, knew the names of every family under their care, and kept a very neat and careful tally of every item or detail that would require his direct attention.

Her letters every month were brusque and formal, rather business-like, and undeniably cold. He could almost smell her disapproval oozing in every ink stroke. Not that he was lax in his duties, for he was quick to respond to anything that was required of him, and, as was evidenced by his recent activities, he had no qualms about getting his hands dirty as the case required.

The problem was that Katherine despised him as much as he loathed her. She disapproved of everything he did and made no secret about it. While he was being insulting and demeaning of her here, she would be doing the exact same thing with her friends in London.

If she had any friends.

He couldn't have said if she did.

He doubted it.

A resounding knock came at the door, and both men craned their necks ever so slightly to try to get a glimpse of the arrival. Rosemont, Nathan's rather smart butler, soon came into the room. "My lord Whitlock, there is a rider here with an urgent missive for you."

Derek groaned and rubbed at his eyes with one hand. "Bring him in here, then, Rosemont."

"Very good, sir," he said with a quick bow.

In short order, the rider, who was rather windswept and breathless at the moment, came before Derek and handed over the letter.

"How far have you come?" Derek asked as he looked up at the young man.

"From London, sir."

Derek made a noise of discontent as he saw the seal on the back of the letter. It was his own. A letter from Katherine, then. That was odd, as her letters always came very promptly on the fifth of each month. Today was the seventeenth. "Cursed old bat," he muttered as he broke the seal.

"Oh, is it from your wife?" Colin asked, grinning from his lounging position.

Derek threw a vicious glare his way. He opened the letter and quickly perused the remarkably short note in Katherine's very neat hand.

To the Marquess of Whitlock:
Dear Sir,

A situation has arisen that requires your attention and attendance for the sake of propriety and appearance. It is a matter of some urgency. I therefore must insist upon your immediate presence in London. I shall expect you to arrive by the twenty-second day of this month.

May this letter find you well,
Lady Whitlock

Derek snorted, rolled the letter into a ball, and tossed it rather accurately into the fire. He was most certainly not going to come all the way out to London just because she told him to, and was most especially not going to do so without knowing exactly why he was going. If she didn't think to put the reason into a letter, it couldn't have been so imperative as to actually require his immediate attention.

"Oh, for heaven's sake, Derek, why do you even read them if you're just going to toss them into the fire?" Colin asked, watching him with interest and amusement.

"Because the witch would know if I didn't read them," Derek said defensively. He settled back into his seat, and looked up at the rider, who looked more than slightly shocked at his actions. "Tell Katherine that I will come down when I want to, and not when she demands it."

"If you please, my lord," the rider said with the barest hint of a stammer. "I know she probably didn't mention it in the letter, but I happen to know that her mother, Lady Dartwell, passed away just last night."

Derek's feet skidded off of the ottoman he was resting them on. "She what?"

The rider nodded. "Lady Penelope, sir. She had been quite ill for some time and she finally passed last night."

"How do you know this?"

The man's cheeks colored ever so slightly. "I happen to be acquainted with a maid in that house, sir, and she told me herself."

He swore under his breath. Now he had to go. "But why didn't Katherine say so?" Of all the cursed things that could have happened, it had to be a death in the family. Not that he was remorseful, for he was really looking forward to a world without his mother-in-law in it, but there was no way he could avoid going to London to support his wife.

"From what I can tell, sir, she knew how you felt about her mother and she didn't want you to come. But she knew she could not refuse to send for you, as is proper."

He groaned and pushed off of the chair. "Yes, yes, all right, I'll come."

"But Derek, if she doesn't want you there and you don't want to be there and you didn't like her mother anyway…" Colin began, scrambling from the sofa.

"Shut it, Colin," he growled as he removed himself from the room. "She's my wife, whether anybody likes it or not, and her mother has just died. What sort of lout would I look like if I didn't show up?"

"The sort of lout every man of sense is!"

"Begging your pardon, milord," the rider interrupted as he followed them. "Should I tell her ladyship you are coming?"

Derek thought for a moment. "No. Let us leave it for a surprise, shall we?" He grinned and jogged lightly up the stairs. "Pay the man, Colin, and Rosemont, if you would see he gets some food, and then see if one of the carriages can be prepared and sent out front?"

"Of course, my lord."

Colin rolled his eyes and paid the man from his pocket. The rider looked confused, but took the coins. "The marquess never carries coin," Colin explained. "He has a bizarre aversion to his pockets jingling." He clapped the rider on the back, and indicated he follow Rosemont down the hall to the kitchens. Then Colin dashed up the stairs after Derek.

"Derek! Why are you going to surprise her? I thought you said Katherine hates surprises!"

"She does," he heard from the bedroom Derek had been using. Then Derek's head appeared with a wild grin. "That's the whole idea!"

Out of the library nearby came Duncan, who looked perplexed as to the commotion. "What's the fuss, Colin?"

"Someone needs to stop him!" Colin cried, flinging out a desperate hand. "Derek is going to London to be with Katherine!"

Duncan came out of the room entirely and stared at Derek in disbelief. "What? Why?"

"What's going on?" Geoff's voice asked as he came up the stairs behind them.

"Derek is going to see Katherine," Duncan said, still looking dazed.

Geoff's face became a mixture of horror and revulsion as he looked to Derek. "What? Why?"

Derek glowered at the lot of them, then waved at a passing servant. "Grab some more of the staff and have my things packed as soon as possible, would you? I need to depart quickly."

The footman nodded instantly. "Of course, my lord." He moved off in search of more servants, leaving the men alone again.

"You're really going to the viper's lair?" Duncan asked, looking worried and unconvinced.

"Yes, I am. And don't worry, I have appropriate medicines," he retorted as he brushed passed them for the stairs.

"They don't make Katherine medicine," Colin insisted as he followed. "I know, I checked."

Geoff sniggered into his hand behind them and Duncan grinned, but Derek only shook his head. "I should probably punch you, but since I know the truth, I won't."

"What if this is all a trick on Katherine's part, knowing how you despise London?" Duncan asked.

Derek stopped suddenly and all three men behind him came to an abrupt halt as they crashed into each other. "I never considered that," he muttered, his brow furrowing. "She is the devil incarnate. It wouldn't be surprising if she were to be conniving as a fox."

"But if her mother died…" Colin trailed off, confused that for once he was sounding like the voice of reason.

"Yes, you're right," Derek said with a nod, moving once more. "Even Katherine wouldn't kill her own mother just to swindle me. I think she rather liked that biddy."

"What if she is using all of this just as an excuse to get you to come to her?" Geoff brought up as he followed Derek and the others outside.

Derek turned with a sardonically quirked brow. "You really think my wife is that desperate for my company, Geoff?"

Colin and Duncan snickered as Geoff flushed a little.

"Well, I don't know, maybe she's secretly in love with you, and…"

Derek crossed himself and spat upon the ground, effectively cutting him off. "God forbid, Geoff. Keep your curses to yourself, will you? I've already got a pox, I don't need anything else."

Colin was laughing so hard tears were streaming from his eyes. Duncan, who was less prone to laughter, only grinned broadly with mirth. Geoff looked ready to burst into rampant laughter that was only held in check by the hand covering his mouth. Only Derek looked un-amused, and that was only because their joke was his reality. It wasn't that humorous to him.

"Rather sporting of you lads to be so understanding," he began, but he was cut off by an approaching coach nearing the house. They all stood back as it pulled up, the proud Beverton crest on the side. In a moment, Nathan stepped out, looking bright and eager and sickeningly happy.

"What a welcoming party to greet us," he said with a grin as he stepped forward and shook hands with all of them.

"Yes, it's quite a relief to find the house so intact," came a tart, but rather amused voice from within the carriage. Moira stuck her head out and prepared to disembark, but Nathan quickly moved to help her down. She glanced up at him in irritation, but he only smiled and took her hand. Once she was settled, she smiled up at the lot. "My, you are a sight for sore eyes, and you all look much more attractive now than you were when I left you. I have had no one to look at but Nathan for a whole month, and let me tell you…"

"That will do, Moira," Nathan overrode, giving her a look, to which she responded with a bright smile, which made him smile, which made her kiss him.

"See?" Derek said, turning back to Colin, who looked a little green at the lovesick couple. "Not all wives are bad."

"No, just yours," came the quick retort. "That seems quite enough."

"What's that?" Nathan asked, looking back and forth between them, having disengaged his lips from his wife's.

"Derek is going to London to be with Katherine," Geoff said, grimacing a bit.

Nathan's eyes shot to Derek's, his mouth gaping a touch with abhorrence. "What? Why?"

"Nathan," Moira scolded, flicking a quick, but rather painful slap of her hand across his chest.

"Another reason to avoid getting wives," Colin muttered to Duncan, who bit the inside of his cheek and nodded.

Moira glared at them both. "I don't see anyone asking you to turn her into one," she snapped. Then she looked back to Derek. "I think it is good of you to go see Katherine, Derek."

"Oh, it's not for pleasure, Moira. I have been summoned."

"Summoned why?" Nathan asked, rubbing his now tender chest a bit.

"Her mother died." He shrugged. "She seems to think it requires my attention, and as I am not a complete waste of a husband, I have seen fit to agree."

Moira stiffened ever so slightly, then turned to the servants now unloading their luggage from the coach. "Put those things back," she ordered kindly. "We are going to be off again in a moment."

Nathan seized her arm as she went to get back in the carriage. "What are you doing, Moira?"

She gave her husband an impatient look. "I am going to London."

"Why?"

She rolled her eyes. "I fancied a visit with the king, Nathan. Honestly, I am going to help Katherine."

"You don't even know her," Nathan protested.

Moira shook her copper hair slowly. "No, but I do know what losing a mother feels like and no one should have to face that alone."

"She is a witch, Moira, I swear," Derek said, stepping forward, sensing the equally horrorstruck expressions of his friends behind him.

"That's enough, Derek. Even witches need friends sometimes. Besides, I am no angel myself. Perhaps we can learn from each other." She quirked her brows then got back into the carriage.

Nathan turned to Derek and gripped his shirt in a fist. "So help me, Derek, if my wife starts resembling Katherine in any way, I will shoot you between the eyes."

"I will shoot myself for you," Derek vowed.

Nathan nodded once and released his friend. "Good luck."

"Don't tell me you are going to hide yourself in your house the entire time," Derek protested as Nathan entered the carriage. "What am I going to do without sentient company?"

"We'll come, don't worry," Nathan assured him with a grin. "I wouldn't leave you to the harpy alone. Ow!" he cried as Moira punched him again.

"The list grows ever longer," Colin muttered to whoever would listen, which happened to be everyone.

"Oh, Colin," Moira called, leaning over to look at him through the window.

"Yes?" he asked, almost wincing.

She grinned at him. "You do know that you are my favorite, yes?"

He returned her smile with a flirtatious one of his own. "Yes,

Lady Beverton. It never ceases to delight me."

She winked and nodded, sitting back. Nathan looked at her in a sort of enraged puzzlement, then signaled to the coachman to drive on, and the remaining men could hear Moira's delighted laughter over the sound of the wheels.

"Blast," Colin sighed, watching them leave.

"What?" Geoff asked, looking amused at the forlorn look on his face.

"I am so weak and susceptible to the charms of women. It's such a tragedy."

"I know just the cure for that," Derek said with a wicked grin. "You are coming with me."

Colin gasped in horror. "I most certainly am not!"

Derek nodded, still smiling. "You are. You can stay at your own house, but you are coming to London. All of you are."

Duncan and Geoff looked surprised, but said nothing. Colin looked to them for help, but they only shrugged and nodded their acceptance.

"This is a bad idea," Colin said as he turned to go back into the house and get his things. "This is a very, very bad idea."

Derek grinned as his friends went to prepare for departure. Spending time with Katherine was rather akin to begging for someone to beat upon him with iron hot tongs, but if his friends would be in town to distract him, then it would not be as bad as it had the potential to be.

The fact that Katherine could not stand his friends was merely a delightful bonus.

Chapter Two

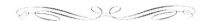

Katherine Chambers, Marchioness of Whitlock, was not happy.

Which seemed to be her normal state of being as of late. But it would not *be* her normal state of being if people would only do as they were told and stop thinking they knew better than she did.

"No, no, no," she said firmly, overriding the small man with watery eyes that was before her at the moment. "Mother was very firmly opposed to flowers indoors at all. There will be no flowers."

A small whimper escaped the man as he frantically scratched out whatever he had written in that little book of his. "What about at the gravesite service, my lady? A small wreath of roses, perhaps?"

Katherine sighed and put a gloved hand to her brow. "No, Mr. Perkins. Mother had a severe dislike for roses being used for anything other than a wedding. No roses. You may have something small and somber, but no color. White only. Nothing fancy, mind you. It is a funeral, not a coronation."

"Yes, milady," he stammered out, bowing out of the room, for which she was especially grateful. Another minute of his simpering and she would have been strongly tempted to strangle him.

She had almost done so anyway, and *that* was certainly not something her mother would have approved of.

"I don't think flowers would have been so very bad," her father said quietly where he sat across the room with his book. "It might have brought some light into things."

Katherine removed her hand and looked over at her father, looking so small in his massive chair, his spectacles sitting so preciously upon his nose, his already very thin hair looking more frail than usual. "Father, you know how specific Mother was about things. She gave me charge of her arrangements, and I will follow her instructions to the letter."

He shrugged lightly. "As you wish, Katherine. You know best. But when I go, I do hope you will have some flowers there."

"Of course, Father. A whole garden, if you wish it."

He smiled just a touch, a mere shadow of his former smiles, and went back to his book.

Katherine watched him for a long moment, wondering just what life would become for him now that her mother was gone. Harry Bishop, Viscount Dartwell, was not a powerful man, nor a wealthy one. He had married well, but without affection, and his wife, Lady Penelope, had seen fit to manage the household and everything else regarding his life, which suited him just as well as he would much prefer to sit quietly alone and read.

As their fortune was not one of great standing, but their bloodlines were rich and old, they had arranged for their two daughters, Aurelia and Katherine, to marry into equally noble families with larger incomes. One of the great crowning achievements of Lady Penelope's life had been seizing the heir to the dukedom at Ashcombe for her younger daughter, Katherine. Only slightly less of a success had been the arrangement of the match between her eldest daughter to Nigel Whittinham, the heir to a rather extensive baronage.

Engaged at the age of three, Katherine had never known anything but her future as the marchioness of Whitlock, and beyond that the duchess of Ashcombe. Lady Penelope had been determined that her daughters would be perfect wives and marchioness, duchess, or baroness, as the case may have been, and the lessons had gone accordingly. Every lesson had a purpose, every activity was fraught with matronly duties, every opportunity to test and examine was exploited. By the age of thirteen, Katherine knew more about running a household and the duties of a marchioness and duchess than she suspected many ladies currently in those positions did.

Satisfied that her life was situated just as perfectly as could be, given their unfortunate circumstances, Lady Penelope had prided herself on being advisor to her two daughters, and such was her influence over them, her advice was heeded. She had never dealt with her husband unless forced to, and the viscount had not minded that either. If he were advised, he would merely suggest they ask his wife, and send them on their way. He had learned long ago that his decisions were not well favored by his wife, and the fewer reasons to let her find fault with him, the better.

Not that she failed to find fault anyway, as faults seemed to magically appear before her, as Katherine well knew, but such was Lord Dartwell's love for peace that he would relent all he could to maintain it.

He had not run his own house or lands for more than thirty years. He would have no idea how to do anything.

Katherine swallowed back her worry and straightened in her seat. *A duchess never worries. A duchess never slouches.* She was forever hearing orders barked in her head, and in her mother's tone. Echoes of her childhood coming back to her, reminding her of her duty.

She nearly snorted at the thought. Duty, indeed. Her duty as the wife of the laziest man in England to ever inherit any title at all. Her husband was never to be seen in her company, and she was grateful for it. He had no idea what sort of pressures she dealt with running his affairs, and maintaining the honor of his family's name. She was the most capable marchioness she had ever met, and the fine order she kept things in made her husband appear to be very organized and attentive when in reality she highly doubted he even read the letters she sent him.

She could not remember the first time she had met Whitlock, as they had both been very young, but she remembered many visits that had been forced upon them throughout their lives, and they had been a torturous experience for them both. The only quality that Derek Chambers had to recommend himself to anybody was the fact that he was far too good looking for his own good. If one had only seen him, and knew nothing else, they would probably think him the most handsome man that ever lived. But the moment he opened his mouth, or they caught glimpse of his mind, what little there was of it, they would recoil in such horror that he might have been a leprous hunchback with no teeth.

Lady Penelope had made no secret of her dislike for her son-in-law, and he equally made no attempt to hide his aversion to her. Katherine had heard her mother say on many occasions that had he been anything other than the heir to a rather extensive title and one of the finest fortunes and situations in all of England, she would not even have matched him with a milkmaid. Katherine suspected it was the worst insult her mother could conjure up.

What astonished her was how all of her servants, and indeed, all of her tenants at all of their estates were so overwhelmingly adoring where Whitlock was concerned. They practically worshiped him. She failed to see how any set of people so industrious could be so very blind. He could do no wrong in their eyes. Everything he did, and everything he was, was ideal, and he was so kind and so generous and so wise, and she had even heard that one of the tenants in Derbyshire had named their son after him.

She could not imagine anybody who knew him wanting to do such a thing.

Katherine sighed, sending a stray strand of her dark hair into her face. She glowered at it. *A duchess always looks her best, regardless of the situation.* There was no place for stray hairs. She stood from her chair and went to the nearest mirror, and was relieved to find her hair otherwise immaculate. She carefully affixed the troublesome strand back in place, and then met her own dark eyes in the mirror. She looked rather drawn today, but once upon a time, Katherine had been a beautiful girl, the envy of many.

"Is your sister coming over today?" her father asked from his chair.

Katherine closed her eyes briefly. Therein lay the worst of her current problems. Aurelia was a constant source of aggravation, and the dire situations of late had only heightened it. Though Katherine outranked her quite soundly, Aurelia seemed to think that her position as elder sister still meant something. Nothing Katherine did was ever good enough, which was ridiculous, as Katherine always did everything perfectly and to the letter.

It did not help that Aurelia's husband practically worshipped the ground upon which she walked. He thought her God's gift to the world, and especially to himself. He agreed to everything she said, obeyed her every whim, and made sure that she never wanted for any comfort at all. His chief purpose in life was to make sure that he kept his wife happy, and Aurelia was more than pleased to let him do so, and frequently made sure that he would. She then followed her orders to him with her attempt at an adoring look, which never ceased to make Nigel return it with one of his own.

It was a nauseating sight.

"No," she said, finally answering her father's question. "Sir Nigel wanted to take the family to see his mother today and as the dowager baroness has yet to see Alice, she decided to pack up the whole family for a few days."

"But they will be here for the services and the reception?"

"I assume so, Father. Aurelia would never pass up the opportunity to dramatically mourn for the public who come to pay respects."

Her words had come out rather acerbically, and she bit down on her suddenly clamped lips. *A duchess always minds her tongue.* That had been the hardest one for Katherine her entire life. She always wanted to say the horrid things she was thinking, and when it came to certain people of her acquaintance, namely her husband and sister, she usually did.

"I apologize," she said with a shake of her head. "That was..."

"Rather true, I think," her father finished in his light, carefree tone as he turned a page.

Katherine gave him a sharp look, which he did not see as he had yet to remove his eyes from his book.

"Your sister performs on many occasions, and not very well, but I don't think that we should hold that against her," he continued, sounding as though he were commenting on the weather or the state of the roads rather than his oldest daughter. "If she has shed any tears of genuine regret or joy in her entire life, I will call myself the King of England and let them pack me off to the asylum."

Katherine covered her mouth as a very un-duchess-like snort escaped her, followed by a series of giggles, and only then did her father look at her, smiling yet again.

"I miss your laugh, my girl," he said as she composed herself. "It is quite possibly my favorite sound in the world."

"Yes, well," she managed, swallowing briefly, "a duchess must be composed at all times, and a snort is most definitely not a sign of composure." She noticed the dimming of his smiles and moved over to place a hand on his arm. "If I could find a way to laugh delicately, then I would do so."

"I don't want you to change it," he murmured, adjusting his spectacles and going back to his book.

Katherine sighed and patted his arm once, then went to exit the room. "I am going to call for some tea in the drawing room. Would you like me to have something sent in here to you?"

He shook his head, still reading. "No, thank you, my dear. Your mother would forbid any food or drink being brought in here. I will wait until dinner."

Swallowing back a lump on her throat, she nodded and went to the drawing room, and rang for tea. Then, assured that she was alone, she leaned forward and set her elbows on her knees, and her face in her hands.

Her father was so lost already. It seemed he could barely think for himself; how could she possibly go back to her home and leave him to his own devices? She had been here for four days already, had taken charge of everything as she was accustomed to, and he had very rarely said anything of his own opinions, which saved her the trouble of asking.

But the strain of preparing for a funeral for the woman who had raised her, who had taught her everything she knew, who had made her the woman she was today, and having to run two households was draining any sort of energy she had.

She would be lost without her mother as well.

Her mother had been her chief advisor, whether she had asked for it or not. She had known the Whitlock estates inside and out just as Katherine did, though it had been quite some time since Katherine had actually asked her for advice concerning her own affairs. She had made it her business to know everybody else's business, and because of that, she always knew everything.

She needed her mother to tell her what to do.

They had never been particularly close, that was simply not in Lady Penelope's nature. She could not have even said if she loved her mother, or vice versa. Oh, they certainly cared for and about each other enough, but the relationship had never been friendly. It had mostly consisted of pupil and teacher, with the odd smattering of "darling" and "Mother says". It had been a very strict upbringing for her, but one could not deny that Lady Penelope was well versed in decorum, propriety, and duty.

And now Katherine was as well.

And it had served her well.

She was well respected by all, she was invited to absolutely everything, her tenants and servants knew her well and always seemed pleased to see her. She had never had any sort of scandal or gossip surround her, and there had never been any fault in her behavior for anyone to see. Katherine, Marchioness of Whitlock, was a woman that commanded respect and attention, and that was something she was remarkably proud of.

But on days like today, she felt as though the weight of the world rested on her shoulders, and even her lifelong training to be the perfect marchioness and duchess had not prepared her for this. Funeral arrangements, meeting with the solicitor concerning her mother's will, seeing that the proper mourning garb was donned by staff and family, not to mention overseeing her own household from all the way across town, and dealing with her sister and her infuriating need to have her own way regardless of the sense of it.

And then there was the little matter of her husband, and the fact that she had sent for him.

But he would not come. He did not respond to her summons, and she had received no word to prepare for his arrival, not that she had expected him to reply. He rarely did when it concerned vital matters of their estate; he would never send a response about something as trivial as a death.

At least that was one matter she would not have to deal with at present.

Even so, a raging headache that reminded her of him was forming behind her eyes, and she did not have the time to have a lie-down and let it pass.

The maid came in with a tea spread, and the tray and cups rattled horribly as she set it down.

"For heaven's sake, Sally," Katherine snapped, leaning back to upright and adjusting her sheer black gloves. "If you cannot bring in the tea silently…"

"I beg your pardon, milady," the maid said with a bob. "It were only due to the state we're all in, what with my Lady Penelope…"

"Yes, yes, all right," she interrupted waving her off. "I do not need to hear your excuses, just your word that it will not happen again."

"It will not happen again, milady," Sally replied dutifully, bobbing a curtsey again.

Katherine took a calming breath. *A duchess is firm, but respectful with the help. It keeps them loyal.* "I can appreciate the struggle the staff is having with the death of my mother," she said in a controlled voice. "We must all adapt as best as we can." She tried for a smile, and saw the maid relax ever so slightly. "But even so, we must not lose composure or fail to do our duties."

"Yes, milady."

Katherine nodded. "Thank you, Sally, that will be all."

Sally bobbed yet again and exited, leaving Katherine blessedly alone.

Katherine poured out tea for herself, and absently put in one sugar and a touch of cream, which was exactly the way her mother took her tea. Which meant it was the way everybody took their tea. Too much sugar was a sign of frivolity and too much cream was missish, but to take tea without either showed a deplorable want of sophistication. And, above all else, *a duchess is the height of sophistication.*

She sipped her tea slowly, letting the warmth course through her and feeling the tension leave her little by little. Gradually, calm and sense returned to her mind and her strength returned to her.

Yes, her mother was still gone. Yes, now she would have much greater responsibility to bear. Yes, she would have to adjust most aspects of her life around the change.

But she could do it.

She was Katherine Mary Alexandra Bishop Chambers, Marchioness of Whitlock. She could do anything.

With a satisfied smile, she set her tea back down and allowed herself one of the tarts that had come with the service. Generally, she never took tarts, despite her affinity for them. There was not a rule for that, but Katherine rather liked her figure, if she allowed herself a small moment of vanity. Even in the horrid black gown she was wearing, she looked quite fetching. One tart would be quite enough for today.

A scarce few moments after Sally had cleared away the tea service, she was back, and looked far more anxious than she had been previously.

"B-begging your p-pardon, milady," she managed, bobbing so shakily Katherine wondered what was wrong with the poor girl.

"What is it, Sally? Do not stammer, it is frightfully unbecoming."

Sally nodded and took a deep breath. "If you please, milady, there is a gentleman that is here to see you."

Gentleman? The very idea took Katherine by surprise. If she had said the undertaker or that dreaded florist again or the solicitor, that was one thing, but a gentleman? Who would come calling on her here at her father's house while she was mourning?

"A gentleman?" she asked, rising from her seat and brushing off her skirt. "What gentleman?"

"Well, milady, he says he… that is to say, he claims he is your…"

"Husband," finished a low, sardonic voice that Katherine knew all too well.

"Whitlock?" she gasped, her body going cold.

He stepped into the room, his brown-blonde hair the tiniest bit tousled, his green eyes dancing, and grinned rather brashly at her. "Hello, wife of mine."

Perhaps a second tart would have been wise after all.

Chapter Three

"*What* are you doing here, Whitlock?"

He had the effrontery to look astonished. "Why, you sent for me, dear Katherine. I thought, surely if my wife needs me in London, I must obey!"

"That is highly unlikely. You don't know how to obey."

He snorted. "I do, too. Whether or not I choose to do so is another matter entirely."

Katherine gritted her teeth and took in a would-be calming breath through her nose. "Do not be impertinent, Whitlock. Why are you here?"

He still smiled. "Ah, but impertinence is my natural state of being, dear wife, and I don't know how to be anything else."

"*That* much is obvious."

"I do so love it when you fight back," Derek said with a sigh as he moved further into the room and sat rather inelegantly in a chair near her.

"I did not ask you to sit down," she forced through her clenched teeth, her hands fisting at her sides.

"No, you didn't, and it was terribly rude of you," he scolded, propping his feet up on her mother's tea table.

Breathe, Katherine. Breathe. "Remove your feet from that table, sir."

"Why?" He looked down at his feet, then back up at her. "They seem quite at home here."

Keep breathing. Keep breathing. "This is not your home."

"No, thank heavens. My home, our home, I should say, as you live there too, is much nicer than this. And I can put my feet wherever I please without comment over there."

Katherine had to literally restrain herself from reaching out to strangle him. She doubted there was a rule that went *a duchess does not strangle her husband*, but she felt quite certain that the sentiment was implied in one or two of the others.

"I say, Kate, are you quite well? You look ready to burst into flame." He looked around, then back at her. "Do I need to scoot this uncomfortable chair back a bit? I'd rather not get ash on this ensemble. Duncan chose it for me with such care…"

"Why," Katherine said loudly, overriding him as her nails bit into the palms of her hands rather painfully, "are you here, Whitlock?"

He paused momentarily and gave her an amused grin. "You are repeating yourself, Kate."

"My name is Katherine."

He shrugged. "Katherine, Kate, it makes no difference. After all, what's in a name? A chamber pot by any other name would still smell…"

"Whitlock!" she screeched, her cheeks flaming further.

"At any rate," he continued, as if she had not said anything, "as I said before, I came because you asked me to come." He cocked his head and looked at her with interest. "Although, now that I think of it, you didn't ask at all, did you? You insisted upon my presence. That is a rather different matter. The tone of your writing was rather severe, Kate."

"I do not think my manner of writing has anything…" she started.

"Oh, of course, it does," he interrupted with a slice of his hand, as if he were actually cutting something of hers off. "If you insist upon something, it would seem as though I have no choice in the matter at all, which is quite silly as I always have a choice, seeing as how you married into the title that I was born to."

Her mouth dropped open in shock. She had done more for the title *he* was born to than he had ever done for it. "How dare you…"

"But if you were to *ask* me to come, very nicely, very politely," he continued, his eyes seeming to hold a certain flame of impudence to them that she very much would like to scratch out, "I might consider acquiescing. But as you have never asked me politely or nicely in the ten years we've been married…"

"Five," she bit out, inordinately pleased to be both interrupting him and correct in doing so.

"What was that, Kate?" he asked, cupping his ear slightly.

"It has been five years that we have been married, Whitlock, as you well know."

He shook his head. "Only five? Goodness me, it feels more like ten. Regardless, in all of the *five* years, you have never asked me. Only orders, only demands." He shook his head. "It was quite remarkable that I accepted at all."

"Surely you knew I never meant for you to accept it."

He put a shocked hand to his chest and coughed in mock surprise. "What? My own wife does not want me to come down to London to see her? But she summoned me!" He stood and paced about as if he were confused. "And she didn't mean it. Oh dear, oh dear, what shall I do?"

"Leave now before anyone knows you have come?" She did not even try to hide the note of hope that rang through her words.

He winced and shook his head. "Alas, my dear, the Earl of Beverton and his wife have already come down, and Mr. Gerrard, Mr. Bray, and Mr. Harris as well. I am afraid that they all know I'm here, and as it was I who invited them, I cannot very well abandon them. Unless you wish me to *un*-invite them, which I suppose I could do, although I doubt the new countess would appreciate the slight as the men might, knowing you as they do."

"I do not have time for this," Katherine said as she threw her hands up and went to the door of the room. "If you would care to notice, I have a funeral to arrange." She could have cursed herself for the way her voice broke on the word funeral.

Instantly, Derek's expression turned somber, and though she would never admit it, Katherine was grateful. Her husband might have been a cad, a louse, irritating beyond all reason, and suspected of actually causing the pox, but he did have some sense of decorum, however infrequently he chose to employ it. And someone, probably his mother, had trained him in manners. With other people, at least.

He waited a moment, and then he came over and bowed slightly before her. "I apologize, Kate. My sincere condolences on the loss of your mother."

She snorted once. "Sincere? You did not even like Mother."

"No, nor did she like me. But I am genuinely sorry that you have suffered a loss. I even forced myself into mourning." He showed her his sleeve, where a black band was indeed tied.

Knowing she could not argue that, and feeling strangely touched by a simple mourning band, she nodded. "Thank you."

He nodded as well, then shrugged slightly. "I came because, like it or not, we are married, and my wife has lost someone close to her. I am here to be the dutiful husband and support her."

Kate blinked in confusion. She did not know that he had a serious expression that was not mocking.

"I… I don't know what to say," she admitted bluntly, which was highly unlike her.

Something that was almost a smile tweaked at the corner of his mouth, but it was gone so fast, she thought she must have imagined it. "What can I do for you?"

His request very nearly stole her breath away. No one had asked her that in so long she could not have said when. The burning in her eyes intensified and she wanted nothing more than to get out of his sight. "Leave me alone?" she whispered, looking up at him.

He nodded once and took a step back. "If that's what you wish. I assume you want to remain here until the services are completed?"

She nodded quickly. "Father needs me. He…" She trailed off and did not finish. He did not need to know the details.

"Of course. If I can be of any service to him, please send for me. And I mean it, Kate. I'm here to be of use. Use me."

She swallowed, more than a touch unnerved by his sincerity. It had to be a ruse. He wanted her to use him? "As what?" she asked with a small snort, attempting to return to the safety of bickering. "A stable shovel? Or perhaps a pin cushion?"

Now he grinned. "Ah, there's my wife. I almost forgot with

whom I was speaking. If you will kindly remove your fangs from my person, I will go back to our house, which comfort I left to come and see you."

Not seeing any need to reply, Katherine inclined her head and gestured for him to lead the way out.

"Services will be held when?" Derek asked as he took his hat from the butler.

"Day after tomorrow. At eleven."

He nodded. "I will come here at ten."

"You do not have to, Whitlock."

He leveled a rather impressive glare at her. "I did not come all this way to *not* attend the funeral services of the mother of my wife, no matter how heinous her taste in hats was in life."

Katherine opened her mouth in outrage, but Derek only tapped his own hat and showed himself out.

"Goodbye, Kate. See you in two days!" he called as he departed, then began whistling cheerfully.

She watched him go with narrowed eyes, her hands still balled. "Katherine," she muttered at his retreating back. "My name is Katherine."

With a small noise of irritation, she whirled and went to find something useful to do, her feelings of kindness towards him gone as suddenly as they had come, and just as fleeting.

The next few days were going to be a very, very long indeed.

It was not as though Derek meant to be so averse to London, for it truly was a city of much amusement and entertainment, he considered as he tipped his hat to a mother and her two daughters that passed. Their shared giggles and whispers at his actions brought a small smirk to his face as he jauntily continued on.

Yes, London had much to offer those who chose to visit or inhabit it. But there were two reasons that Derek ever ventured into London apart from his own amusement and responsibilities.

His wife was the first, and he had already dealt with her and had come out less scarred than he had predicted, which was always a pleasant surprise. The second was his father, the Duke of Ashcombe. That was his task at hand.

His father was a good man, and a rather well-respected one. His opinion was sought after in the highest circles, his fortune was rather extensive, and his heritage impeccable. For these reasons, the duke was unnaturally focused and driven on maintaining all appearances of respectability and accomplishing one's duty.

This was not an issue for Derek, as he had a great deal of pride in his family. It did mean, however, that he came under rather close scrutiny from his father and much of the pressure in his life, what didn't come from Katherine anyway, came from him.

It could not be completely construed as being the duke's fault, as he had not come from the direct line, and due to the lack of heirs there, his grandfather had inherited upon the previous duke's death. Many had believed that this particular branch of the family would never amount to anything more than a gentleman's status, and not very wealthy ones at that. The doubts of Society had only fueled Derek's great-grandfather, and ever since then, it seemed that the one task that was paramount for the family was to prove them all wrong.

It didn't matter that it had been so many years ago that very few people even knew about it. The insistence on maintaining bloodlines and power, and garnering respect and admiration from all, was ingrained in every future duke's mind from the time they were small.

Marriages were arranged to ensure that future heirs would have the highest breeding that England had to offer, because the very idea of a future duke marrying someone of their own choosing was enough to terrify the existing ones. And Derek had not been old enough to know what all of that had meant until he had already been well acquainted with Katherine, and had learned the importance of his duty.

And it was not until much, *much* later that he thought enough about it to resent anything.

With a sigh, Derek approached the grand London home of his parents, and faintly he wished that they were only his parents and nothing else, but wishing was fruitless at this point.

He knocked firmly, waited only briefly, and was then let in by the family butler, Wooster, instantly.

"Hello, Wooster, how are you?" he asked, handing over his hat and gloves.

"Very well, my lord, thank you."

"How is your knee?"

The old man grinned. "Still there, I think."

Derek laughed and clapped him on the back. "That's a relief. You keep up with all of Mrs. Tabbit's remedies and you may be challenging me to a footrace soon enough."

"Yes, my lord, I think I shall."

"Very good. I have come to see my parents, are they available?"

"They are, sir. I believe the duke is in his study."

"Thank you, Wooster. I shall take myself down there. You go on and sit down somewhere," Derek said with a smile as he left the entryway, knowing full well that the butler would do no such thing.

The door to the duke's study was open slightly, but Derek knocked anyway. Rule number seventeen in this house growing up was *Always knock when seeking entrance.*

"Come," the voice of his father was heard within, and he pushed the door open.

"Whitlock!" his father cried in surprise, a smile forming on his still relatively young face as he rose from his desk.

Derek bowed as perfectly as he had ever done. "Your Grace."

He turned to where his mother sat, looking as regal as she always had, and still beautiful even after three children had grown. "Your Grace," he said, taking her hand and placing a kiss on her knuckles.

"Oh, Derek, it is so good to see you," she returned, rising to give him hug.

"You as well, Mother," he replied with a smile, giving a fond kiss to her cheek.

"What brings you to London?" his father asked as he came over to shake his hand.

Derek gave him an odd look as he took it. "Katherine's mother passed away, sir. I should have thought you would have seen it in the paper."

"Ah, yes, poor Lady Dartwell," the duke said with a nod as he returned to his desk. "Do give our condolences to Lady Whitlock, will you?"

"I shall tell Katherine, thank you," he said pointedly, which earned him a quirk of a brow from his father. "But will you not be paying your respects at the reception in two days?"

"Oh, I do not know that we..." the duke started.

"Ashcombe," his wife broke in gently as she took her seat once more. "I think it would mean a good deal to Lady Whitlock if we went. And it would show respect for the family and for our son."

The duke frowned slightly, then sighed. "Very well, then, my dear. We shall attend the services for Lady Dartwell."

"If you wish, sir," Derek said with an incline of his head.

"Now that you have come, Whitlock, I need your assistance," his father said, indicating that he sit.

"Oh?" Derek asked, dreading the request that was forthcoming. "On what matter?"

"Your brother."

Derek almost groaned and sat back. Of course the subject was going to be David. It was his father's favorite topic to rant upon, as he thought David was the biggest wastrel to ever inhabit nobility.

"What has David done now?"

"It is what he is *not* doing!" his father bemoaned, looking rather troubled.

"And that would be?" Derek tried for a patient, concerned tone, but really, nothing David did was actually shocking to anybody except his father.

"He adamantly refuses to marry!"

That was surprising, even to Derek. He licked his lips slowly, then said the first thing that had come to mind. "Ever?"

His father's eyes narrowed. "Are you amused, Whitlock? I can assure you, this is not a laughing matter."

Derek straightened ever so slightly at his father's stern tone, even though he was very much a grown man now. Fathers can have that effect on their sons. "No, sir, I am not amused. I was merely seeking clarification."

His father still looked suspicious, so Derek forced any sign of amusement or humor out of his expression. Only then did his father continue. "He has not spoken of the future, but at present, he claims his only inclination is to enjoy himself."

Quite frankly, Derek thought that was a very good idea. David was still young, there was hardly any need for him to be rushed off to the altar and bound to a woman for the rest of existence when he could be enjoying freedom of thought and purpose.

But Derek knew far better than to say any of this aloud, and arranged his features accordingly. "I see," he said carefully, desperate to avoid saying anything he would regret with regards to either party.

"I do not think you fully grasp the severity of the situation, Whitlock!" his father said, his voice rising. "This is the future of the family we are speaking of here."

"Ashcombe…" his wife warned, but he would not heed her.

"Unless Lady Whitlock provides you with an heir, David will inherit after you! Do you really want to leave the dukedom up to chance?" the duke asked loudly, his fist banging the desk.

"I hardly think that the timing is as important as the lady in question," Derek tried, his mind working as fast as it could bear to. "Have you not arranged something for him?"

"No," his father groaned, sitting back. "You were the only one we arranged a match for. Diana did well enough with marrying Lord Beckham, though I wish he was placed a bit higher than Bow Street."

Derek did not comment on that, as he rather liked Edward and his choice of profession.

"But David could have his pick of any number of ladies in Society," his father continued, growing more earnest. "We have drawn up a list of suitable candidates for him, and he will not even look at it."

"A list?" Derek asked, feeling a little peeved. "You are not going to let him choose as you did Diana?"

"Why should I? Diana was not going to come into anything. She was a catch for any man of nobility, she did not need to do the catching."

Derek didn't think his sister would appreciate being likened to a fish, but then, he had no inclination to tell her.

"I think you should trust that David will do his duty when he is ready to take it on," Derek said calmly, hoping he could smooth things over. "He has a good deal more sense than you give him credit for."

"Are you saying that I do not know my own son?" the duke cried, his fist tightening.

That was exactly what Derek was saying, but there was no polite way to phrase it.

"What's all the commotion in here?" came the drawling, unaffected tones of David, who entered the room without knocking.

The glare that their father offered David was one that would have made stone gargoyles cower and flee. "You must marry, David. Now."

David's brows rose in surprise. "Right this minute? But I'm not suitably dressed for a wedding."

Derek had the bizarre urge to laugh, which would have gotten him shot, or worse.

The duke looked ready to explode, but somehow maintained his furious demeanor without variation. He looked to Derek, who couldn't help but to swallow a little hastily. "Take care of this, Whitlock."

He indicated with his eyes and his head that the two should leave, and Derek got to his feet immediately. David did not move. Derek looked to his mother, who said nothing, but her eyes had widened significantly. He turned back to his brother and took his arm. Thankfully, David responded to him, and in short order, they were out of the study and back to the relative safety of the rest of the house.

"Hello, Derek," David said finally, with a wry grin, his green eyes that matched Derek's in an almost eerie fashion twinkling. "Feels a bit like our childhood, doesn't it?"

Derek couldn't resist smiling just a touch. "A lot, actually, except for the topic."

David nudged his head onward and they moved into one of the front drawing rooms, where each flopped into chairs. "I don't know why he thinks I need to marry now."

"Nor do I," Derek admitted with a sigh. He hesitated, then asked, "You do want to marry eventually, don't you?"

"Of course," David said with a snort. "But I want to fall in love with the girl. *Before* I marry her. No offense."

Derek waved it off. "None taken. I would have liked to do that myself."

"And I don't think I'll care very much at all for what her bloodlines are, thank you very much," David said in a grumbling tone. "In fact, I think I'll fall in love with a merchant's daughter."

Derek laughed out loud. "That will really impress him. He might kill you."

"He would never kill me, he thinks too much of the family." David paused a moment, then said, "He might hire someone to kill me, but he would never do it himself."

"Why do you intentionally provoke him?" Derek asked, truly curious. The duke was a powerful man, and a rather intimidating one. It hardly seemed a prudent thing to do, even for a rebellious son.

David shrugged. "Because I can. Because I am tired of him running my life. Because, despite what he thinks, he is not God."

"He could disinherit you, you know."

Again came the shrug. "Huzzah. Then I really would be free. I don't mean to be his wastrel son that is always disappointing, but you must admit, you are the preferred son."

Derek was shaking his head before David had finished. "I am the heir, nothing more."

"And I the spare."

"Don't say that."

"What? It's the truth. Do you really think that if Diana had been a boy I would even be here?"

As much as he hated to admit it, Derek knew it was more than likely true. Their parents were companionable with each other, but never affectionate. And each had always been so focused on duty, honor, and family and blood that they wanted to force their children into similar tendencies.

Unfortunately, none of them were quite as determined.

"You are not a spare," Derek said firmly. "You are my brother, and I will support you in whatever you do."

David smiled and nodded. "Thank you, Derek. Now what about getting some decent food from that delightful chef our parents have employed, eh? I'm famished!"

Chapter Four

Two days later, Derek found himself beside his wife and her father in the parlor of their family home, and he was bored out of his mind. Katherine, ever controlling and interfering, had demanded that, as she and the other ladies had not been present for the service, they would hear exactly what the minister said during such before they received their callers.

He wasn't sure he could bear hearing it again. He hadn't expected the service to be amusing or light-hearted, given the circumstances, but he had never in his life been to a funeral or reception that had been so monotonous. Or that had been so devoid of emotion. Not a single person present was crying.

Well, except for Katherine's sister, Lady Aurelia, who was in the adjacent anteroom sobbing rather unconvincingly into her rotund and ridiculous husband's now drenched waistcoat. But he was holding her and patting her shoulder, and looking rather subdued, which seemed a decent fit for the act.

The minister, a rather small, balding man, was now reading some psalms or some such from his Bible, and, though Derek appreciated religion as much as any good Christian, he really would rather have skipped the whole thing. What was the sense in trying to be uplifting here? If Lady Penelope were going to Heaven, he would gladly go to Hell when his time came.

Derek nearly groaned when he saw the minister turn the page and continue reading on the next. Would this day never end?

At long last, the minister bowed his head and waited for judgment to be passed upon him.

Katherine, looking pale and drawn, pressed her lips together firmly. "And that is exactly as the service proceeded?"

"It is, madam," the minister said with a nod. "After which the grave site service commenced."

Katherine nodded and looked at her father, whose expression was too vacant for any sort of reaction. She turned to Derek. "Was that what he said?"

Derek snorted. "More or less."

She glared fiercely. "Was it more or was it less, Whitlock?"

He shrugged and scratched at the back of his neck. "I slept through it, I have no idea." He sheepishly smiled at the minister. "Sorry, it was a rather long procession from the house to the church, and I am not used to walking such distances."

The minister bit the inside of his cheek, but waved his hand a little dismissively. Katherine's frown grew, but she turned back to the other man. "Thank you, Mr. Clarke," she said softly, for once not sounding as though she disapproved. "It was exactly the way Mother had wanted it."

Now *that* did not surprise Derek at all. He did rather expect that the old bird would have been affronted by the lack of attendance, but as she had not been anybody's favorite person in the whole course of her life, he wondered just who she would have expected to come. He further suspected that she wrote the entire boring service out herself and gave specific instructions on what was to transpire and how it was to do so.

Such was the behavior of Lady Penelope.

May she rest in peace.

He nearly snorted at that. Peace? Ha!

Mr. Clarke shook hands with them all, and then waited for them to leave the parlor. It was time to receive the guests who had come to pay respects.

Derek expected that, given the number of friends Lady Penelope had, this would take all of ten minutes, perhaps fifteen, and then he would be free of this madness.

If it was a good day, even less.

Ever a puppet to duty, he stood obediently beside his wife as a surprising number of people proceeded past them to murmur insincere condolences and far too many handkerchiefs dabbed at completely dry eyes.

To his surprise, his parents came up and dutifully expressed condolences, but said nothing much further. Katherine thanked them for their attendance, which was more than Derek did. They took his hand as well, but moved quickly on. They had never been very emotional people, and mourning for someone they would not miss was not in their repertoire of feelings.

More and more people came by them, murmuring their faux sympathies, and just as Derek was wondering how long he was going to have to stand here and be somber-faced, Nathan and Moira appeared.

He almost grinned in relief, which would not have been appropriate at all.

He sensed Katherine stiffening ever so slightly, but she was far too principled to object to an earl and countess, no matter how she disliked Derek's friends.

"Lady Whitlock," Nathan murmured with an incline of his head.

"Lord Beverton," she said tightly, her mouth stretched in only what the most optimistic of people would have considered a smile.

"My condolences on your loss."

"Thank you for coming."

Nathan nodded and moved on to Derek, who allowed himself to smile.

But before he could say anything, Moira had taken hold of Katherine's arm. "I know we don't know each other, Katherine," she said earnestly.

Derek coughed to cover his sudden laughter at Moira's use of Katherine's given name, knowing how his wife would be shocked and appalled by it.

"...but if you need anything, I hope you will let me know," Moira continued, as if she had not just severely breached Katherine's beloved sense of decorum.

"Thank you, Lady Beverton," Katherine said stiffly.

Moira gave a comforting smile and patted her arm again, starting to move away. But then she hesitated, and before anybody could even blink, she had thrown her arms around Katherine in a rather awkward looking hug.

Oh, that was not going to go over well. "Nate," Derek hissed, seizing his friend's sleeve, "what is she doing?"

Nathan shrugged. "You know Moira. She does whatever she wants."

"Well, it's going to drive Katherine absolutely batty and I'm going to have to deal with it." And it was going to be terrible. Awful. Horrifying. The stuff of nightmares. He was apprehensive already.

Nathan gave him a rather sardonic look and pushed his hand away. "Why don't you try to stop my wife, Derek? I'm certainly not going to. I know better."

"I know it feels dark right now," Moira whispered to Katherine as she held her close, "but it gets better. I promise." Then she let go, smiling gently, and took Nathan's arm. She glared at Derek, and he returned it with a completely lost look of his own. What, did she really think that *he* had killed Katherine's mother? Other than that, which was actually a rather intriguing idea, he had no idea what he could possibly have been in trouble for.

"Be nice," she mouthed, looking rather severe.

Nathan snickered quietly, and escorted her away.

Derek glowered after them, wishing they would have stayed. Pleasant conversation would be difficult to come by for a while. But thankfully, he and Nathan and Colin had arranged to meet tomorrow morning at his home for a quick breakfast before meeting the other two of their friends at Dennison's Stables, Moira's family business.

Kate would not appreciate the company in the morning, which was, of course, all the more reason to do it.

He turned slightly to look at her, dreading what he would see, and sure enough, she looked as if she had suddenly smelled something rather pungent, but her eyes were also shimmering with unshed tears. Surely she was not so offended that she was brought to tears?

No, that was ridiculous. Not even Moira could offend someone to that degree.

Well, perhaps Colin, but he was sensitive.

"Kate?" he asked quietly.

"Katherine," she snapped, blinking rapidly.

He rolled his eyes. She was just fine, tears or no tears. "Whatever. Would you like to retire now?"

"I would like *you* to retire now," she muttered under her breath. Then, louder, she continued, "But I will leave it up to my father to decide when we are finished. After all, it is his wife that was buried today."

Unable to help himself, Derek responded, "Technically, it's only her body. She's not down there at all. Just bones and muscles and flesh."

She looked up at him with a half-disbelieving, half-aghast expression. "Are you completely without mental capacity or do you just manner yourself after a pig?"

"Katherine," her father said softly, as if just now realizing there was a conversation occurring around him.

She looked over at him, and it pleased Derek to no end to see the slight fear of reprimand in her eyes. But her father did not even look at her, so she turned back to Derek again.

"Do not be unfeeling towards him, Whitlock," she hissed. "He may remain here however long he chooses. If you would like to leave, then be my…"

"I would like to retire now," Lord Dartwell announced in his quiet voice.

They both turned to look at him in surprise. "You would?" Katherine asked, looking confused.

He nodded. "What's the use? No one really misses her. They're only here for the food."

Derek had to bite his lips together to keep from grinning or laughing, and quickly clasped his hand behind his back, as he also had the sudden urge to poke Kate in the shoulder.

"Besides," he continued, "I'm hungry myself." And with that, he turned and walked away.

Derek very properly offered his arm to Katherine, who very reluctantly took it. "Have I ever mentioned how much I like your father?" he asked rather brightly.

"Shut up, Whitlock," she muttered.

A satisfied smirk crossed his lips, which faded as he saw that Sir Nigel and Lady Aurelia were crossing over the room to meet them. Of all the people in the world he couldn't bear to converse with, these two were at the top of the list. Sir Nigel never said anything worth hearing, though he seemed to think his whole purpose in life was to grant his wife's every request, and to speak to anybody nearby about whatever he could think about for however long he could think about it.

Aurelia was not much better. Everything should have been her idea, everybody should do things to her satisfaction, every fashionable item would look better on her, which Derek knew for a fact that it would not, as Aurelia more often than not looked as though someone had tried to stuff a pig into a dress. He also had no doubt that people were much wiser than he gave them credit for, as nobody ever asked Lady Aurelia's opinion on anything.

He held his breath as the approached, as if that would make them avoid speaking with him.

He had no such luck.

"Whitlock!" Nigel cried joyously, as if they had not just spent the last two hours in the exact same places, and if those places had not revolved around the funeral for the mother of their wives.

"Nigel," Derek answered with a nod, trying to hurry Katherine along just a little bit more, though she seemed to be moving a touch faster on her own.

"Whitlock, it is *so* good to see you," Aurelia gushed, very nearly hauling her husband along to keep speed with them.

"And you as well, Aurelia. May I say how lovely you are looking this morning?" He bit the inside of his cheek as he felt more than heard Kate groan next to him. He knew better than to say such things, but really, sometimes Aurelia said the most delightfully insipid things that it was worth asking just to hear it.

"Oh, I daresay," Aurelia replied, pretending to blush, and not very convincingly, "this is a *mourning* dress, Whitlock. Nobody looks lovely in a *mourning* dress, not even pretty Katherine. Look at how that black color simply washes her out! Ugh, I cannot even begin to imagine what it must feel like to look so pallid."

Kate stiffened next to him, but still said nothing, which was much to her credit. He didn't even like his wife and he felt his ire rising.

"The service was quite good, didn't you think, Whitlock?" Nigel asked peering around his wife, which took some effort, given that he was so large that peering around anything took effort, and Aurelia was hardly small.

"Oh, but it would have been *so* much better if I had been in charge of things," Aurelia broke in. "Nigel told me there were no flowers, no music, and the minister who spoke? So drab and little and hardly worth looking at. I should have chosen that Mr. Emery who is the clergyman over where we live. He is quite attractive."

"Everything was just as Mother specified," Katherine managed through her teeth. "Down to the minister."

"Yes, well, Mother would not have known if things had been different, would she?" Aurelia said without concern. "After all, we were the ones who had to attend, not she. No, I should have done the whole thing. It would have been quite a triumph."

"Right you are, my love," Nigel said with an adoring look that was so gruesome that Derek actually winced.

"I didn't know that funerals were meant to be triumphs," Derek murmured, mostly for Kate's benefit, and, sure enough, one small corner of her mouth ticked, ever so slightly.

"Oh, Whitlock," Aurelia said on a rather annoying high-pitched giggle. "You are such a silly man. Now, if you do not mind, I should like to speak to my sister for a moment."

Derek shot a look at Kate, who looked back at him with almost panicked eyes. "Oh, but your father has decided to retire, and Katherine must as well," he said quickly, wondering what was possessing him to take his wife's side.

"Oh, Father can wait a few more moments, and so can Katherine," Aurelia said, taking her sister's arm and separating both of them from their husbands. "Just a little sisterly chat for a moment. It will not take long, I promise. You and Nigel can talk while we do so, it has been *so* long since you have been here, I am sure there is much to catch up on."

With an odd sense of reluctance, he let Kate go, fearing very much for the state in which she would be returned to him. Then he turned to the man he was left to converse with, and he wondered who would be in a fouler mood when all this was over.

"Aurelia, I really do not think that now is the time to…"

"Katherine, I do not care what you think now is the time for," Aurelia overrode in a tone so serious, and so very unlike her normal timbre, that Katherine actually did not think of interrupting. "There are more important things at stake at this moment than you can even bear to think of."

Knowing her sister's tendency towards the dramatic, Katherine only offered a small, "Oh?" and waited for the rest to unfurl. When it became apparent that Aurelia expected to hear more of a response than that, she added, "What things?"

"Your reputation, for one. And your husband's for another."

A cold feeling swept through Katherine's frame. She had spent the last five years very carefully managing each and every detail of her life, and quite a bit of Whitlock's, so that there was nothing but respect and admiration surrounding their names. She was not foolish or naïve enough to think that people believed theirs was a romantic marriage; she knew full well that the public was aware of their distaste for each other, but perhaps not to the full extent.

But if somehow, someway, she had made a false step somewhere, and now all of her work would be for naught, that would be a disaster tantamount to the world crumbling beneath her feet.

"What is it?" she whispered in fear.

"I was standing over near Lady Greversham, who looked absolutely appalling, did you see that hat she had on?" Aurelia shuddered, as if the mere recollection gave her chills. "Horrifying. I would never be seen in anything so outré."

"Aurelia," Katherine bit out as patiently as she could, which was not very. She should have known that the severity in her sister's demeanor would not last.

"Oh, yes, yes, sorry, distracted by the horror. As I said, I was standing near Lady Greversham, who was conversing with Miss Milhern and Mrs. Cardew. And the gossip they were spreading, and at our lovely wake service, I know," she said, holding up a hand to ward off Katherine's apparent offense, which was not even forthcoming, "they should not have been so rude, and I had half a mind to turn about and scold them most soundly, but I was in too much of a state to do so. At any rate, they were whispering in the most horrid fashion."

"About what?" She could almost not even bear to ask. What could she possibly have done to draw comment from these women?

Aurelia quirked one brow, and smirked. "Your husband."

"Whitlock?" Katherine asked slowly, her mind feeling very sluggish.

"Unless you have another husband, that would be the one, yes."

Katherine ignored the snide comment for the time being. "No, I mean, what could Whitlock have done? He is so well liked by everybody." Except her, but that was no matter.

Aurelia huffed with impatience. "He *came*, Katherine."

"To the funeral?"

"To *London*. Honestly, Katherine, do you know anything of people?"

"Apparently not. Why is his coming to London cause for comment? He does so every year."

"Yes," Aurelia said, drawing out the s for a long moment, "but he does that at the same *time* every year. He is here suddenly to be with you."

"For our mother's *funeral*," Katherine said, taking on Aurelia's repeated need for emphasis just this once. "It has nothing to do with me, I can assure you."

"Does it not? Everybody knew our mother detested him, and

that Whitlock was only barely polite to her face. Why would a man as powerful as he come down to London purely to attend the funeral of the woman for whom he held the greatest contempt?"

Katherine's mouth worked for a few moments, her mind ever so slowly working through the wasteland that used to be her thoughts. "What are they saying?" she whispered.

"That the marquess has finally come to produce the heir to his dukedom."

The breath was stolen from Katherine's lungs as the words pierced her. She would almost prefer that the gossip be about something awful, some lie that could be refuted by a few well-placed individuals with proper knowledge of fact. Speculation on what her husband was doing in London on short notice was one thing; predicting that he was come to do his husbandly duties and sire an heir was entirely another.

It was positively mortifying. She did not doubt that people wondered when they would start their family, but she hardly expected it to be an item of such great concern and conversation. Did they think that when she and Whitlock finally produced children was any of their business, or that their level of intimacy was something to be speculated? Children would come when they were ready for them, and not a moment before.

And she did want children, very much. But she could hardly bear the children of a man she detested so completely without some serious reflection and preparation before even contemplating taking on such measures. Perhaps it was silly of her, but she wanted to enjoy raising her children. She wanted to be able to ensure that Whitlock would make a good father, and that he thought she would make a good mother.

At the moment, she was not convinced of either.

A duchess never shirks her duty, no matter how distasteful.

She groaned at that particular rule of her mother's, but knew it was true. Her main duty would be to ensure that the duke's line continued on, and the only way to do that was through her husband.

She was only three and twenty, surely they could worry about children later.

But if the members of Society were going to discuss it amongst themselves…

"Katherine!"

She shook herself as she realized that her sister had been attempting to get her attention for some time now. "Yes?"

"Good heavens, where is your mind at the moment?"

Even Katherine did not have a good response for that.

"I asked you how long your husband is going to be in Town."

"I do not know," she admitted, gnawing at her bottom lip. "We have not discussed it yet. I have been a little occupied with…"

"Well, you had better ensure that he remains for some time, or else worse things will be spoken of concerning the two of you, and of you in particular."

"Of me?"

"Darling girl," Aurelia said with a mocking laugh and a roll of her eyes, "I never imagined that you could be so very stupid as far as these things were concerned. Do you honestly believe that people will consider a lack of his attentions to you something to do with him? No, no, they will be very severe with you, Katherine. Whether or not you two decide to become adults and produce some children, which you really should, dear, it's not good for you to be so occupied with business affairs, is beside the point. Appearances are everything. If you cannot manage to keep your husband around for more than a few days…" She trailed off and shrugged. "Have you seen your husband, Katherine? There is not a woman in London or any other part of the country who would hesitate to do what you will not."

"That is nobody's business but my own," Katherine protested in a hissing voice, though her stomach clenched at her sister's words. She knew it was true, and she was quite certain Aurelia herself would have done it. "Whitlock and I are…"

"Taking far too long," Aurelia interrupted with a flapping of her pudgy hand. "I do not very much care or mind such things, Katherine, as you well know. I am discretion herself."

Katherine almost snorted in spite of her turmoil.

"But I can only do so much to stem the tide of rumors," she continued. "I will do what I can, I assure you, but the rest must come from you. Keep Whitlock in town however you can, and then nobody will think that you have been putting him off in favor of furthering your own influence in Society."

"Is that what they think?" Katherine asked, putting a hand to her throat and feeling suddenly very queasy.

Aurelia pretended to look surprised. "Did I say that? Oh, dear, I had not intended to reveal such a horrible falsehood. Well, I suppose it is better that you know than for it to remain a secret any longer." She heaved a sigh and looked back over to their husbands. "Well, I certainly feel much better having discussed this with you, Katherine. My burden is so much lighter now. Shall we return to our husbands?"

Katherine did not, and could not, respond as her sister led her back to where the men stood waiting. She ignored the trite comments on Aurelia's part, as it was in her nature to think herself so kind and generous when she was anything but, and her derogatory comments on the subject of her husband were the most commonplace things in her collection of rants.

She groaned in her mind at what now lay before her, atop everything else. What would Whitlock say? How would she even bring up the subject? Her cheeks were flaming at the mere thought of how that conversation would go, how would it be when she actually had to do it? She could not even bear to look at him as she approached, though the moment her hand was transferred back into his arm, she knew that he was in just as foul a mood as she was. For the very first time in her life, and she highly suspected the last, she was grateful that Nigel had married her sister. One could always count on him to be dull and rambling and maddening in his tepidity.

With the swiftest farewells ever known to mankind, Whitlock nearly shoved her out of the room, himself impossibly quick to follow, and then they waited for their coach to be readied and loaded. It was time to return to their own home. If the rumors Aurelia had spoken of were true, she could not stay away any longer.

Tomorrow, Katherine decided. She would discuss the subject of his staying with Whitlock tomorrow. Today she needed to think.

Chapter Five

$\mathcal{A}$fter what was quite possibly the worst night of sleep she had
ever received, Katherine thought it prudent to give up the charade of
attempting to continue sleeping and go down for some breakfast.
Perhaps having a little something in her stomach would aid her mind.
It needed all the help it could get.

She had run through every scenario she could in her mind,
practiced at least thirty different ways to approach the subject of his
stay, and tried to produce no less than seven very sincere and
innocent expressions, and none of the attempts had been worth very
much. She would have to tell him something at some point, and it
was going to have to be soon. Time was not something she had the
luxury of taking for granted.

At the moment, she found that what she lacked more than time
was courage, which was a strange sensation. There was not much that
actually made her want to cower in a corner somewhere.

Leaving her room in the black mourning gown she detested, and
with her hair pulled tightly back as she always kept it, she made her
way downstairs. She caught sight of the maids and asked, "Jemima,
has Lord Whitlock been down to eat yet?" She fought the urge to
cross her fingers and hoped desperately that he had not.

"Yes, milady," the girl responded with a quick bob. "He and the
Earl of Beverton and Mr. Gerrard are just finishing in the breakfast
room."

Blast. She did not want to see Whitlock *and* two of his friends this morning. Colin Gerrard was one of those people that one either loved or hated, and Katherine was not one that loved him. The Earl of Beverton, on the other hand, was generally a very pleasant man, though Katherine knew that his opinion of her was formed by his association with Whitlock, and therefore, he was somewhere between terrified she would lash out and bite him and disgusted by the very sight of her.

The feeling was mutual. She further did not wish to see the earl this morning, for his wife had called every day since *she* had arrived, and some days twice, and had left a card every time. At this rate, she would have a stack of the countess's cards that was larger than her own.

But now she had to face that woman's husband as well as her own, with the addition of a loon at that.

She would merely have to ask if Whitlock would speak with her privately, that is all. Surely he would grant his wife that request.

With a final release of breath, she pushed open the door and found the three of them laughing uproariously about something, and she knew instantly that there would have been no preparation she could have made that would have given her more ease.

It took them all a moment to notice her approach, but once they did, her husband stood hastily, and was quickly followed by the other two. Well, at least they had manners. For the moment.

"Good morning, Kate!" Derek crowed aloud. His friends bowed politely, but he refrained, no doubt hoping to garner a response.

He did. She stiffened and fixed her cold, dark eyes upon him. "I prefer Katherine."

"Well, I prefer Kate," he stated as he and his friends sat back down. Colin looked excited about the potential fight that was brewing. Beverton, on the other hand, seemed remarkably ill at ease.

"It is not your name," Katherine said through clenched teeth as her hands tightly balled into fists.

He shrugged and replaced his serviette into his lap as he reached for another biscuit. "It's not your choice. I will call you what I want to call you and you will just have to deal with that."

"I will not answer." Her voice was starting to grow shrill, and

Katherine knew she was reaching a breaking point. It galled her that he knew how to taunt her so very well.

He offered her one more careless shrug. "Then I will continue to call you Kate and worse until you do."

A sound so high she nearly could not hear it escaped her. "Insufferable man!" she screeched.

"Impossible woman!" he mimicked near perfectly with a smirk.

"Aren't mornings with Derek and Katherine the best?" Colin sighed to Beverton.

Katherine gathered up what control she had remaining, and said, "Might I have a word with you in private, Whitlock?"

He grinned rather impishly. "Going to scold me, are you, Kate?"

"Katherine."

"Whatever. Chamber pot, remember."

"Yes, I remember," she snapped. Then she took a steadying breath. "I need to speak with you. Alone."

"That's not likely," he said as he tossed a grin to his friends, which Colin returned and Beverton did not. "I'd like to keep my head firmly attached to my body and all of my limbs too, if I can help it."

"So little confidence in your own strength?" she retorted before she could stop herself. *A duchess never reacts in haste or retaliation*, came the scolding voice of her mother in her head.

That was one of her least favorite rules. Katherine was always reacting in haste and retaliation where her husband was concerned. It was the only way to behave around him.

"Bravo, Kate," Whitlock said with a small amount of applause. "That was a brilliant retort. But as I was going to say, I will not be removing myself from this sumptuous breakfast, nor will I ask my friends to. Therefore, if you wish to speak to me you will either have to wait until I am finished or say it here in front of these two gentlemen."

"Derek, I can…" Lord Beverton began, but he was silenced with a glare, and then chanced a look at Katherine, who was surprised by his actions. Perhaps having a wife had changed him.

Katherine looked back to her husband, who obviously had no idea what she needed to speak to him about. If he did, there was no way he would have even suggested that she do this here and now in front of his friends. But if that was what Whitlock wanted, then that was what Whitlock was going to get.

"Very well," she said slowly, knowing that she should not, but would, enjoy every single moment of his discomfort, in spite of her own mortification, "then I will tell you now, with your friends present."

A quick lifting of his brows was all the satisfaction Katherine needed as Whitlock's always so carefully composed features shifted to complete surprise. Oh, this would be sweet indeed.

"I need you to stay in London for at least another two weeks," she told him, folding her hands in front of her.

He recovered his surprise and snorted. "Whatever for? I've already been here three days, which is entirely too long as it is."

She offered a very small smile, which made his eyes widen, just a touch, with worry. "I need you to stay because people think you have come into town to get me with child."

Colin choked on his drink instantly, Beverton closed his eyes and put a hand to his forehead, and her husband merely sat there stunned, though his face went shockingly devoid of color. "How do you...?" he started to say in a very weak, very hoarse voice.

"My sister overheard some of the ladies yesterday," Katherine said, enjoying this far too much to even feel mortified any longer. "You know Aurelia, she never lies about gossip."

His harsh swallowing told her that he did know that. After a moment, he said, "So I need to stay because..."

"Because otherwise people will think me incapable of sustaining your attention or they will think you unable or unwilling to further your bloodlines," she finished, waiting for his response.

He closed his eyes and shook his head for a moment, and then he looked back at her. "How long, did you say?"

"Two weeks," she repeated, feeling victory nigh at hand. "And you would not have to come later in the year, if you wished."

"It's a trick," Colin muttered aloud, not caring that she could hear him. "It's all a trick, Derek, don't listen..."

"Shut up, Colin," the other two men said at the same time. Then

Beverton continued, "Derek, Moira and I will stay as long as you want. She's enjoying herself very much."

Her husband nodded, then looked back to her. "Very well. I will stay another two weeks from today. Maybe that will quiet the rumors for some time."

But not forever.

The unsaid words hung in the air, and Katherine and Whitlock held each other's gaze, each sensing what the other was thinking at the moment. The time would have to come soon.

Oblivious to everything, Colin snorted. "Well, I, for one, am not staying," he announced.

"Who asked you to?" Katherine snapped as she flicked her eyes to him.

That earned her a grin from Beverton, who gave her the barest hint of a nod in approval. Perhaps the earl would grow on her with time.

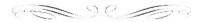

Derek ignored them all as his mind raced. He spent his whole life held to a high standard of behavior, and had been proud of the fact that his reputation was spotless and without comment, save for his unhappy marriage, which was not so surprising as many other people had them as well. But now…

He looked back to Kate. He would only think of her as Kate now, it was too much fun. She was watching him carefully, and for once, her eyes on him did not make him want to cringe.

He should have met with her in private.

"I think we should talk in private," he told her, his voice hoarse still.

"What?" Colin gasped in horror. "Why?"

"Colin, if you want to be welcome in anybody's house any further, you need to stop talking," Nathan ordered firmly. "In fact, I think we have stayed long enough. Let's leave some breakfast for Lady Whitlock, and Derek, we will meet you at the stables."

Derek nodded, but Kate shook her head. "Thank you, Lord

Beverton, but it is not necessary. I have quite finished with what I have to say, and I think my husband needs the distraction."

Derek looked at her in confusion. Was she actually being nice to him?

She looked far too smug, and he felt his heart resume normal pacing. No, she was just being Katherine the Terror, everything on her terms, in her way. For all he knew, she had started the rumors herself just to spite him. "Well, I was going to oblige you," he sneered at her, feeling rather angered by her cavalier attitude towards the whole situation, "but if you would rather I go, then absolutely, I will do so."

"I do want you gone," she told him, her eyes flashing, but at least the smugness had vanished. "I never wanted you here in the first place."

"Then you shouldn't have sent for me!" Derek yelled, knowing full well that he was not nearly as composed as he preferred to be in her presence, but not particularly caring at the moment. How dare the Society of London think they could gossip about what did or did not go on within his bedchamber? He had quite enough to be going on with.

"We have already been over this!" she returned, her cheeks coloring with indignation. "I never meant for you to come!"

"Then why the hell did you even write, Kate?" he bellowed, shooting to his feet, upending his breakfast plate all over Colin, who squawked faintly in protest.

"Some of us," she retorted loudly, "maintain an air of sophistication and respectability and decorum regardless of how distasteful the subject may be."

"Oh, come off it, Kate!" Derek said in disgust. "Sophistication and decorum? Nobody would have known if you hadn't told me about the great tragedy of your mother's death. You had no cause to even inform me, and order me here I might add, if you didn't want me. Lord knows I wouldn't have come on my own for that hag, believe me."

"You go too far," Katherine whispered as her eyes clouded with a sheen of tears, but Derek was beyond caring.

"Forgive me for that," he said sarcastically with a dramatic bow to her, "since you have *always* been so kind and deserving of considerate treatment, and never say things beyond the bounds of respectability. What a horrible example I will be for our children."

"If we ever have any," she spat, even as her face paled at his words. "At the moment, I do not know if I would rather bring anything with your bloodlines into this world or spend an eternity being the brunt of every joke and gossip in London."

"Well, you don't see me carting you off to bed, now do you?" he retorted as he headed towards the door. "The world has enough harpies in it without your help."

"How dare you!" she screeched, rooted in place as she was, watching him go, and his friends following, both of them entirely silent.

"Oh, I dare whenever, however, and with whomever I please, Kate," Derek said with one last look at her, his tone low and dangerous, "and I do not need to refer to you or to any other person on this earth to do so." He turned away, and muttered, "Bloody whore," under his breath to his friends, neither of whom found it amusing.

"Derek," Nathan hissed as he took his hat and gloves from the maid, "that's hardly called for. What if she heard you?"

"Then may I joyfully rot in hell," he barked as he brushed passed them both and headed for Dennison's stables, walking briskly and recklessly, not caring if either of them followed behind.

"Well, it *is* a beautiful animal, but I just don't think…"

"What did you *do*, Derek?"

All of the men silenced at once and froze at the terrifying cry of one Moira Hammond, Countess of Beverton. Slowly, they all turned to face the approaching threat, who was marching very purposefully towards them, her expression murderous.

"Moira?" Nathan asked tentatively, but she silenced him with a look.

"Darling, I will speak with you in a moment. Currently, I only have business with Derek." She flicked her gaze to him, and the other men around Derek each took a large step away from him, as if to protect themselves from the fire in her eyes.

"Hello, Moira," Derek offered with a half-smile, his voice steady, even as his knees trembled just a touch.

"What. Did you. Do." There was no hint of a question in her voice, and Derek could not help but swallow involuntarily.

"When?"

"Just now."

His brow furrowed. "I've been here, Moira. We came over early to check on your stables and the horses."

"Before."

"Before?" He had a nagging sense about what she was trying to get at, but he would feign ignorance as long as he could. Much as he liked, respected, and, yes, feared Moira, he was not about to discuss his wife with her.

"Would you like me to elaborate and refresh your memory, since you have obviously lost the ability to recall your actions this morning?" Moira asked, folding her arms, her blue eyes lancing into his green ones.

"Please."

"Derek," Nathan warned softly, looking at his wife with anxiety, but Derek ignored him.

Moira snapped her brows together. "I went over to your house just now, as I have every morning and afternoon, to call upon your wife and ask after her. I, unlike so many others, present company included, feel sorry for her and for what she must be going through." Her tone was harsh and scolding, and Derek rather imagined this was what her children would experience when they came along and misbehaved. She would be a very good disciplinarian. "When I was told, yet again, that she would not see anyone as she was still mourning, I asked if the butler thought there was anything I could do to lessen her grief. He confided to me that he did not know, as Lady Whitlock had been crying in her room since breakfast, and nobody had seen her since."

A small, guilty feeling started in Derek's chest and with each beat of his heart, it stretched further and further outwards until it encompassed just about every part of him. "Well," he said uneasily, "perhaps she simply wanted some peace and quiet and to not be disturbed. She is in mourning, after all."

"That is why she stays at home, Derek," Moira said with a slow shake of her head, her eyes never leaving his. "Why is she staying in her room, Derek?"

"I don't know," he lied, trying to appear confused.

Moira flicked her gaze to Colin first, who flushed a bit and looked away, then to her husband, who steadily met her gaze, but it was clear he was uneasy. For a long moment, she continued to stare at Nathan, and he at her, as if they were communicating silently. Then Moira looked back to Derek. "I think you had better tell me, Derek."

"I don't think it is your business, Moira," he said tartly, though without malice.

She snorted. "Nor is it Colin's or Nathan's, and yet they know all. And you had better tell me yourself, or I will have Nathan tell me later."

Derek's eyes widened. "He wouldn't…"

"Oh, he would," Moira interrupted with a smile that was not kind. "He doesn't approve of whatever it was, and even if that were not the case, I have ways of making him talk that I cannot employ with you."

Fighting the impulse to look to Nathan for confirmation, Derek swallowed and gave in with a nod. He very briefly told her what had transpired that morning, and, along with the occasional add-in from Colin, who possessed a keen memory for exact words, the story was told without variation.

When he had finished, it seemed that everybody stood yet further away from him. He glanced around and found Duncan and Geoff, who had not been privy to the details looking at him in shock. Colin and Nathan had no expression at all.

"Well," Moira said finally, as she glanced to Nathan, who nodded his affirmation of the details, "that was enlightening."

"Was it?" Derek could not help but asking.

"Yes. Now I understand why Katherine cannot stand you."

Though the group had been silent before, the air became quieter still at her words, and nothing in all of creation moved.

"I beg your pardon?" Derek asked softly, his voice taking on that dangerous tone that seemed its habit of late.

"Oh, don't you think you can put on airs with me," Moira said with a shake of her head, her eyes bright. "I do not care how rich you are, how important you think you are, or that you have any title at all, let alone a high ranking one. If I could slap you right now, I would do so. But I don't think I could stop with just one, and I am really not in the mood to be hauled off by my husband for beating the sense out of you in front of all your friends."

A number of his friends choked back a laugh, but they were all stifled rather quickly.

Derek put his tongue over his teeth for a moment, and focused on breathing. "What gives you such righteous indignation, Moira?"

"The notion that you would treat Katherine in that way, that you think so little of her and her situation to attack her in such a way. I know I don't know her," she said as she raised a hand to the protests that she somehow knew were rising in him, "but did you even think what it meant for her to come and face you after hearing those words?"

Derek suddenly felt his throat tighten, and he could not have spoken should he have wished to.

"Knowing how the two of you feel about each other," Moira continued, "I can only imagine how it must have felt for a woman who is as proud as she is to come and tell you that she needed you to stay. Did she really say that it was about your reputation?"

He nodded slowly, his mind working as though through mud.

A smile flickered across her lips. "I doubt she really thought that. Everybody knows how Society feels about you. It wasn't about you at all, or at least, very little. She told you it would involve you because she couldn't admit that she would be the only one affected, and considering the arrangement you have, she would be left here all alone to deal with the shame and the gossip and the rumors."

Derek opened his mouth, but Moira went on without giving him opportunity to answer.

"She just lost her mother, Derek. Her *mother*. Yes, she was, by all accounts, a horrible woman, and nobody else misses her, but did you ever consider that Katherine might? I don't care if she is the spawn of Hades, she deserves a little understanding from her *husband*, of all people."

"Moira," Nathan said softly as he watched Derek.

"I'm almost finished," she assured him, still looking at Derek as well. "I'm not saying that she is blameless, Derek. But the fact remains that at this moment, your wife, whom you consider a tyrant and a cold-hearted witch, is upstairs in her room, refusing everything and everyone. I am asking you to put aside your need to spite her just for a while. Show her that there is a man with a heart inside her husband."

Derek could not move, could not breathe. He had never felt more ashamed of himself in his life. While he knew perfectly well that he was exactly the same height and weight and stature that he had been only moments before, at the moment he felt about three feet tall and barely the weight of a blade of grass. She could have knocked him over with a whisper.

He felt Moira's hand on his arm and found himself looking into those eyes of hers again. "I wouldn't say these things if I didn't like you, Derek," she said with a smile. "You know that, right?"

He nodded almost mechanically, but he did know it, and he liked Moira in return. He could not say it at the moment, though his throat worked as if it wanted to anyway.

"But don't think I won't smack you later," she said, her grin turning impish. "A good whack on the back of the head can do wonders for a man." She looked around at the lot of them, then winked at her husband, who smiled broadly. Then she turned on her heel and left without looking back.

For the longest time, nobody said a word. Then, because he could not stand silence, Colin said, "I don't know that I will ever understand women, nor wives in particular, but I think that Moira might be the most terrifying woman I have ever met, including Katherine."

"And how I love her," Nathan sighed proudly as he watched his wife stride away.

"Shut up, Nate," his friends replied in unison as they went back to the horses.

Derek joined them, but he knew that Moira's words would haunt him for quite some time. He vowed silently to himself that he would try harder to attempt to see beyond Kate's prickly shell.

But he couldn't deny that he was more than a little nervous of what would happen if he did not fight back when Kate tossed her harpoons at him.

With a tender rub to the back of his head, as if he could feel the threatened slap from Moira, he pushed the thoughts of his wife out for the time being.

They would come back later, as would the guilt.

If it ever left at all.

Chapter Six

$\mathcal{K}$atherine very studiously avoided contact with anybody after her appalling behavior with Whitlock. She shut herself up in her room for the remainder of the day, went to sleep rather early, and woke rather late the next morning.

She slowly made her way downstairs, desperate to avoid her husband at the moment. She could not bear the awkwardness that would stem from yesterday's words. He had been cruel and had hurt her deeply, but she had not been kind either. If she had been more composed, as a duchess always should be, then he would not have reacted so strongly.

A duchess has no regrets; she never has cause for them.

Well, it was a good thing that Katherine was not a duchess yet, for she had quite a few regrets, and could not begin to imagine how many of those would have to improve before she ever became one.

"Good morning, ma'am," the butler, Harville, said with a fond grin. Of all the servants in the household, he was one that seemed to take special care where Katherine was concerned. Most days, his smile was the only one she received.

"Good morning, Harville," she replied with a smile.

"A bit late getting the day started, are we?" he asked, flirting with the line of propriety for a servant, but Katherine always allowed him a bit of leeway.

"A bit, I am afraid," she admitted. "It has been a rather exhausting few days."

He nodded soberly. "That it has, ma'am. Is there anything I can do for your ladyship this morning?"

"I am quite hungry, but I imagine that the marquess already had breakfast cleared," she said with regret as her stomach growled.

Harville shook his head slowly. "His lordship was up and about quite early, ma'am, and did not eat. He did leave instructions that we were to hold breakfast for you, if you should wish it."

"He did?" Katherine asked in surprise as she rocked back on her heels a little.

Harville nodded with an odd twinkle in his eye. "Yes, ma'am. Looked rather troubled about something, if I may be so bold."

"I daresay he was," Katherine murmured, her eyes far away. Whitlock probably had many things on his mind, now that he had to stay in town for his reputation. And yet, he had taken the time to ensure that she would have a decent meal this morning, though he would take none.

Could that have been a sort of apology, or was he simply taking control of the household now that he was here to do so? It was impossible to say, but she would like to think that he was not as unfeeling as he had seemed the day before.

"When did the marquess return yesterday?" she asked Harville, who was still watching her. "I did not hear him."

"He came in just after dark, my lady. Did not take dinner either, as it were. He asked after you, but then he spent the remainder of the evening in his study." Harville gave an uncharacteristic shrug. "I am afraid I cannot say much more than that."

Katherine considered his admission carefully, but opted to not assume anything on the part of her husband. It had been a very trying day for both of them, and one could hardly expect him to be in good spirits after what she had told him.

Perhaps they could simply avoid each other for the remainder of his stay, and then no more fights would ensue.

"Shall I call for breakfast for you, ma'am?" Harville asked, bringing her out of her thoughts.

She shook herself and smiled. "Yes, please, Harville. That would be lovely, thank you."

He nodded and moved away, then turned back. "Oh, and Lady Beverton called for you yesterday afternoon, and already this morning."

"Again?" Katherine asked before she could stop herself.

Harville nodded once more. "Yes, my lady. I am afraid she is very determined."

"So it seems." Katherine sighed and closed her eyes for a moment. The countess would not give up, it seemed. And she could not, in good conscience, put her off forever.

A duchess is always gracious, particularly with nobility.

Her mother's words in her head made up her mind for her. "Harville, would you please have a note sent over to Lady Beverton and inquire if she might come for tea this afternoon?"

Harville's bushy brows shot up, but he nodded. "Yes, of course, my lady." He bowed and moved away, leaving Katherine alone on the stairs.

She groaned just a touch and made her way to the breakfast room. The sooner the headache of this meeting was over and done with, the sooner she could get back to her solitude and peace of mind.

Instead of waiting for what was actually considered by the general public as tea time, Katherine was stunned to find that the countess of Beverton was waiting for her in the drawing room no more than two hours after she had finished breakfast.

Well, what must be done might as well be done soon.

Releasing a long breath, and steeling herself for what was destined to be the longest visit of her known life, Katherine pushed open the door to the room and fixed a polite, albeit not very friendly, smile on her face.

Before she could say a single word of greeting, Lady Beverton was speaking.

"My dear Katherine, it is so good to see you!" she said as she came over and took her hands.

Her dear Katherine? They had met once, how could she be her dear anything, and why was she calling her Katherine without invitation to? It went against every rule of formality. Even so, she was determined to be civil. "Thank you, Lady Beverton. I trust you are well?" she asked as she gestured towards the seats.

"Very, I thank you," Lady Beverton replied as she sat down and began to pour tea for them both. "I confess, I did not think you were *ever* going to send for me."

"It would be impolite not to, given your… rather extraordinary amount of requests." That was a polite way to say it, Katherine considered with a mental nod.

With a light shrug, she handed Katherine a cup of tea. "Not so extraordinary at all. I merely wish to be of use."

"Lady Beverton…"

"Moira, please. I am still getting used to this whole Lady Beverton business," she said with a merry laugh.

Katherine restrained a sigh, but relented. "Moira, you called every day. Multiple times."

"Yes, I did."

"Why? What are you trying to do?"

Moira gave her an odd look. "I should think that is obvious. I mean to be friends with you."

Katherine choked on the tea she had just been starting to sip, and somehow, between coughs, managed to force out, "You do?"

"Of course," Moira said with a smile, as if it were the most obvious thing in the world. "Our husbands are friends, and so should we be."

"I… do not have much to do with my husband," Katherine answered as she shook her head, nearly recovered from her surprise.

"Yes, so I have heard." Moira frowned with displeasure. "I don't approve, but it is not my place."

It certainly was not, Katherine thought to herself, wondering when this visit would be over. The woman was maddening and presumptuous and had absolutely no idea of anything to do with Katherine. *A duchess has infinite patience, as not everyone is as refined or as sensible as she is.* Well, she thought with a mental snort, she would need infinite patience with Moira. She carefully sipped her tea again, wishing she knew a polite way to get the woman to leave.

"If Derek weren't such a pickled salmon, you two might get somewhere."

For the second time in not as many minutes, Katherine choked on her tea, but not so badly as before. She carefully set it down on the saucer and set both back to the table, then turned to face Moira fully. "I beg your pardon?"

"Oh, Derek," Moira said with a wave of her hand. "He is just so... I'm not even sure there is a word for what he is. But I don't like it."

Choosing her words carefully, Katherine said, "Most people think I am the one to blame for the way we are."

Moira sniffed as she sipped her tea, then shook her head as she swallowed. "Yes, I know that, too, but there are two people in a marriage, not one, and people had best remember that." Her expression looked so deadly that Katherine almost felt sorry for everyone Moira was currently thinking of.

"They have good reason to," she admitted softly, her fingers absently picking at her dress.

"Well, then we had best set about to fix that, hadn't we?" Moira said as she reached over and took Katherine's hand in her own.

"Moira..."

"Katherine, I know that you have an extremely tough exterior, and it does you credit. But going about your life determined to exclude everyone is only going to come back to bite you in your backside."

Katherine almost hiccupped with the bluntness of her words. Her mind raced as she tried to think of any duchess rules that applied to that, but she could not find any.

"But we will talk about you later," Moira said as she sat back. "I want to discuss Derek. He is not a very good husband, is he?"

"He does what is expected." Katherine lifted one shoulder lightly, finding herself remarkably at ease. Perhaps Moira was not so bad after all.

"And that says much about him, doesn't it?" Moira commented dryly, bringing Katherine back to topic. "I have been married for a month now, and we have a lark of a time. But of course, we were friends before we fell in love. Even so, if Nathan did only what was expected of him, I would never have married him, you can be certain of that."

"I did not choose to marry Whitlock," Katherine said bluntly, but without spite. What would be the point of it? She had accepted her fate when she was a child, and wishing for anything else would have been a waste of energy and mental capacity, and would serve no purpose.

A sad smile graced Moira's lips, albeit briefly. "No, of course not, but nor did he choose you. Fact of the matter is, dear Katherine, you two are married and you might want to start acting like it before one of you kills the other. Or before I kill Derek," she added as an afterthought.

Katherine laughed out loud, which surprised her. "Why kill him?"

Moira grinned at her laughter, but her eyes were serious. "Because he does not treat you like a wife ought to be treated. I don't accept such things, especially not from my friends and to my friends."

Now it was Katherine who gave a look. "He does not even like me, Moira."

"Do you like him?" she asked, her pale blue eyes fixed intently on her.

She shrugged, even under the power of Moira's gaze. "Not really."

"Then we ought to change that," Moira replied matter-of-factly. "I like Derek, in spite of his many flaws, and I do mean many, and I like you."

Katherine laughed without mirth. "How can you like me? Pardon me for saying so, but you don't even know me."

"No, but I am determine to like you and there is nothing you can do about it. I feel quite certain that I will like you very much indeed."

Katherine was unaccountably choked up by that admission. How could Moira know that at all when all she knew of Katherine was what Derek had told her? That could not have been flattering.

And yet, as she looked at Moira, she could tell that she was sincere, and it moved her beyond words. When she could manage to, she smiled. "I would like that, Moira," she said softly. "I would like to be your friend. I do not have many. None that come to mind, actually."

Moira set her tea aside, and threw her arms around Katheı and held her close. "Now you have one," she whispered with fierc determination.

Katherine squeezed her eyes shut against the sudden desire to cry on Moira's shoulder, willing the tears back. She could not completely stem them, but she could hold them off until later.

With a small sigh she sat back, and offered Moira a truly genuine smile, even as she sniffled and brushed at her eyes. "Well, what are friends supposed to talk about?" she asked with a laugh, feeling considerably lighter than she had in days... years, in fact.

Moira's eyes twinkled. "All sorts of things, I expect. But the first thing I want to discuss are these tarts! Where in the world did you find them? I would get so fat eating this with every tea!"

The two spent the next hour and a half giggling like school girls over the most ridiculous things, and by the end of the visit, Katherine could quite honestly say that she, at last, had a true friend.

That alone was enough to bring tears to her eyes.

There could be no avoiding it now.

Derek groaned as he entered the house, knowing that tonight Kate would still be awake. He had been able to avoid his impending confrontation last night, as she had been to bed early. Tonight, however, that would not be the case. He was back earlier than expected, and he quite honestly had nowhere else that he could go.

He trudged up the stairs, his mind still grumbling about the fact that he had to apologize to his wife for something that they were both to blame for. She was not in any hurry to apologize to him, so why should he do so first?

He was quick to shove those thoughts out of his mind, as the image of Moira stomping towards him was enough to remind him just how guilty he really did feel.

Reaching the door to Kate's bedchamber, he paused, needing to collect his thoughts.

Then he heard something he thought he would never, in his entire life, hear. Within Kate's room, someone was crying.

His brow furrowed in confusion. He had not expected this at all. He rapped on her door softly. "Kate?" he called.

"Don't...call me Kate," came the would-be strong retort from within, still choked with tears and sniffles.

"Kate, are you all right?" he asked carefully as he listened more closely.

"I am fine," she insisted harshly.

He didn't believe that for a moment, and pushed open the door. "Kate?" he called softly as he entered. She was sitting on her bed, facing the window, her back to him, but she wiped at her face insistently.

"Don't call me Kate! And don't... do not come in."

"Too late, I am coming in," he said as he closed the door behind him. "I'm calling you Kate and I'm coming in."

She turned her tear-streaked face and glared at him. "Can you never be serious?"

He lifted his hands, then dropped them uselessly at his side, feeling more than a little lost in the face of her tears. "You're right. I'm sorry."

She turned away from him. "What do you want, Whitlock?"

"I came to apologize for my behavior yesterday," he said as he approached the bed cautiously. "It was inexcusable and rude and in appallingly bad taste, least of all because we had company. I should have met with you in private and perhaps we could have discussed things calmly, but considering our past, I doubt it."

Still not facing him, she hiccuped and put a hand to her mouth, but nodded, which he took to be an acceptance of his words.

He sighed and took a seat in a chair across from her bed. "Kate, is there anything I can do for you? Anything at all?"

She turned and looked at him, her expression full of confusion and suspicion. "Why?"

"Because, Kate, I am your husband, and I think I should start acting like it," he said firmly, but he paired it with a kind smile. He was amazed he could even manage one.

She looked uncertain, and he thought she would put him off, then his duty would be complete and he could tell Moira he had trie But then, in a small voice, she said, "Do you… do you think we coulc just talk for a moment?"

Surprised beyond measure, he shrugged. "Of course, if that is what you want. Did Moira come to see you again today?"

She sniffled and nodded. "Yes. I invited her for tea. I thought it best, as she had called so many times."

Derek almost swore, thinking that must surely be the reason for her distress after all, and sighed heavily. "I'm sorry about her. She is absolutely impossible to deal with."

"I like her," Kate said bluntly, sniffling one last time.

His brows nearly shot through the roof. "You do? I thought she would drive you to distraction."

Kate smiled a bit. "She did at first, but you cannot help but like her, can you?"

"No, I suppose not," he admitted with a chuckle.

"She says she is going to kill you."

"Yes, she told me that, too."

Kate tilted her head to one side, and looked confused still. "She says she is determined to like me," she said slowly. "She wants to be my friend."

"I thought she might," he muttered dryly, but still smiling.

"Do you… do you think we could ever… be friends, Derek?" she asked in a timid, choked voice, forgoing all formality she had ever employed by addressing him by his given name, which, oddly enough, made him happy.

Her voice was so small, so full of tears, and it strangely hurt Derek to hear it. If she had asked him only yesterday, he would have laughed in her face. But then, she would never have asked yesterday. "I think we could, Kate. If you were not so impossible…"

"I beg your pardon?" she protested.

"…and I were not so stubborn…"

"That's better."

"…then yes, I think it's possible that we could," he said with a nod, and much to his surprise, he actually meant it. This Kate before him, the lonely, innocent Kate who was not constantly aggravating him, who did not control every aspect of his life without consulting him, who did not make him want to tear his hair out or climb walls or spit fire like a dragon, she would be someone he could gladly associate with. If this was who he married, he could see things growing much brighter in the future. If it was the other, then he was doomed.

"I would like to try," she said simply, sitting up a little taller.

"Very well, then, we shall try." He stood from his chair and bowed, then stuck his hand out towards her. "Hello, my name is Derek, Lord Whitlock."

She gave him a confused, slightly amused look and took his hand. "Hello, my name is Katherine, Lady Whitlock."

He gasped in mock surprise. "We share a title? How extraordinary!"

She quirked a brow and shook her head. "Are you always this droll, my lord?"

He shrugged. "Rarely. I'm usually quite a bore." He paused at her surprised giggle, and fought a smile. "I wonder, Kate, if I may ask you to join me for breakfast tomorrow morning. I should like to make sure that my new friend has pleasant table manners, as I find bad table manners a sign of deplorable willpower and I could never be friends with somebody who uses the wrong fork."

"No, I should say not. What a travesty," Kate said seriously, surprising him with her quick reply, but then, he knew she was witty. Sharp, but witty. "I would be happy to join you for breakfast. What time?"

He pretended to consider it for a moment, then tilted his head. "Would eight o'clock be too early?"

"No, indeed, for I happen to be an early riser."

"As am I," Derek said, a little curious now.

"Eight o'clock at breakfast, then." Kate smiled, giving him a nod.

Derek snapped out of his thoughts and bowed once more. "Very good. I shall see you then, Kate." He smiled at her, then left the room and shut the door quietly behind him.

His curiosity was certainly piqued as he made his way to his o chambers.

What else could he have in common with his wife?

Chapter Seven

$\mathcal{A}$t eight o'clock sharp, Katherine hesitated outside her own breakfast room, feeling absolutely ridiculous in doing so, but she could not be certain which husband of hers she would be greeting this morning. If it was the man she had arranged this meeting with last night, it would be amusing. If it was the husband she was used to, it could be a disaster.

Still, she was willing to attempt cordiality and friendship, if he was. She had meant what she had said the night before; she did want to try. Moira's words to her had penetrated some long-forgotten piece of her, and she realized that she had been lonely for a rather long time. She had been so focused and driven on doing her duty that she had shut the entire world out.

Now she wanted something else, something that once seemed far out of reach.

The door to the breakfast room opened, and there stood Derek, who was very properly dressed for breakfast, she was pleased to note. He bowed to her, the barest hint of a smile on his face, even as his green eyes danced.

"Good morning, Kate," he said, offering her his arm in such a proper fashion that it almost seemed mocking.

She fought a smile and took the proffered arm. "Good morning."

"I trust you slept well?"

She nodded. "Very well, thank you. You?"

"Like the dead." He winced as he pulled the chair out for her.
"I'm sorry, that was…"

"Just a phrase," Katherine said with a wave of her hand. "You
need not think everything regarding death or funerals is insensitive.
I'll not take offense."

"Really?" he asked in surprise, dropping his overly proper act.

"*A duchess never takes offense where no offense is meant,*" she quoted
with a smile.

He quirked a half smile and looked at her in slight confusion as
he moved to the opposite end of the table. "What's that from?"

"Mother's rules for proper duchess etiquette," she responded,
feeling a little embarrassed. She had never told anybody about the
rules that had been governing her entire life, nor where they had come
from. It hardly seemed appropriate to do so.

Derek's brows snapped together and, for a moment, he looked
a trifle upset. "Did she have many of these rules?"

"Hundreds," Katherine replied softly, wishing he would pick a
new topic.

"Hmm," he murmured softly, but said nothing further, still
looking unhappy. But then the food was brought in and his
expression cleared.

"So," Katherine asked as she started on her meal, "what have
you done with yourself of late?" She almost winced at the
awkwardness of that statement. She had never been very good at
small talk. She was far better at fighting with her husband than she
was at trivial conversation with him.

He quirked a brow in amusement. "Of late? Or since our
wedding?"

Relief washed over her. "Both, I suppose." She offered him a
tiny, apologetic smile. "I am afraid that I really do not know you all
that well, even after all this time."

He nodded, still amused. "Sad, isn't it? But I suppose now is as
good a time as any to start."

And so they began to talk of themselves, very simply, without
detail or embellishment. Katherine learned that her husband might
not have been quite so lazy as she had previously thought, as he had

spent the last few months helping Beverton with his estate. When asked he about her, she was embarrassed at not having much to tell him. Since their marriage, she had been here, working and managing and dictating the affairs of their estates. That was all she ever did.

He looked ready to comment on that when Harville came in with a letter and handed it to him. He took it with confusion, looked at the seal, and then frowned.

"Urgent, did you say?" he asked, not looking up at Harville.

"Yes, sir. That is what I was told."

He muttered something under his breath, but nodded. He looked up at Katherine with regret in his eyes. "I apologize, Kate, but I have to read this. Will you excuse me?"

"Of course," she said with some surprise. She had not expected him to be polite; she assumed he would simply leave. The fact that he bothered to ask made her question if perhaps he was not quite the imbecilic animal she had thought she had spent the last five years married to.

Perhaps.

He stood back from the table and walked past her, then stopped and took a few steps back so that he was in front of her again. "This was nice. I think we should eat together more often. What do you think?"

She knew she looked as surprised as she felt, but she managed to say, "I think that is a very good idea."

He smiled. "No need to sound so surprised, I do have them occasionally, Kate."

He walked out, but not before she called, "It's Katherine."

"Chamber pots," he responded in kind, and for once, it made her smile.

But only a little.

Derek groaned and sat back in his chair, rubbing his forehead, hating his father at the moment.

The note he had received from the duke during breakfast was

even more upsetting than Derek had imagined it would be, and he had a very vivid and accurate imagination where his father was concerned.

Of course, it had to do with David.

And, of course, the duke was counting on Derek to fix things.

It was getting to be ridiculous. David was no more reckless or irresponsible than any other gentleman of his age and station, and he was a good deal more sensible. In fact, David was one of the most intelligent people that Derek had ever met, but intelligence and normalcy was not something that mattered to their father. He only wanted them to appear far superior to everyone else.

He sat forward again and picked up the note, trying to decipher just what his father wanted him to do, in between the parts about fearing for the future and the rather dramatic imagery of washing his hands of the waste of space his son was becoming.

Even then, it was not very clear.

Against wisdom and habit, he dropped his head to his desk and banged it a few times, hoping it would either give him a new idea to relieve the situation, or kill him instantly so that he would not have to do anything about it at all.

A soft knocking at his study door brought his head up. In all of his haste to have done with whatever his father wanted him to do, he had neglected to close his door entirely. Confused as to who would be seeking entrance, he sat up taller, his head starting to throb from impact most painfully. "Come in."

As if the multitude of surprises of late could have gotten any more shocking, Kate entered, looking oddly timid. "May I?"

Gathering himself and hopefully hiding his shock much better than he thought he was, he nodded and stood. "Of course, Kate."

"I do not mean to intrude upon your privacy," she said slowly as she took a seat.

"I wish you would," he replied as he sat back down. "My privacy is rather annoying me at the moment."

She looked at the note on his desk rather pointedly. "Not good news?"

He glanced at it as well. "Not at all. It's from my father, and..."

He trailed off, hesitating. One day of attempted friendship with his wife was not enough to entitle her to know the details of their private lives. He could not even be sure that he liked this woman, let alone if he trusted her.

"I do not want to pry," she said, guessing his thoughts rather adeptly. "I just… I heard you banging on the desk, and I wondered if I might be able to help."

"With the injuring?" he snapped, more as a reflex than anything else. "I manage to do quite well on my own, Kate."

She frowned and her mouth opened to retort, but she quickly closed it, then shook her head and stood. She moved towards the door, and Derek sighed in frustration.

"No, don't go," he said, getting to his feet again.

She stopped and looked at him, rather superiorly. He prayed this was not the return of Kate the Tyrant. The last twelve hours had been unusually temperate for being at home, and he would rather they stay so mild. It was far less stressful.

"I apologize," he told her, spreading his hands out just a bit, wondering just how often he was going to feel the need to apologize. "Again. Old habits. Please." He gestured back to the chair she had just vacated, knowing that she would probably snap at him, and he would be lucky to escape with that hand still attached to him.

Kate nodded and returned to her seat, again with the surprises.

Reeling from the sudden change, as the old Kate would never have done something so forgiving or decent, he slowly sank back into his chair, careful to not stare at his wife and wonder when she was going to burst into flames.

"Did it help?" Kate asked after a moment.

He looked at her oddly. "Did what help?"

Something that could almost be called a smile flicked across her face, and he suddenly remembered that his wife was a beautiful woman. It was easy to forget, as she was so often looking severe and disapproving, and always kept that dark hair of hers so tightly pulled back. But he recalled a day, right around five years ago, when he had married her, when for the first time in his life, he had been grateful to marry her. She had been stunning even though he hated her. That, of course, had faded and even now it was a blurry memory, but he remembered her smile, small and slight and hidden, and how it had caught him right in the chest.

Rather like it did now.

"Banging your head against the desk," Kate said, tilting her head just a touch.

"Who said anything about it being my head?" he asked with a grin.

"One, you have a red mark on your face, and two, it has been something I have considered doing a time or two."

"You wanted to bang your head against the desk?" he laughed. "When?"

"Whenever I get letters from the estate in Derbyshire," she said, still wearing that almost-smile.

"Oh, yes," Derek groaned, nodding. "Mr. Frazier and his blood... erm, blasted reports," he amended quickly, feeling that he should probably curb his harsh language around her.

She nodded, her eyes looking almost amused. "If I never read another report of his about every detail of every farm, I will consider myself fortunate."

Derek sat forward and smiled. "Did you ever get his notices of his..."

"...mother's gout?" they finished together.

"Yes," Kate said, tucking an invisible strand of hair behind her ear. "It was awful."

"I know," Derek said with a chuckle. He sighed and gave her an appraising look. "Nathan and Moira want us to come to a party at their home this evening. Would you like to go?"

She thought for a moment. "I would, but I am still in mourning."

He shrugged. "So don't dance, if it should occur. It is only a small party, not a formal audience. It hardly counts. Besides, I think Moira would like to have you there."

"Really?" she asked in a voice that was almost too sincere for him to believe it came from her.

"I think so," he said with a nod, enjoying this side of her. "She doesn't show it, but Moira does not have many friends. She is still new to Society, and things are difficult."

"Then yes, I think we should go," Kate said firmly. "It is important to support her." Then she gave him a serious look. "But I still would like to know if I can help with whatever is troubling you."

Derek considered thanking her, but refusing the offer. But as he looked at her and saw an honest willingness to help, he gave in. What was a wife for, after all? And so he opened up to her for the first time in his life, and found her to be discerning and receptive and really rather wise in family matters, and the rest of the morning and part of the afternoon was spent trying to determine the best course of action for keeping David out of trouble and keeping his father satisfied.

And by the time they broke to change for the party, Derek thought that perhaps this friendship idea would not be so difficult after all.

They caused a small stir as they entered the ballroom of Nathan and Moira's house, where a good many chairs had been set up and already people were milling about, but all had frozen as the Marquess and Marchioness of Whitlock had been announced together. Then the titters and whispers started, and Derek sighed.

"Well, that should give them something to gossip about for a while," he muttered.

"How very shocking we are," Kate muttered right back. "To think, we, a married couple, appeared at something together. How dare we. And I in my mourning gown? Appalling manners, all around."

Derek bit his lip, wanting to snicker, but knowing he shouldn't. Then he caught sight of a truly horrible thing. "Oh dear," he murmured to his wife as they moved into the room. "I believe Baroness Rudin intends to sing again."

Kate's head snapped up and she looked where he indicated. "Blast!" she hissed. "Perhaps I will suddenly find myself violently ill. Catch me if I faint away, won't you?"

"Kate!"

"What?" she asked, looking up at him. "You cannot possibly expect me to listen to her caterwauling like a drunken sailor and applaud the performance. I have heard better vocals from dying cats."

Derek choked on more laughter. "Kate, stop. I will never maintain composure during her attempt to perform now that is in my head." He tilted his head as he considered her in a new light. "I had no idea you were funny."

She gave him a look that was so coy, he had no idea she could do so. "There are many things you do not know about me, Whitlock." She looked around, and then sighed. "Now if you will excuse me, I must find Moira and then spend the rest of the evening avoiding Lord Pembrook and his noxious fish breath."

Derek allowed her to move away from him, and turned to put a fist to his mouth, hoping to stem the fits of laughter that were threatening to burst out of him. But really, he was truly flabbergasted. Kate was funny? That was a twist of irony he had never expected. What else was she hiding underneath that buttoned up demeanor of hers?

"What's the fuss, Derek?" Colin asked as he, Duncan, and Geoff approached him.

Derek took a calming breath and turned. "My wife," he announced, "is funny."

The stunned expressions on each of their faces nearly set him off again, but he had felt that same shock only moments before.

"Oh, come off it, Derek!" Colin said after a moment, starting to smile at what he thought was a joke. "Katherine doesn't have a sense of humor!"

"No, no, she does, I swear," he said with a very serious shake of his head. "It's the strangest thing." He proceeded to tell them all exactly what she had said as proof, and he knew they were convinced when even the mostly stoic Duncan had to put a hand to his lips.

"Well," Geoff said, when he had recovered, and started to move away, "I think I might stand by Katherine during the musical portion of the evening. It might be extremely entertaining."

"Watch out for her claws," Colin told him, demonstrating with his hands, and earning himself a smack on the back of the head from

Duncan, which was akin to getting punched by most men.

"Leave off Katherine," Duncan said firmly as he and Derek followed Geoff. "She's funnier than you are."

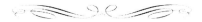

Across the ballroom, having no success in locating Moira, Katherine decided to look for her out in the hallways. Hosting one's first event could be very trying, and though she had not much experience, she had been an unofficial hostess a time or two, and those were demanding enough.

She entered the darkened hallways and let her eyes adjust to the change from the brightly lit ballroom, then slowly made her way along, hoping she would not get lost. That would certainly be something for comment if it ever got out, how the Marchioness of Whitlock wanders around other people's houses, even when in mourning.

She almost laughed at the thought.

"Did you see that the Whitlocks came in *together* just now?" said a female voice not too far away. Katherine pushed herself into an alcove behind a suit of armor, and waited, holding her breath.

Another voice snorted in derision. "Rather brave of him to go anywhere with her, I should think," came the unmistakable voice of Lady Greversham, one of the most notorious gossips in all of London. "And she is supposed to be in mourning. That girl is going to turn out to be just like her mother; puffed up and ridiculous and severe, only prettier."

"And she will have no one to regret that she is gone once she dies," the first voice snickered.

"I doubt," came a third voice Katherine did not know, "that the marquess has yet done the deed, as they say, with his wife, no matter what the rumors say."

"Oh, heavens no," Lady Greversham said in a disapproving tone. "Can you imagine? He could not get within ten feet of her without being burned or bruised. No, the day they produce a child of any sex, heir or not, is the day that pigs will fly. The dukedom will pass to the younger brother, unless they will accept illegitimate children of the marquess."

"Are there illegitimates?" one of them gasped.

Lady Greversham tsked. "No one knows, to be sure, but you could hardly blame the man if there were."

"Do you think their marriage has even been consummated?" the third woman hissed, the three of them almost past Katherine's hiding spot now.

The other two snickered. "I am quite certain it has not. Which means the marquess could have the marriage annulled, if he should choose. The scandal might be worth it, if it means finding a new bride."

"And he would have his pick," Lady Greversham said importantly, her voice fading as they turned the corner. "All of London would line up for him, and I do mean all…"

When she could not hear them anymore, Katherine stepped out from her hiding spot, her knees weak, her eyes watering, and her lungs burning.

So that was what people thought of her. Though they had not seen her, though they would never know she had heard them, their words wounded her as though they had been flung in her face like mud.

Things were far worse than she had imagined.

She could not stay here any longer, not even for Moira.

Somehow, she made her way back to the ballroom without seeing another person, and she only prayed that her countenance was not too distraught, though she knew that if anybody looked closely enough, they would see her distress. But if what she had just heard was true, no one would look at her anyway. No one would care.

She saw her husband instantly, standing and talking with his friends, and she cursed the fact that he was never alone. She approached, unnoticed by anyone, and touched his arm. "Whitlock, can we leave?"

"What's that, Kate?" he asked with a smile, turning to face her. Then his smile vanished and he looked at her with concern. "What is the matter?"

She shook her head, feeling the eyes of each of his friends upon her. "Can we go, please?"

"Kate," he whispered, stepping closer, "we have only just arrived. We cannot possibly…"

"Please, Derek," she begged, her voice breaking as more tears rose to the surface.

He stopped talking and looked a trifle stunned, but instantly he nodded. "Yes, of course… Of course, we can." He turned to Nathan. "Sorry, Nate, but we have to leave."

"It's quite all right," Nathan responded, still looking at Katherine with concern. "I am certain that…"

"Katherine?"

She closed her eyes as Moira's voice met her ears. Then her arm was seized and she opened them to find Moira directly beside her, looking worried.

"Katherine, what happened, what is it?"

She shook her head again. "I have to go, Moira, I'm sorry, but I…"

"What happened?" Moira asked again.

"I do not wish to create a scene," Katherine whispered, as tears continued to threaten.

"You aren't," Derek assured her, taking her other arm gently. "Duncan is blocking everybody's view, and nobody ever looks at Colin anymore."

"It's true," Colin said with a sigh, for once not against her. "You are in luck, Lady Whitlock. They are getting my more popular side at the moment."

She tried to smile, but could not manage it. "I just…" She broke off with a sharp inhale as she saw Lady Greversham enter with two companions, and she knew immediately those were the women she had heard. Worst of all, they were women who had been one-time friends of her mother. As if she were hearing the words for the first time, she felt as though a knife were slicing through her, and her hand fluttered to her throat.

"What is…?" Moira began, but then she saw where Katherine

was looking, and stopped. "Oh," she said in a very low, very dangerous voice. "Don't say another word, my dear. I will take care of this." She immediately gave Katherine a tight squeeze of a hug, and then marched directly over to a very pretty blonde not too far from them.

"Oh no," Nathan groaned, swaying a bit.

"What?" Derek asked, looking around, but still holding onto Katherine's arm.

"That is my sister-in-law Caroline," Nathan muttered, shaking his head. "She has a vendetta against Lady Greversham and only needs an excuse to act. She and Moira have become thick as thieves. I think you had better leave now before those two hatch a scheme that will probably make us all very proud, and the rest of Society exceptionally appalled."

"Say no more," Derek said with a raised hand. "I trust we can leave the resolution of anything unpleasant to you lot?"

"Oh, yes," Geoffrey agreed, nodding. "You can be sure we will find some way to blame Colin for this."

"I'll take it," Colin chimed in at once. "I need all the attention available."

Katherine nodded gratefully at the group, but could not say more. Thankfully, Derek led her out a side door quickly, his grip on her arm the only thing holding her up. The closer to the carriage they got, the harder it became for her to keep her emotion contained. It was going to all come out in one panicked, sobbing mess, and if she could avoid completely breaking down before her husband, it would be a miracle.

Derek was grateful he knew this house so well, as it enabled him to get Kate out of that ballroom and away from the public eye swiftly. He had no idea what could make his strong wife break like this, but he found himself rather enraged, and he didn't understand it. All he knew was that he needed to get her home and get to the bottom of this.

Their carriage arrived rather quickly, for which he was grateful. He helped Kate in, then climbed in after her, and they were off.

Derek watched Kate carefully, waiting for an explanation. She stared out of the window, holding herself as stiffly as possible. But he could see her chin and her lower lip, and both were trembling. He couldn't take it.

"Kate," he said as gently as he could. "What happened?"

For a long moment, nothing happened. Then her shoulders heaved and gasping, panicked sobs started racing out of her. Stunned beyond action for a moment, Derek sat across from her, staring helplessly. Then his sense returned to him, and he moved to the other side of the carriage, not sure if he should touch her or hold her or leave her be.

"Tell me, Kate," he pleaded quietly, deciding to take her hand in his.

"I'm… trying, you… idiot," she gasped, raising her free hand to her throat, as if it might help her breathe.

Derek almost smiled at her retort.

Gradually, she was able to tell him exactly what had happened, and, as he thought, he was disgusted. He was half tempted to turn the carriage around, go back to Nathan and Moira's, and bring down all of the power and influence of the name of Ashcombe, Whitlock, and Chambers upon each of those women.

What Derek did not expect was the rest of the things came out of Katherine. Soon she was talking about not being able to be a proper duchess, how she would never live up to the standards she needed to, how she didn't know what she was going to do without her mother to turn to for help, how she could not possibly be a mother herself when she did not even like the man who would be the father of her children, a point which made Derek flush slightly.

"And… and…" Katherine tried, still gasping. "And I am *not* a bloody whore!" she cried, bursting out into fresh tears again.

Derek's heart stopped. "You heard that?" he whispered.

"I have *never* been unfaithful to you," she said, poking a finger into his chest. "I would never do that to you or to our family name. I have never even considered it for a moment." Her jaw quivered and her eyes flooded once more. "And nobody would want me anyway. Nobody does. Not even you."

"I didn't mean it, Kate." He immediately decided to forgo his pride and pulled her against him, knowing she would probably shove him away. "I'm so sorry. I should never have said anything of the sort. I know you wouldn't. I know, I know."

"I know I make you miserable," she sobbed, surprising him once more by burying her face against him. "I will try to be better, I promise I will."

"I know, Kate," he soothed, rubbing her back. "I will be better, too, I swear."

She nodded, sniffling. Just when he thought it might finally be over, she burst out with, "And I hate black crepe! I look terrible in it, and I do not want to wear it. It is depressing, and morbid, and uncomfortable, and I hate it!"

"Then you don't have to wear black crepe, Kate," Derek said in a placating voice, wanting to laugh just a little.

"I do, too," she huffed, pushing against him finally. "Society says…"

"Hang Society, Kate. Don't wear it. Wear whatever you want. I will buy you dresses in twenty-seven shades of purple, brown, grey, and any other dark color you want, in whatever fabric you want. It doesn't matter. Your mother is not here to be scandalized." He broke off and winced, releasing her as she sat back to look at him. "Was that too insensitive?"

"It was insensitive," she said slowly, but a small smile briefly graced her lips, "but it was also remarkably true." She sniffled, and thought for a moment. "I choose to not wear black, or crepe."

"Very good," he praised, nodding in approval.

She grimaced suddenly and shook her head back and forth, as if she were trying to shake something from her hair or she just had a chill.

"What?"

She shuddered. "I think I just heard my mother turn in her grave. It was… rather unpleasant."

Derek hesitated only a moment, then released the laughter he had been holding in all night. Kate smiled and wiped at her cheeks, sitting back against the seat.

"Better?" he asked on a sigh, as he matched her pose.

She nodded. "I'm so sorry for doing that, Whitlock. It was…"

"Call me Derek," he interrupted on a whim.

She gave him a look. "What?"

"You have called me Derek twice now when you were feeling particularly emotional. I like it," he admitted with a shrug. "My friends call me Derek, and I think you should too. I am your husband, Kate. When we are alone, just like this, or at home, call me Derek. When it is just the two of us, I don't want us to be the marquess and the marchioness. Let's just be Derek and Kate."

"Katherine," she muttered, but with a smile.

"Chamber pots."

She snickered finally, the last of trace of her tears vanishing. "All right. Derek it shall be."

They sat with their backs to the carriage seat for a moment, and then Derek nudged her shoulder with his own, grinning. "I hope you're done crying for a while. It was quite a shock to me. I didn't even know you *could* cry until yesterday, Kate."

She nudged him right back with a smile of her own. "Shut up, Derek."

Chapter Eight

$\mathcal{D}$erek was actually rather pleased with the way things were going with Kate. Breakfast this morning had been quiet, but not unpleasant. They'd avoided the topic of last night's emotional outburst, and he'd not missed the gratitude in her eyes when he started rambling about the food.

It was becoming obvious to him that her upbringing had been even stricter than his. Eventually, he hoped that she could break free from it, as he could not have a warm and friendly relationship with both Kate *and* her dead mother, who seemed to rule from the grave. He wished he knew severe enough curses that could reach her there, but alas, he did not.

Walking through the halls on the main floor of his home, he wondered where Kate had gone to now. He'd gone down to the kitchens after breakfast, finding the meals at home not to his liking, and discussed bringing in additional help for their young and inexperienced chef. He could hardly get rid of the man when Kate craved his pastries so fiendishly, if his reports and suspicions were correct.

And he wanted Kate to be happy.

Which was a bit of a strange thought.

A sound met his ears then, and he stopped in his tracks to listen. Was that…singing? And the pianoforte?

His thoughts trailed off and his mouth gaped. There was only one person in this house that could possibly be playing in the music room, and that was his wife. But Kate was not musical, was she? He would have known that, wouldn't he?

He moved quickly and quietly to the music room and stopped outside of it, listening closely. He could hear quite clearly through the door, but the words were a little muffled. Not that it mattered, he could tell immediately that not only was his wife secretly musical, but she was also very gifted. Never in his life had he heard someone play with such feeling, and he prided himself on being a sort of connoisseur. Secretly, of course.

He turned the handle to the room as softly as he could, wincing as it creaked, his whole frame tense. If he could steal a few moments of witnessing unobserved, he would consider himself fortunate. Kate would never be so open and vulnerable as to perform, and, as he had never heard her in their five years of marriage, he highly doubted that it was something she did often at all, even for herself. If it had been a part of her life, she would have done so regardless of his being at home or not.

At last, the door opened enough for him to be able to see her, and his view was worth the effort of secrecy.

Though he had just seen her at breakfast, though he knew exactly how she looked, though he was not even certain that he even liked her, he had to catch his breath at the sight of her. She had never looked so at peace, so full of some private joy as she did at the instrument, her eyes closed as her fingers danced and her voice rang throughout the room. This was no tyrant wife of his; this was an innocent young girl in the bloom of her youth, full of hope for the days ahead.

For some reason he dared not identify, he found his throat inexplicably tightening and his eyes burning. Such a reaction was unwarranted and unprecedented from his wife, but then, he could not be certain the woman before him even *was* his wife.

When she had finished the song, he pushed open the door further, partially entering the room. "Kate?"

With a slight gasp of surprise, she shot up off of the bench and stepped away from the instrument as if it were a wild animal. "Derek! I'm sorry, I just…"

"Sorry?" he interrupted, coming into the room fully and looking at her in disbelief. "Sorry for what? Kate, that was beautiful!"

She looked startled for a moment, as if ready to deny it, but then she only blushed and ducked her head. "Thank you."

"No, really, Kate, I am very impressed," he said with real honesty, and not caring that she would see it. "I had no idea you could play."

"I can a little," she admitted, adding in a light shrug. "But it is no matter. It's only a bit of entertainment, and quite superfluous. It serves no purpose."

"Not everything has to have a purpose, Kate. All the purpose it needs is that you find pleasure in it."

She looked up at him, tilting her head ever so slightly. The confusion in her eyes made him ache just a little. But she made no move to comment further, so he thought it best that he leave her to it. The compliment had been paid, and that was all he had intended to do.

"So you like music, then?" she asked just as he had turned to leave the room.

"I love music," he confessed, turning back. "But that is entirely a secret, and I think only you know it. We must keep it that way."

She nodded sagely, presumably storing that information into her head. He hoped she would not use it against him. "Do you really think that was good?" she asked in a quiet, curious voice.

"I know it was," he responded immediately. "You have a gift, Kate." At her doubtful expression, he frowned. Surely a woman as confident and composed as his wife would be well aware of her talents.

Unless...

"Kate, did nobody ever listen to you play?"

She shook her head. "Mother did not like it. She agreed that I could learn for the sake of accomplishment, but she..." She bit her lip and hesitated, but at his smile, she continued. "She did not feel it was a good use of my time. Nobody was permitted to listen. I never performed."

"Well, pardon me for slighting your mother *again*," he said with a brief smile, "but I think you should play often, any time you feel like it, and for however long you wish. If you enjoy it, that is."

"I do," she admitted softly, but he could hear the emotion behind it.

He nodded, smiling fondly. "Then play on, Kate, without reservation or purpose. Just play. And, if you will permit it, I would love to listen whenever you wish."

"You would?" she asked, her eyes widening in surprise.

"I would."

She looked surprised, and a little pleased, which triggered a warm, almost glowing sensation somewhere in the vicinity of Derek's chest. "I think I would like that very much," Kate told him shyly.

"Excellent," Derek said with pride and animation, for she really was furiously talented. "When should the first concert be?"

Kate looked back at the piano, then at him again, her eyes dancing with excitement. "What are you doing right now?"

He laughed and moved to take a seat near the instrument. "Not a thing."

"You don't have somewhere better to be?" she asked as she took her seat, somehow looking more timid and uncertain than ever before. How many times had someone said that to a much younger, more innocent Kate who only wanted to show what she had accomplished?

"No," he said honestly, his heart leaping to his throat at the tender vulnerability in her gaze. "No, I do not."

If confusion were an illness, then Katherine would be so severely infected that she would have to be quarantined for the safety of any around her.

In all of the twenty-three years of her life, she had never known that one could feel so utterly bewildered, and the idea that it was her husband who was bewildering her was the most bewildering part of all.

She had known this man her entire life, had severely disliked him, hated him, really, for most of that time, and the feeling had been completely mutual, and she had not minded that. Now that they were becoming friends, however, she found that she did not know her husband at all.

To be fair, he did not know her either, nor had he ever seemed inclined to do so before this. But yesterday they had spent a good amount of time in the music room as she played and he critiqued, and quite intelligently at that, and it had been the most enjoyable morning she had spent in a long time.

He'd asked her about acquiring a new chef and she perked up at that. Though she had never spoken of it, the meals were not particularly palatable in their home. But as she did not usually care, she hardly felt right to complain. And the tarts in particular had always been delightful, which he assured her would still be at her disposal. He seemed quite adamant about that part, actually.

And he'd asked her about the new chef. Not informed her what he would do, but asked and consulted with her. Like a true married couple would.

With all of that, she had begun to think that perhaps things just might work out between the two of them after all. And she had to admit, but only to herself and only to the very most private part of her, that his calling her Kate was not the irritation it had once been. She would like to be Kate. Kate was open and honest and fresh, while Katherine was stuffy and haughty and held herself with far too much pride.

Someday she would tell him. Someday she would stop correcting him. But for now, she would only do so in her mind.

But this morning her thoughts were whirlishly dancing around the subject of her husband. She never knew quite how to behave around him, even when things were innocent. And why was he being so attentive with her? It was not yet certain if they were even going to succeed in this friendship of theirs. It had potential, if they would work at it, but nothing was certain. Still he treated her with more kindness than anybody except her father had done, and they had not fought in a number of hours, which was a record for their marriage.

All of these things jumbled about in her mind as she now hurried along the busy streets of London, making her way to the one place she never thought she would go for advice.

"Katherine?" a rather imperious voice called from a window in the building before her.

She looked up and almost sighed in resignation as her sister was trying to force the top half of her body out of the open window, and having quite a bit of difficulty in doing so. "Hello, Aurelia."

"What are you doing here?" Aurelia tried to hiss, though her voice carried quite a good deal.

"I came to speak with you," Katherine said plainly. There seemed no point in trying to hide it.

"Have you really?" Aurelia asked in surprise, and not a little suspicion. "On what topic?"

Katherine looked around, and saw that very few people were heeding them at all, which she hoped was a typical thing for members of her sister's neighborhood. "My husband," she replied at last.

A scheming light entered her sister's gaze and she smiled down at Katherine. "It is about time, I daresay. Do come in."

"Thank you," Katherine muttered dryly as her sister removed herself from the window.

In short order, the two sisters were ensconced in Aurelia's rather hideous drawing room and a tea was before them. A plate of biscuits stacked so high it looked impossible that it had been carried up from the kitchens as it now sat on the tray, and Aurelia made no attempt to restrain herself from devouring them.

"Where are the children?" she asked politely as she sipped her tea.

Aurelia waved a pudgy hand dismissively. "Damien and Vincent are up in the school room, and the girl is upstairs with the wet nurse."

"The girl?" Katherine felt her ire rising at that. Alice was a beautiful child, only a few months old, and rather sweet tempered, and if her sister changed that, Katherine would be enraged.

"What else am I supposed to call her?" Aurelia asked with an incredulous laugh.

"Oh, I don't know, perhaps Alice? As that is the name you gave her."

Her sister's eyes narrowed. "Really, Katherine, you ought to have checked your attitude before entering. This is my home and I may refer to my children however I wish to. Honestly, I think Mother's ghost might be inhabiting your body at present." She reached for another biscuit, giving her a disapproving glare. "And besides, it is not as though that child adds anything to the world. She will not amount to anything, I know. I had so hoped for another son. I have no idea what to do with a girl."

Fighting for control, Katherine took in a steadying breath, then released it slowly. "If you care so little for Alice, then why did you even have her?"

"Why, for my own amusement, of course!" Aurelia cried in surprise, taking a large bite of biscuit. "You did not honestly think that I went through all of that out of love or admiration for Nigel, do you?" She laughed at her own words. "Good heavens, but that man is an idiot. I declare, I do not know how I put up with him at all."

"He does wait on you hand and foot and treat you as if you were royalty or deity," Katherine pointed out with no small amount of sarcasm and distaste.

Her sister missed the spirit in which the words were said. "Oh, I know," she gushed with a smile. "And it is for that reason alone that I keep him around. It is vastly amusing. But as far as conversation or wit or anything useful, he is perfectly a waste. Husbands are such bores, don't you think?"

"I hardly know," Katherine said with more honesty than she had meant to. "My husband is a trifle difficult to understand."

"What is there to understand?" Aurelia laughed as if it were the most ridiculous assertion she had ever heard. "What was it that Mother said? 'Our duty as women is to make sure that our husband is well respected and his estate envied, but every intelligent being of sense knows that the real power in the world lies with the wives'." Aurelia grinned at the memory and nodded. "I do not think she ever spoke truer words to us, do you?"

Actually, Katherine did not. "Not in the case of my husband, I can assure you. He is a mystery."

"Dear Katherine," Aurelia said as she sat forward and put her tea down, watching her sister in a sort of triumphant amusement, "haven't you learned how to milk your husband for all he is worth yet?"

"My husband is not to be 'milked', Aurelia," Katherine muttered with no small amount of irritation. "He is not a cow. And he does not worship the ground I walk on as yours does."

Aurelia trilled a laugh that was not at all amusing. "Then you are not doing it right, dear. The man should be eating out of the palm of your hand."

"If he did that, I would be likely to be bitten."

"For heaven's sake, Katherine," Aurelia groaned dramatically with a roll of her eyes as she sat back, "how long have you been married anyway? You know nothing of men. But then, if you did, you would not be here to ask me for help."

Katherine chose not to point out the fact that she had not asked for help at all, and would never do so. If all husbands were to be handled in the manner that Aurelia did hers, then the entire world would be doomed.

"And I do not know why you have so brazenly come to call upon anybody when we are in mourning," her sister said in condemnation, tsking rather noisily. "It is entirely shameful of you. And you are not even in black!"

Aurelia seemed quite unaware of the fact that at the moment, she was wearing a rather ghastly looking yellow gown with no hint of mourning colors at all. Katherine opted to remain silent on this subject as well.

"I can assure you," she continued, "that I have been quite unable to venture out of doors at all. Poor Mama."

Katherine nearly choked on her tea that she had taken up again. Their mother would have blanched terribly at being called Mama. It was always to be Mother and nothing else.

Regardless, Katherine was quite certain that Aurelia did not venture out of doors at all unless it was to be well worth the efforts in doing so, whether in mourning or not.

But she allowed her sister to ramble on for the next three years, or so it felt to her, before she conveniently recalled an errand that had to be done, and made her escape. She moodily made her way back to the house, only to be met by Derek as he returned as well.

"Kate!" he said pleasantly as he stood back and let her enter first.

"Good morning, Derek," she replied with a smile and a nod as she stepped into the house. She carefully removed her gloves and bonnet and handed them to Jemima with a nod of thanks. Then she turned back to her husband. "Have you been with the solicitor all this time?"

"Yes, unfortunately," he responded with a small scowl. "I hate those meetings."

She wrinkled up her nose in distaste. "I don't know many that enjoy them. But is it all resolved?"

He nodded. "Yes, it was about the Shropshire tenants. Apparently, they have not been receiving adequate attention from the manager down there."

"Mr. Everett?"

"The very same."

"Oh dear," Katherine murmured as she walked towards the sitting room, Derek at her side. "And Mrs. Goodrich has been so ill of late, I hope that she has not suffered more because of Mr. Everett's inability to do his job."

Derek looked at her in surprise.

"What?" she asked, ducking her head slightly, knowing her cheeks would be growing pink under his gaze. "I may not know all the London gossip, but I do know our tenants quite well."

"Apparently," he said, smiling still. "At any rate, we have sent inquiries and Randall is going to start looking for a new manager, just in case."

"Very prudent." She gave him an approving nod as she sat on a sofa. "Mr. Randall has excellent taste in character."

"That he does. So what have you done all morning?"

She sighed and tried to smile. "I just returned from visiting my sister."

The look of horror and disgust that crossed his face made her laugh. "Good heavens, why?" he asked as he took his own seat in the chair that she had always thought of as his. It was worn, but not terribly so, and had a large and comfortable back to it. She had often times caught him sleeping in this chair in this room, and every time in the past she had slipped out as quickly and quietly as she could, praying not to disturb him, as she did not wish to speak with him. Now, however, she was taking pains to do so.

How confusing things had become!

"Kate?"

His voice brought her out of her reverie. "I'm sorry, what did you say?" she asked him.

He grinned. "What great disaster or horrific event prompted you to risk a visit to your sister?"

"I hardly know anymore," she muttered darkly. "It seemed the only viable option at the time. But next time, if there is a next time, I'll think it through a good deal more carefully."

"Now that is an impressive glower," he commented with an odd sort of amazement. "What did Aurelia do this time?"

"She calls Alice 'the girl'." Katherine shook her head, feeling her agitation rising again.

"That beautiful child that is so different from her brothers she has to be adopted?" Derek asked in astonishment. "That Alice?"

Katherine nodded earnestly. "She says that Alice will never amount to anything, so she did not see why she should take pains towards her. Derek, I almost slapped her."

"I think you should have," he said, his expression dark. "If she doesn't want Alice, then we'll take her."

"We will?" Katherine gaped, stunned by his admission.

He gave her an incredulous look. "You don't think I am going to sit by and let her ruin that child, do you? No, our niece will always be allowed to come here as often as she likes without invitation or warning. I daresay the nurse they have set her with will appreciate the break from your sister's household."

"Thank you, Derek," Katherine whispered, her eyes tearing up.

"Oh dear, don't cry again, Kate," he said with a teasing smile. "It's rather difficult to get you to stop once you start."

"My apologies," she laughed as she wiped her eyes. "And it's

Katherine."

He gave her a look. "Don't make me say it, *Kate*."

She grinned, then remembered what she had actually wanted to tell him. "Oh, but I forgot to tell you the best part!"

"I tremble with excitement," he muttered, but with a smile.

She quirked her brows knowingly. "My sister thinks you should be eating the crumbs from under my shoes."

Derek raised one brow slowly. "Have I ever told you," he announced, emphasizing each word carefully, "that I absolutely despise your sister?"

"She is quite a viper, isn't she?" Katherine returned with a crinkle of her nose. "I have never been especially fond of her."

She received a curious look for that, to which she snorted rather indelicately. "Oh, please, I lived with her for seventeen years of my life, you don't think I know her better than you?"

Derek chuckled. "Then why did you go speak to her, if you dislike her so much?"

"Who else am I supposed to speak to?" she asked.

He shrugged. "How about me? I am your husband, after all."

She rolled her eyes, but smiled. "Don't be ridiculous. I cannot possibly speak to you *about* you."

"Well, why not?" he asked with a mischievous grin. "I am an expert on the subject." But then he took on a very serious face and nodded. "No, I suppose you're right. Hmm. Well, I don't want you speaking to Moira about me."

"Too late," she replied with a smile of her own.

He sighed heavily and shook his head. "All right, well, you need a better option. How about my sister?"

She raised her eyebrows in surprise. "Lady Beckham? We are not especially well acquainted."

"All the more reason to speak with her," he said without concern. "She is wonderful, you'll love her. And she knows me very well." Then he winced. "On second thought, I don't want you speaking to her either."

Now it was Kate who grinned mischievously. "Oh, I am definitely going to speak with her."

Derek groaned, and waved a hand in surrender. "Fine, fine, but please, try to remember that I am available to talk if you need it. I can safely promise an answer to at least half of your questions concerning me roughly thirty-five percent of the time."

She snickered, then cocked her head slightly and looked him over. "Do you think we can talk without fighting?"

"About me?" he asked, then snorted. "Probably not, but I am willing to risk it."

"Why do we fight so much, anyway?" she sighed, sitting back, even though it was not proper posture.

"Because it's fun?"

"Be serious."

"I am being serious. I love fighting with you."

She laughed out loud at that. "Why?"

He grinned rather cheekily and spread his hands out as if the answer were obvious. "Well, because you are so very good at it, that's why."

"Derek," she scolded, trying not to smile.

"Kate," he replied in the same tone, mirroring her expression.

"You are ridiculous," she said in resignation, shaking her head at him.

He shrugged one shoulder. "I know. But you like me, admit it."

She laughed once. "Hardly."

"Come on, Kate. You know you want to," he taunted with a grin.

"Do I?"

He nodded emphatically. "Yes, you do."

"Oh, very well then," she sighed, as if surrendering. "I like you. Are you satisfied?"

A rather bright grin crossed his features. "Really?"

Katherine fought the urge to smile and shrugged. "So you say."

"Very well, then. You like me," he pronounced proudly, as if he were a king granting a knighthood. Then the childish grin was back. "In fact, you wonder how you ever lived without me."

"And now I am leaving," she said, pushing to her feet and heading for the door.

"Where are you going?" he cried in dismay, looking rather

petulant.

She turned with a half-smile. "As you suggested, I want to visit your sister."

"Oh no," he moaned, jumping up from his chair. "I'm coming along."

"What? Why?"

"Somebody needs to keep Diana in check."

Katherine frowned and looked up at him. "Won't her husband do that?"

Derek gave her a rather dark look indeed. "You do not know Edward." He turned and took her bonnet from Harville, who seemed to have a bizarre ability to sense whenever anybody was going out.

"Thank you, Harville," he said as he handed Kate her bonnet.

"Shouldn't we send a note over?" she asked as she put it on and tied the ribbons.

"Why?" he asked with a laugh. "She is my sister."

Katherine gave him such a look that he suddenly turned his laugh into a series of violent coughs. "It is polite, Derek. That's why."

"Diana will not expect me to send a note," he said with a roll of his eyes as he escorted her out, taking his hat and walking stick from Harville with a nod. "She would be very surprised if I did so."

"Yes, but she would expect me to send one, I am sure," Katherine said with a bit of worry. "It is proper and polite, Derek. *A duchess always obeys the polite order of things.*"

"Who is a duchess here?" he asked rhetorically, looking about him. "Besides, the only rule any duchess needs is this one; a duchess can be whoever she wants to be, whatever she wants to be, wherever she wants to be, without consideration to anybody else."

"That is not one of the rules," Katherine said with a glare.

"No, I would imagine not," he allowed thoughtfully. "But as a future duke, I think that I am entitled to creating a rule for the wife of a duke." He looked down at her with a small smile. "What do you say to that?"

"I will need to think about it," she murmured, looking away.

He took her hand and looped it through his arm as they started to approach people, who tittered at the sight of the two of them out and about together, and sighed. "By all means, think about it, Kate. But just to clear the air, I will not be testing you on whatever those rules of a duchess are. I couldn't care less. My previously stated rule is the only one that I care about."

Katherine did not respond, but she did not think that he had expected her to. She could not honestly have said that she thought that he would ever approach her about the proper behavior of a duchess, but she supposed that some part of her had expected somebody would at some point. Perhaps she had been wrong.

It was certainly something to consider.

But if she did not have to obey the rules of a duchess, how would she conduct herself?

Who would she be?

Chapter Nine

"Derek! How unexpected. And Katherine, too! This is a surprise indeed."

Katherine blushed as the beautiful dark-haired woman before her appraised her with the green eyes that seemed to be an uncanny Chambers family trait. "I am so sorry, he would not let me send a note to inquire if we could come, though I told him it was polite." She glared up at Derek for effect, which brought an amused smile to Diana's face.

"Yes, a note would have been polite. But as it is my brother, I don't expect it," Diana said, still looking at Katherine with interest.

"Ha! See, Kate? I told you she wouldn't expect it!" Derek crowed, jabbing her in the shoulder with a finger.

"Katherine," she muttered, batting his finger away.

"Kate," he scolded with a warning look.

Diana looked supremely interested in them now, and her smile grew just a touch. "Just because I don't expect you to be polite, Derek, doesn't mean that it would not be nice. One could always use a little warning before guests show up."

"I told you," Katherine accused with a glower, feeling strongly tempted to jab him back, but decided against it. One should not be so childish in front of practical strangers, even if they were related by marriage.

"But you like surprises!" Derek cried, looking at his sister with a sort of betrayed air.

Diana held up a finger for clarification. "I like *pleasant* surprises, Derek. Unless you are bearing gifts, you are rarely one of those."

Katherine allowed herself to smile widely. She liked Diana already.

"I knew this was a bad idea," Derek grumbled as he shifted uncomfortably. "Come on, Kate, let's go and visit some people who actually like us."

"Oh, no, I am staying right here," Katherine replied, taking off her bonnet for effect.

"Yes, I would like her to," Diana agreed. She took Katherine's arm in her own, and smiled at her. "You do not need to send a note, Katherine. You are welcome to show up at any time without warning." Then she glared at her brother. "From you, I will require three days' notice."

Derek smirked at her as he removed his hat and gloves and handed them off to a servant. "I am going to speak to the only person of sense in this house, if you ladies will excuse me."

He moved to go past them, but Katherine stopped him with a hand to his arm. "I thought you were going to sit in with us."

"And be abused by the both of you?" He snorted and shook his head. "I think not."

"But you said you needed to keep Diana in check," she reminded him, enjoying the way his eyes widened in warning the moment she finished.

"He said *what?*" Diana cried, looking at her brother in indignation.

Derek broke free from Katherine's arm and moved on. "Beckham!" he called, moving rather swiftly away from them. "Beckham, where are you?"

Katherine watched him go for a moment, feeling just the slightest bit uneasy about being left alone with Diana when she knew very little about her. She had been counting on Derek to be a soothing influence, which seemed odd, considering his temperament, but he knew his sister and obviously loved her, so he could make things a bit easier for her.

She heard a quiet snickering from beside her and glanced over at

Diana.

"I'm sorry," she said between laughs. "I just love to give my brother a hard time. It is so easy to rile him up." She sighed and smiled brightly. "Come, you look hungry. I'll order us some luncheon."

With a fairly strong tug, Diana pulled her down the hall to a rather comfortable dining room, which must have been reserved for family only, as it was not very formal at all, and would not be able to sit more than eight comfortably. She felt oddly pleased to be so included.

"So, Katherine," Diana said without preamble once they had food before them, "what brings you to visit me today?"

Katherine's brows raised just a touch at the directness of her tone, and the bluntness of her question. No false expressions of delight, no attempt at small talk, nothing but the truth and the root of the situation. Yes, she thought she might like Diana very well.

"I needed someone to talk to," she confessed softly, looking down at her hands.

"And you thought of me?"

She chanced a glance up at her sister-in-law, who was watching her with some confusion, but without any judgment or censure. "I didn't, actually," Katherine admitted with an apologetic smile. "It was Derek's idea. I went to my own sister this morning, which is not a very wise thing to do."

"I can imagine not," Diana said with a wrinkle of her nose. "I know your sister, Katherine, and you must really be in a sorry state if you tried her first." She winced, which made her look very much like her brother. "I'm sorry, that was rude. What I meant was that I do not think that your sister would be a particularly able advisor." Diana frowned at those words as well. "That doesn't sound polite either. What I am trying to say…"

Katherine laughed a little and covered Diana's hand with hers. "Don't make yourself uneasy, I understand."

Diana grinned. "Thank you. I hope you don't take offense at my wondering why you should go to her."

"Not at all," Katherine said with a shake of her head. "It was my own fault for thinking I could get any sense out of her."

"Who would you confide in before?"

"My mother." She shrugged and attempted to eat something, but she could hardly taste it. "It seems odd, I know, but she had always been the person who advised me. Whether it was good advice or bad, she allowed me to regain some balance, and she always had a ready opinion on how to proceed. Now…" She trailed off and took a bite of her food, knowing that her silence would say what she could not find the words for.

"And you cannot confide in Derek?" Diana asked carefully.

"I don't know," she murmured, toying with her fork absently. "Our relationship is complicated, and he is part of the problem, and…" She heaved a sigh and shook her head. "I am feeling so lost, I don't even know which side is up. I don't know what to do, and nobody is giving me direction."

"Well, Derek is a very good listener," Diana suggested as she lightly buttered a roll, "when he wants to be. But I am always willing to listen and advise or simply sit here and let you ramble on with whatever thoughts are swirling about your head. I am sure that your friend Lady Beverton feels the same way, knowing what I do of her."

"Yes, but she doesn't know Derek that well. She's only known him for a few months. I need someone with a bit more insight into the man I married."

"Oh dear," Diana said as she wiped her mouth with the serviette in her lap. "What has my brother done to cause such a conundrum in your life? You two have been married for five years, I should think that nothing would surprise you anymore."

Katherine smiled. "We are trying to be friends," she told Diana as she began to eat the meal before her in earnest.

"Now that is something I never expected to hear," Diana laughed. "I know he loves sparring with you, I wonder at his giving that up. How is it going?"

"Rather well, actually," she admitted just a little grudgingly. "But it's confusing."

"I can imagine." She smiled faintly. "After all this time? What a mess."

Katherine nodded, sighing a little. "I am so used to him fighting with me, and being insulting and rude and insolent and irritating. That is the man that I married, the one who does everything in his power to avoid me and stay out of my sight."

"Is that why he's never in town?" Diana asked in surprise.

"So I assume. I don't blame him, I can be quite tyrannical, no doubt you've heard about it." She glanced up at Diana, but found her expression suspiciously blank.

Undeterred, Katherine went on. "We have grown accustomed to our battles, and now… it is this other, more friendly side of Derek that I am having trouble with."

"Why is that?"

"Because he has never been this way with me. We have always been at each other's throats, all the time. Even before we were married, we spent our annual visits in either a war of muttered insults or complete silence. So I have to ask myself, which is my husband? The man I have known or the man I am coming to know?"

Diana sighed and set her serviette on the table. "I think this conversation is better suited to a sitting room, Katherine. Are you finished?"

Though she was not, she was not going to waste a moment of possibly gaining insight into her husband from an expert on the subject. "Yes, I am."

Diana nodded and the two of them made their way to the sitting room a few doors down. Though not expensively furnished, the room was neat and clean, rather well-ordered, and altogether pleasing to the eye. Katherine suspected that was the very nature of Diana and her husband. Simple, unadorned, but rather elegant at the same time. It was refreshing.

"I think that I need to tell you about how we grew up," Diana said softly as they took seats near the large window in the room. "Perhaps that will allow you to see Derek in a more honest light."

Katherine nodded somberly, and found herself somehow both eager to learn and content to listen at the same time.

"Derek is the firstborn, which of course you know," Diana began, keeping her eyes fixed on Katherine intently. "In our family, firstborns are held to a rather high standard. As our family inherited our title by a death in the direct line, all of the dukes since have been determined to prove that we are deserving. My father is the most determined of all. I don't know if you are aware of my father's irritation with my brother David or not."

"I am," Katherine said quickly. "Derek and I had a discussion about him only a few days ago."

"He confided in you about that?"

She nodded. "It seems rather a lot to ask of an elder son to take charge and control the younger, particularly when the younger son has no responsibility."

"Ah, but you forget; my father is very determined," Diana said with a raised finger. "We all were bound by the same rules and restrictions as Derek, purely to ensure that our behavior was impeccable at all times. David does not like rules; I do not like rules; Derek does not like rules. But unlike David and myself, Derek obeyed without a fight. He is a very obedient son, and he works very hard to please. Even as a boy, he was being trained up and tutored to be a duke. If he had been an only child, perhaps he would have become the very likeness of our father."

Diana broke off with a bit of a mischievous smile. "Thankfully, David and I took it upon ourselves to prevent that." She sighed and the smile faded slightly. "But it did not stop him from inheriting the same determination to prove his position. He feels very strongly about our family name and our heritage. Does he feel as strongly about things as our father? No. Derek has a genuine love and concern for people, regardless of who or what they are."

Katherine only nodded, her mind whirling. Had she and Derek really had much of the same upbringing? Granted, she had not the luxury of siblings who were full of joy and laughter, but it seemed they had both been groomed for the positions they now held.

"He will be a wonderful duke," Diana continued with a fond smile. "Better than our father, I am sure, because Derek cares for more than his title and position and the opinions of others. Derek feels things far more deeply than he appears to, and he always has. You said that he is being rather warm and friendly to you, more than you expected?"

"Yes," she replied quietly. "I never anticipated he would try so hard to make a friendship between us work. It was my idea to be friends, and if we are to have any sort of working marriage, we ought to be able to remain in the same room with each other for a few minutes."

"Yes, I think that would be a requirement, particularly if you want the family to continue on at all," Diana said with an impish smile that was so well suited to her that Katherine suddenly had a glimpse of what she must have looked like as a child.

She blushed in response to that, but it faded nearly as fast. "But he is so changed from who he was even a few days ago. I am not sure which man is really Derek."

"I would venture to say that he is both," Diana replied. "But the heart of Derek is in the man you are beginning to see. I imagine that before now he viewed you and your marriage as one more responsibility he had to bear, and since our father was not to always be overseeing this particular part, Derek could control it. He could resent it, he could do whatever he liked with it. Now that he has been forced to view it in another light, I think he is seeing that there is another way it could be done. I think you ought to trust this version of Derek, rather than expect something nefarious to come out of it."

Katherine winced at the implication. "Was it that obvious?"

Diana flashed a friendly smile at her. "Not really, but I know my brother, and I think I am getting quite a good read on you. You have never had someone you could confide in, so I daresay trust is difficult for you. I only wish that I had been able to come to those annual meetings between you and Derek before you were married. I think you could have used some ballast."

"Will you be my ballast now?" Katherine asked softly, tears pricking at her eyes.

"Of course, I will," Diana said instantly, reaching over to hug her. "Between Moira and myself, I think we can steer the two of you towards calmer waters."

"That would be nice," Katherine sniffled as she hugged her sister-in-law.

"Does he really call you 'Kate' all the time?" Diana asked as she sat back, grinning.

Katherine groaned. "Yes, and I cannot make him stop. Although, don't tell him this, I am starting to like it."

The grin broadened. "Are you really? Oh dear, he must never know that. I'm sure he only does it to irk you."

"Oh, I know he does. But I think I could be a Kate rather than a Katherine," she mused, pondering it.

Diana smiled. "It suits you, you know."

"What does?"

"Kate."

She smiled shyly. "Then you may call me Kate as well. But not when he is around."

"No, of course not," Diana agreed, looking horrified. "Then we would have to tell him he was right about something, and the swelling of his head would never subside."

They laughed almost in unison about that, and Katherine sighed, still smiling. "Thank you for sharing a bit about Derek with me. I would like to understand him, and I am trying to allow him to do the same with me, but it's difficult to become someone else."

"I think both of you are just learning who you really are together," Diana said softly. "And you know, Derek would never tell you any of this himself."

"He wouldn't?"

She shook her head. "Derek is all about appearances. It's why no one knows he loves music, why no one knows he hates working outside, and why only I know that he hates geese."

"Geese?" Katherine repeated with a surprised laugh.

Diana nodded, smiling a bit. "He has no fears, but geese make him uneasy. He avoids them in the park, and will go to great lengths to do so."

"He has a fear," Katherine murmured softly as she realized the truth herself.

"He does?" Diana asked in shock. "What is it?"

"Failure."

For a moment, there was silence. But then, "You *do* know him well, don't you?"

"No," she said with a shake of her head. "No, not at all, I am coming to find out."

Again, Diana reached out a hand to cover hers. "Don't sell yourself short, Kate. You know him better than you think you do. On a level that you are perhaps afraid to consider."

They heard male voices then, and Diana looked to the door expectantly. Katherine was relieved to have an interruption, she admitted to herself. Diana's words had struck something in her, and she would need some time to understand just what it was.

"Well, have you ladies talked about me enough?" Derek asked as he came into the room and took a seat in between the two on the sofa.

Diana gave him a look. "What makes you think we were talking about you?"

"Well, it is the only thing you two have in common, and as Kate has already said that she cannot talk to me about me, the logical deduction is…"

"Shut up, Derek," Diana said with a roll of her eyes. "The words 'logical' and 'deduction' do not belong in your mouth together. Edward, couldn't you reason with him?"

Edward smiled an easy smile and shrugged his shoulders as he took the open chair. "I tried, my dear, but you know how Whitlock gets."

"Yes, I do," she scowled.

Edward grinned and nodded at Katherine. "Hello, Lady Whitlock. How are you?"

"I am well, thank you, Lord Beckham," she said with a returning nod.

He waved a hand dismissively. "Please, we are family. Edward will do just fine."

"Edward it is, then," she agreed with a smile. "I am sorry we have never been so informal before."

Again he shrugged. "It is a pity, but the past is the past."

"So help me, Edward, if you start going off about new beginnings again, I am going to throw myself out of the window," Derek warned. It was Edward's favorite topic, and Derek had heard quite enough about it.

"Promise?" Diana asked, perking up with interest. She looked to her husband. "Oh, do go on about them, darling. I've been trying to send him out of a window for *years.*"

Edward and Katherine laughed and Derek only glowered. "I think it is time to leave, Kate, don't you?" he asked in an imperious tone.

She offered him a cheeky grin. "If you would like to leave, then by all means we can, Derek, but just so you know, Diana and I are great friends now, so you had better get used to it."

"God save me," he muttered as he hauled himself to his feet.

"Oh, are you really going?" Diana asked in disappointment, her humor gone. "I never see you anymore."

He smiled down at her and helped her up. "Sorry, Di. Why don't you and Edward come over for dinner soon? We're getting a new chef."

"Yes, and he is very excited about it," Katherine said with a laugh as Edward stood and offered her a hand up.

Diana's eyes widened. "Oh, didn't I warn you?" She leaned closer and whispered loudly, "The only proper way to control a Chambers man is through food."

"Duly noted," Katherine replied.

"True enough," Derek sighed, stretching his arms widely. "Give me a fine meal and I will bow to any bidding."

"Any?" Katherine asked with a skeptical quirk of her brow that sent Edward and Diana snickering.

"Well, within reason," Derek amended, shooting her a dark glance.

She shook her head, smiling, and moved to embrace Diana. "Thank you for humoring me," she said softly. "I hope it was not too much of an imposition."

"Not at all," Diana returned with a tight squeeze. "You are

welcome any time, with or without invitation."

"You as well," Katherine insisted as she released her. "Any time."

"Within reason," Derek said again, glaring at both of them.

The girls rolled their eyes and scoffed at the same time, which made them laugh again. "Do you know, I think we are in trouble, old boy," Derek murmured to Edward as he watched his wife and sister laugh in an eerily similar fashion.

"I have been in trouble for a couple of years now," Edward sighed in resignation. "It only gets worse."

Derek shuddered, clapped his brother-in-law on the back, then gestured for Kate to lead the way out.

"Just a moment, Derek, if I may," Diana said suddenly.

Surprised, he turned to her. "Yes?"

She smiled at Kate, and said, "It will be brief, if you don't mind."

"No, not at all," she replied, looking curious, but accepting as she left the room.

Once she was gone, Derek turned back to his sister. "Yes, sister dearest?"

She punched him in the arm. "Derek, why have you been so mean about her?" she hissed rather malevolently. "She's wonderful!"

"Give it time," he ground out as he rubbed the arm. His sister had always had a rather powerful punch. "She may just be hiding her true self."

"You don't sound very convinced."

"I'm not."

"Derek," Diana said slowly, looking up at him. "Do you like her?"

"Kate? Sure I do. When she is in a mood for it." He shrugged. "I have yet to determine if she is going to attack me in my sleep or not."

Edward looked like he would laugh, but one glare from his wife and the ceiling suddenly became very intriguing to him. Diana looked back at her brother and her eyes were stern. "Derek, I think you know what I mean."

"Leave it alone, Diana," he warned, losing humor. "You cannot meddle in this one. I don't even know if this friendship between my wife and I will work, let alone if it will ever go anywhere further. She may be lying in wait for me to grow comfortable and careless, and then she will strike with a vengeance and all you will find of me will be my coattails and front teeth."

"Derek," she tried again, looking earnest.

"No," he said firmly, kissing her forehead briefly. "No, Diana. Leave it alone. Good bye."

"What if you are wrong?" she persisted as he turned to go.

He growled and whirled to face her. "You know that Shakespeare play, Diana? 'Taming of the Shrew'?"

Her brow furrowed in confusion. "Yes, of course, who doesn't?"

"It just so happens I may find myself in the middle of the sequel, 'Revenge of the Shrew'."

A sudden smile appeared on Diana's face. "Methinks the gentleman doth protest too much."

The glare she earned was so full of warning and irritation, Derek was rather proud of himself. "Methinks my sister is both interfering and insane. Good day." Without a further word to anyone, he turned on his heel and left the room.

Diana turned to her husband with a grin as her now riled brother was leaving.

"What?" Edward asked as he took his wife into his arms. "What are you thinking in that conniving head of yours?"

"Derek just may be falling in love with his wife," she confessed with a light kiss to her husband's mouth.

"He *what?*" Edward cried, rearing back a bit in shock.

She nodded fervently.

"He didn't look like a man in love to me," Edward said skeptically, looking back to the door.

"No, but he does look like a man in denial," Diana allowed with a smirk. "And that is always a good way to begin."

Chapter Ten

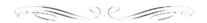

"Tell me more about the duchess rules."

Katherine jerked out of her thoughts and looked up at her husband. "What?"

He took her arm and pulled her back from the street where a coach had nearly run her over. "Shocked, are you?" he quipped with a grin. "I was listening most intently, and I want to know. Tell me."

She scowled up at him and started towards the street again. "You want me to tell you about the duchess rules my mother forced on me as a child?"

"Yes," he replied with a nod.

"No."

"Why not?" he asked as he followed her towards their house. "I married a future duchess, I think I am entitled to know what I'm getting into."

"Did you not tell me only a few hours ago that a duchess can do whatever she wants, be whoever she wants, wherever she wants, and that was all that mattered?" she returned with a raised brow.

"I did, indeed. But the fact remains that there are more rules than just that one in your head, and I want to know what they are."

Katherine frowned just a bit. After the whirl of the day, she really could use some time to herself to think, but talking with Derek could help as well. Diana had said he was a good listener, so perhaps he could genuinely be of some assistance. But what if he mocked her? What if this was to be the turning point that ruined their budding friendship?

"Kate?"

She looked up at him again, and found that they were stopped in front of their home, and Derek was looking at her with a touch of concern, and a good deal of curiosity.

"What will I receive in return?" she asked, swallowing to moisten her dry throat.

"For what?"

"For telling you the duchess rules, of course."

His furrowed brow relaxed. "Oh, that." He thought for a moment, and then shrugged. "I will tell you the rules for being a Chambers."

She had not expected that. She had hoped he would ask what she wanted to know, and then she could approach whatever subject she wanted clarification on. But for him to offer to share something so similar to hers was too intriguing a prospect to pass up.

"Very well," she agreed, turning to enter the house. "But you cannot mock me."

"I wouldn't dream of it," he said in a not very convincing voice.

She almost snorted at that. Of course he would dream of it. And she had no doubt he would actually do so when he heard the rules.

They seated themselves in their drawing room, Derek in his chair, his feet propped up on a nearby ottoman, and Katherine on the sofa near it, wanting to pull her feet up under her. But that would be against the very rules she was about to inform him of, and she couldn't do it.

"I like your sister very much, Derek," Katherine said with a smile as they situated themselves into their respective seats.

He returned her smile with a thin one of his own. "Yes, I thought you might."

"She seems to have a great deal of insight and wisdom."

Derek leaned forward a little and gave her a hard look. "Don't bypass the subject, Kate. I will not be swayed."

"I had no intention of bypassing it," she retorted, folding her arms, her pride a little tweaked.

"Oh, yes you did," he said with a knowing shake of his head. "I saw it in your eyes, you don't want to talk about it."

"Well, can you blame me?" she cried. "These rules were the whole course of my childhood. I heard nothing else. Everything I said or did or learned was turned into a rule. The way I sat, the way I ate, the clothes I wore, the way I chose to amuse myself, everything was controlled and critiqued. There was not a thought in my head that my mother did not put there, and I cannot go a single day without hearing at least one of them repeated in my mind."

Derek's eyes had gone wide and his amusement vanished completely in the face of her outburst. "Are you serious?" he asked softly.

"Entirely." She closed her eyes and tried to still her breathing into something more refined. She had agreed to tell him about the rules, not about her whole childhood. And yet, with one accusation, she had unleashed the full force of it upon him in one great wave. *A duchess maintains control in spite of her emotions.* She took in a slow, even breath and released it just as calmly. Sanity and clarity must be her companions, not madness and incoherency.

"You just heard one, didn't you?"

Her heart stopped in her chest. She opened her eyes and looked at him in surprise, only to find that his feet were no longer propped up on the ottoman, but flat on the floor. He was leaning towards her with interest and concern, his elbows on his knees, hands folded together before him.

"How did you…?"

"Your face," he told her gently, mercifully sparing her from having to continue. "You went from trying to calm yourself to looking as if you were listening very hard. As if you were being instructed."

"I was," she whispered, feeling another surge of emotion swell in her that was sure to end in more tears.

"What was it this time?"

"I…" She shook her head, knowing she could not get it out. Something held her back, besides her emotions. Something impossible to define. What would he say? What would he think?

"Kate," he murmured quietly, reaching out to put his hand over hers. "Look at me."

She did so, knowing that her fear and unease would be rampant in her eyes.

"Trust me. What was it?"

Swallowing back tears, and her fear, she opened her mouth and eventually, the words came. "*A duchess maintains control in spite of her emotions.*"

He nodded in approval and smiled. "Yes, I thought it would be something like that." He sat back in his chair again, his hand sliding from hers, still watching her carefully.

Should she have said more? Did he want a list? She was quite certain she could compile a decent catalog of at least thirty of the rules, but as there were more rules than that, she doubted it would give him the proper scope. She looked down at her hands, which were currently in the process of mangling each other in her lap. She only waited for his further response, wondering when her cheeks would begin to flame, and tried to imagine the best way to leave the room with dignity and speed.

"Mine was 'Never display any overt emotion in public'," Derek said suddenly with a sigh. "Rule Twenty. That can be difficult, as I'm not exactly reserved."

Katherine brought her head up slowly to meet his eyes again, and she saw that, though he was smiling, he was not amused. "Rule Twenty?" she managed to force out.

He nodded. "Preceded by the slightly less specific Rule Nineteen, 'Always exhibit patience'. You see, the rules for a proper member of the Chambers family span a great many things, and are not listed in any particular order. For example, Rule Fourteen is 'Always respect your heritage', which I do, but Rule Fifteen is 'Always carry a handkerchief', which I am always forgetting. I am convinced that my father created the rules as he thought they were needed."

A small smile flickered across her face, and she was more than touched by his attempt to move the topic away from her and onto himself. "Do you pick and choose the rules you obey?"

"Not if I can help it," he said with a shrug. "Ridiculous as they are, some of the rules are quite good. Growing up, we obeyed them all. We had no choice. I spent far too many hours in a school room being drilled on the importance of family and heritage and decorum, and if proper behavior was not exhibited, more rules were passed."

"That sounds familiar," she murmured as she watched him.

His eyes met hers and for a moment, they said nothing. It seemed they had passed similar childhoods, and the idea that neither of them had known it was both shocking and regrettable. Could they have confided in each other at a much younger age and spared themselves the years of hatred?

"How did you handle it?" she asked in a small voice, knowing that he would understand.

"I obeyed, same as you," he replied softly, his eyes growing distant as he remembered. "It was not as though there was a better option. David could always manage to get out of it, and Diana never had the same rules as we did. I didn't have their luxury. I am a firstborn son. I am to be a duke. How else was I supposed to behave? There is a heritage to uphold, a legacy to honor, and a dignity to maintain. Obedience and respect were required."

She sat up a little taller and tilted her head at him. "It means a great deal to you, doesn't it? The family name and the title."

"It's who I am," he said with a fervent nod. "We are the product of those who came before, and our duty is to pass down an even greater legacy to those that will come." He laughed a bit at his own passion, and shook his head. "I'm sorry. No doubt my sister told you that I have an affinity for this sort of thing."

Katherine shrugged just a bit, but made no reply.

He sighed, and looked around. "I take a great deal of pride in what my family has done, what we have become. This house, for example, has been in the family for generations. It's been the home of the Marquess of Whitlock ever since the title was created. My father, grandfather, and great grandfather all inhabited it, and there is a great deal of history in its walls."

"That would be a lot of pressure, I would think."

He seemed to shake himself from his thoughts and looked at her. "It can be. But David and Diana have always been rather quick to lighten the mood for me, and keep me sane. And human. I would be in danger of turning fairly cold without them."

"I wish I could be of more help," Katherine said, almost to herself. "I become so focused on what needs to be done, on what is expected of me, on my duty that I forget about everything else."

"Kate," he murmured gently, sitting up once more, "don't. We're changing, aren't we? I'm not the image of my father, and you are hardly your mother, thank the Lord."

She managed to smile. "But did you ever feel that you were being controlled, Derek? Have you always wanted to be what you are?"

He frowned, thinking hard. "In some ways, yes, I did feel controlled. My father always expected much of me, and broken rules were met with severe punishment, up until the point where I was no longer breaking them. My duty has always been very clear to me. But have I always wanted to be what I am? I don't know. Who else would I be?"

"Exactly," she murmured, folding her hands together in her lap and looking at them. "I don't even know who I am without the endless rules in my head. How else should I comport myself? I had a duty to fulfill, and this was the only way I knew to fulfill it."

"Do you always hear her?"

"Every day. There is always something. *A duchess is the epitome of refinement. A duchess does not give in to idle gossip. A duchess never takes large bites.*" She sighed, and looked over at him. "There is always something," she repeated.

"And you always listen?" he asked quietly, his brow creasing again.

"I don't know what else to do. I don't know how else to behave."

"Judge for yourself." He leaned forward again and pressed his hands together. "I take the rules my father forced upon me and mold them to my own view and sentiments. Are they the same? No, but some of them are similar. You can do the same."

"I don't know," she whispered, shaking her head. "What if I make a mistake?"

"Then you make a mistake, Kate." His eyes were rich and green and earnest as they held hers captive. "Put the old bat out of your head, think about what you want, and then do it! Mistakes or no mistakes, folly or not, just do it."

She shook her head insistently. "*A duchess does not act without…*"

"Oh, hang what a duchess does or does not do, Kate!" he cried, throwing his arms up. "I couldn't care less. I want to know what Kate does, what Kate would do. Not the future duchess. Just Kate."

Katherine was more than a little taken aback by his words, and she was well aware that she showed it. But when he looked at her so earnestly, when his entire being and attention was fixed on her so intently, it was hard for her to make sense of anything. He was just too attractive, and it unnerved her. And his words… Could she forget that she was a future duchess and just be Kate? It seemed so impossible. Her entire identity, the very way she viewed herself, was wholly based on her position as the Marchioness of Whitlock. That was who she was.

"I…" she tried, not knowing what she was even going to say. Her mind had still not conjured up a response to Derek's extraordinary outburst. "I… I don't know."

He sighed softly and gave her a sad smile. "I understand. It will take some time, but you need to understand this, Kate; you are not just a marchioness, or a future duchess. You are a woman, a wife, a future mother, if we are so fortunate. You can't let just one part of you dictate the rest. You are more than that."

His words had stolen the breath out of her lungs, and she found that she had to believe him. Something about his determination, his fierceness for something so unimportant as how she viewed herself, was rather invigorating, and suddenly she wanted to do exactly as he said. There was no way for her to know even how to begin, but she wanted to try.

It was the least she could do.

Maintaining the eye contact between them, she nodded slowly, which brought a relieved smile to his face. "Now that we have *that* out of the way," he said wryly, "let's move on to something more fun. What is the most ridiculous rule you ever had to obey?"

Katherine grinned and found herself turning towards him. "Now that one is easy. *A duchess always washes her face three times in the morning, once at midday, and two times at night.*"

Derek's mouth popped open, and Katherine laughed at his expression. "You cannot be serious," he said, a smile starting to form.

"Oh, but I am," she assured him. "There was a nightly inspection and the maid would have to verify that I had washed the requisite number of times."

"How could your mother possibly know how often a duchess washed her face?"

Katherine shrugged and shook her head. "I haven't the faintest idea. I never questioned it, though I thought it was the most absurd thing I had ever heard."

"You can stop washing so often now. I grant you leave to wash only as you wish to." He smiled broadly, no doubt thinking himself a very amusing fellow.

It really was too bad that he was.

"I already have, thank you," she said with a dismissive sniff. "It was the first rule I broke after we were married." She did not mention that it was one of only a few that she had broken on purpose. Somehow, she was fairly certain that he would know anyway.

"Bravo, Kate," Derek said, applauding her with an amused smile.

"What was your most ridiculous rule?" she asked in turn, hoping he could match her absurdity in upbringing as well.

"Rule Twenty-six," he replied immediately.

"Which states?"

"Never be partnered in whist with someone who always loses at whist."

A burst of laughter escaped Katherine, and she quickly covered her mouth, which did nothing to stifle the sound. "I'm sorry," she tried, between giggles. "I am sorry, I…"

"Don't be," he said, waving off her apology. "I'm fairly certain all three of us had the same reaction when that rule was set up. Turns out my father hates to lose and thinks it is somehow beneath our dignity to do so, even at whist. Oddly enough, I seem to obey that rule without any trouble."

"You don't play whist." She was surprised with herself for revealing that little bit of information she knew. She had known it for some time, but had never thought of it, as far as she could remember.

Derek smiled in his surprise. "Exactly. One can never be paired with one who always loses at whist if one never plays whist. It is the perfect solution. But tell me, Kate," he said, leaning forward once more, elbows on his knees again, "is there any time that you don't hear your mother's rules in your head?"

She nodded without thinking, and replied, "When I play."

He looked inordinately pleased by her answer, and his smile grew so much that his eyes crinkled at the corners, their green depths no less stirring for their diminished state. "Truly? There wasn't a rule for that?"

"Only that I do so quietly and without bothering anyone," she answered with a shake of her head. "As I said, she did not care for it, but as it was an accomplishment highly favored in a young woman, she could hardly forbid me from doing so. She merely restricted when and where and how I could." Katherine leaned forward and matched his pose, which she could tell amused him, which amused her in turn. "Sometimes I would play just so I could shut her up."

"A very noble endeavor," he whispered conspiratorially. "And I think you should continue to do so until you no longer hear her." He leaned back and slapped his knee, then rose, holding a hand out to her. "In fact, I think you should do so now, and every night, if you feel so inclined. And I will sit in there for as long as you play and listen to every single note."

She smiled up at him in amusement, confusion, and even with a bit of pleasure. "It may be a rather lot of notes," she told him, looking from his hand to his face a couple of times for effect.

"All the better." He held his hand out a bit further, his eyes teasing her. "My ears have quite remarkable endurance for excellent music."

Shaking her head, she took his hand and allowed him to lead her into the music room, sit her at the pianoforte, and select music for her. Though he was being more than a little overbearing about the whole affair, she found that she didn't mind at all. She would play for him as long as he would listen, and if he could listen forever, than she could play forever.

And if this were any indication of how their marriage would

continue, she would have nothing to find any displeasure in at all.

Much later that night, Katherine crept as quietly as she could from her room, praying that the door would not squeak as she very carefully brought it to a close, but not enough for it to latch. When she was satisfied enough, she tucked a long strand of her dark hair behind her ear and tiptoed down the hall, past the great stairs that led down to the second floor, and the open entryway that had always been a little grand for her taste. She stopped when she had reached the narrow door at the very end of the hall, and opened that as silently as anybody might be able to, then slid inside and shut the door behind her, allowing the darkness to envelop her.

Once her eyes adjusted, she swiftly made her way down the confined, rather pokey stairs and just when she thought her heart was going to pound right out of her chest, she came to an abrupt halt as another door met her. She turned the latch and pushed the door open, and sighed to herself as the soft light from the kitchen fire brought the return of her sight.

With a grin, she scampered over to the shelves and began the hunt for what had brought her here in the first place; the strawberry tarts that had been prepared for her this afternoon.

She wandered along the shelves and searched all of the cupboards, her bare feet growing a little cold on the stone floor beneath them as they stretched on tiptoe as she searched. Though it was a darkened room, the fire added some light, as did the slivers of moonlight that filtered through the trees and into the one window of the room.

"Blast," she whispered as she failed yet again. She pulled her head out from the shelves, and accidentally bumped it on the one above, sending a quick jolt of pain through her. She hissed with the pain, and gingerly brought her head fully out, rubbing the top softly.

Well, she was not going to bed without having one, so she might just have to turn the whole kitchen over from top to bottom until they were found.

"Try the middle shelf about three feet to your left, behind the sugar."

With a shriek of surprise, Katherine whirled around one hand on her mouth, and one at her chest, clutching at her night wrap.

Leaning against the far wall, dressed in only his night shirt and dressing gown, hair slightly tousled, grinning unabashedly, was her husband.

"Well, well," he drawled, his eyes raking over her in amusement, "if it isn't my little wife coming to pilfer the kitchens."

"I... I..." she stammered, her heart still racing frantically in her chest. He quirked a brow at her inability to formulate any words, and she clamped her lips together, focused her thoughts, then managed, "What are you doing down here, Derek?"

"Same as you. I wanted another one of those tarts." His grin seemed to deepen even further, and with it came the disgruntling effect of warmth spreading through her. "Imagine my surprise to find you down here this late at night. And barefoot, at that. Why, Kate, you astonish me."

She turned back to the shelves, even as she swallowed hastily, desperate to preserve some of her dignity. "Middle shelf, you said?" she asked, as if he had not just scared the life out of her.

"Behind the sugar, yes," came his amused voice, a bit closer.

Sure enough, once she moved the sugar out of the way, there were the remaining tarts. She allowed herself a small "Ah ha!" of victory, and turned back around to find Derek standing across the table, hands placed firmly upon it. "Would you partake with me, my lord?" she asked with a quirky grin of her own. "I dare not eat alone."

His eyes twinkled and he inclined his head. "But of course, my lady. It would be ungentlemanly of me to let you consume these poor tarts unaccompanied."

"Well, we would not want that, would we?"

He shook his head rather somberly. "No, not at all."

Like two naughty children, they devoured at least two of the delicious tarts a piece, giggling and shushing each other as if some stern, sallow faced nanny were about to descend upon them. Derek, she soon discovered, was deplorable at hiding his laughter, and he discovered that she had a difficult time maintaining her composure if others could not. It made for several moments of uninhibited snickering that had both in tears.

When at last she was stuffed, and had licked the last of the strawberry from her fingers, Katherine sighed. "What is going to happen when the staff comes back tomorrow and sees that half of this plate is gone?"

Derek shrugged lightly as he carefully placed the plate back on the shelf and replaced the sugar in front of it. "Oh, no doubt they'll come to me with concerns, and I will simply wave it off and say it must have been some hungry vagrant, and they should just make a few more."

Katherine grinned up at him. "This hungry vagrant would enjoy that, I think."

He chuckled and helped her from her seat, then followed her as she ascended the servants' stairs again. "The servants' stairs, too, Kate?" he commented behind her as the darkness fell upon them. "I am surprised at you."

"It's the most direct route to the kitchens," she defended without shame. "And I am more than capable of navigating these stairs without difficulty in the dark, thank you very much."

"So it seems," his voice returned, sounding thoroughly amused. "I can't see a blasted thing and have stubbed at least three of my toes already, while you succeed without any effort. You're not part feline, are you?"

She snorted in a not very ladylike manner. "Hardly. Just practiced."

"Ah, so you venture down to the kitchens by night often, do you?"

She bit back a groan. She hadn't meant to let that little detail slip out. However, now that it was, she saw no reason to deny it. "On occasion, yes. I have done so after our marriage frequently, and I believe I did so as a child, but the intervening years, I rarely did."

"Why is that?" he asked with real curiosity as they finally reached the door, which he opened for her.

She nodded her thanks, then slowed her pace to walk beside him down the hall towards their rooms. "It's quite simple. I had a wedding dress to fit into."

"Even so young?" She peered over at him and he was watching her, his eyebrows raised in surprise.

"You forget who my mother was," she sighed. "I began hearing about my wedding the day I turned thirteen. Preparations started then, and my figure was the chief subject for criticism. I simply *had* to fit my dress perfectly. Therefore, the desserts were entirely removed from the house. Not that it helped much anyway, as the dress she forced me into was too small regardless." She smiled with a touch of humor. "I don't know if you could tell, but I thought I was going to faint clear away before the service had ever begun. Mother kept telling me beforehand how frightfully pale I was and pinched my cheeks repeatedly to get some color back in them. I shudder to think what I really looked like."

They stopped as they reached her bedchamber, and Derek turned to face her outside of the door. "I thought you were a beautiful bride," he told her, his eyes fixed on her face.

"You did?" she asked in surprise, her heart catching somewhere in the vicinity of her throat as those eyes held her captive and unable to breathe.

He nodded slowly, and for the first time, she realized just how close he was to her, how close he had been to her. The air was suddenly too thin, and she could not feel her toes. "It made me so mad," he murmured.

"What did?" She almost couldn't bear to ask, her words nearly stuck in her chest.

"The way you affected me." His words were low and rasping as he took all of her in, and everywhere his eyes touched she felt warm until she seemed nothing but an ember herself.

She swallowed with some difficulty. "I'm sorry," she whispered.

"Don't be," he breathed, reaching out to touch a long strand of hair that had fallen over her shoulder. He played with it, twirled it around his finger, and with each touch, Katherine felt herself slipping further and further on the precarious slope she had found herself on.

"You have lovely hair, Kate," he mused, almost to himself. "You should wear it down more often. It becomes you."

"K-Katherine," she managed, her voice weak and quivering.

"Oh, no," Derek said with a slow shake of his head as he continued to toy with her hair, his eyes now back on hers, and something pulled her closer, lured her in to the warmth she saw in them. "No, you're not Katherine. You haven't been for some time. I don't even know Katherine. All I see is Kate. Try her on for size."

His words danced across her face as they drew nearer, slowly, maddeningly hesitant and tentative, but closer indeed, and she could not find thought, let alone voice to do as he wished. Her eyes had been on his lips as they had moved, and now she somehow dragged them away back to his eyes.

Her confusion must have been obvious, for he only gave her the slowest, briefest hint of a nod. "Say it," he whispered as his fingers in her hair brushed against her ear slightly, sending a chill through her. "Say your name, Kate."

She shuddered involuntarily, and from somewhere deep within, she felt more than heard herself whisper, "Kate."

The flash of pleasure in his eyes was so potent that she almost swayed into him. "That's my girl," he said in a voice so soft she could barely hear him. He was so close, so close she could feel the breath of his words on her cheeks. "That's perfect. You might even like her, you know, Kate."

His nose grazed hers then, the briefest, barest hint of a touch, but it made her eyelids flutter and she could hear the blood pounding in her ears, and some small, stubborn part of her reared its terrified head and from her lips came the breathless words, "Do you?"

Time froze as the mood immediately shifted, and Derek, so near to his goal he could taste it, stilled. Her words, so soft and uncertain, and seemingly called up from her very soul, held him back.

Did he?

He scrambled for an answer, but too late. She pulled back and he heard the slight gasping that escaped from her as she became aware of their position, of how close they had almost been. "I'm sorry," she stammered, stepping away and holding her wrap around her more closely. "I will go to bed now, good night."

She turned to enter her room, as if determined not to look back. He couldn't blame her. He was hardly capable of movement, let alone thought. But as her hair slipped from his fingers, he knew he couldn't let it end this way. He stepped forward and braced the door open just as it was about to close. "Kate," he said in a low voice, his heart still pounding.

She peeked around the door, and again his breath caught. Her wide dark eyes were so entrancing, so luminous in the dark night that he almost forgot what he wanted to tell her. The slightly tumbling state of her rich, dark hair was so alluring that he was more than half tempted to sweep her into his arms. And that skin of hers, the very skin she had scrubbed so often to be a duchess, looked so like porcelain that he wanted to touch it. His wife was a transfixing beauty; he was the world's greatest fool to have ever forgotten.

He cleared his throat, seeing the uncertainty that was almost fear in her eyes. "The next time you go off to the kitchens in the middle of the night, come and get me. I would like to do this again. Very much."

For a long moment, she only stared at him, her eyes searching his, as if seeking the joke in his words. When she found none, the secret smile he so adored appeared on her lips, and she nodded once. "Good night," she murmured, closing the door softly.

When at last he heard the latch click, Derek released the breath he had not realized he had been holding. He ran a hand through his hair and turned to go back to his own rooms. What in the world was happening to him? Not only was he losing the ability to control himself, but he was also getting lost in the rush of thoughts and emotions that were raging within him.

About his *wife*.

He paused and looked back at Kate's door, wondering what she was feeling, if she had felt it too; that inexorable need to be closer, the tug in the heart that drew him in so completely, in spite of confusion or hesitation.

Surely she had.

Surely it had not been all on his side.

He said she would like being Kate. Did he like her, she had asked. *Did* he like her?

Shocking as it was, he finally found himself answering in the affirmative. Yes, he did like her. A lot more than he ever expected to.

And it absolutely terrified him.

Chapter Eleven

*K*atherine… no, Kate, she reminded herself. She was Kate now… woke feeling somehow both energized and drained at the same time. Nightly excursions with her husband to the kitchen might have to become a regular occurrence, if he enjoyed it as much as she did.

And if last night were any indication, he did.

Do you? she had asked when he'd said she would like Kate. What had prompted her to ask such an impertinent question at that moment? She could have kicked herself for her lack of tact. Did *he* like her? She couldn't even say if *she* liked her!

What foolishness.

The way Derek had frozen in place, the stunned look on his face had been more than enough to cool any feelings she might have had.

And what feelings she'd had! The heat had been unbearable, and she found herself torn between two extremes; flee and surrender. She was proud she had done the former, but the idea of the latter was… tempting. But how could she give in to a man who did not even know if he liked her?

His words to her after, the way he had held her door ajar and asked her to come and get him if she ever ventured out at night, those words had rekindled the tiny spark of hope within her.

Hope for what? She could not have admitted, even to herself.

She made her way downstairs to breakfast, knowing that the early moments of seeing Derek today would be very telling. Perhaps he would be waiting for her at the bottom of the stairs, or in the breakfast room, at the very least. But to her surprise, he was nowhere to be found.

Her heart sank just a little. So that was how it was to be, then. A hasty retreat from anything more than a light friendship. Well, she supposed she could hardly complain, given what they had been in the past.

She sat down at the table, a little grumpily. How could she decide how to act around her husband if her husband was not around to be acted upon?

"Pardon me, Lady Whitlock," came the gravelly voice of Harville from her right side, "but his lordship asked me to give you this."

Suddenly into her vision came a silver tray with a note on it, written in her husband's bold handwriting.

Unable to help herself, she smiled up at the butler and took the note swiftly. "Thank you, Harville. That will be all."

"Yes, your ladyship," he said with a perfunctory bow, his lips quirked on one side.

Blatantly ignoring the food that had also just been placed before her, she tore open the note with more eagerness than was probably appropriate, but she could not find the affront enough to care. She scanned the lines quickly, praying they would allow her some insight.

Dear Kate,

I am so dreadfully sorry that I will not be able to have breakfast with you this morning. I woke with every intention of enjoying your company as soon as possible, but a note from my father greeted me first. David has upset him once more, and I must console him as best as I can. I do not know how long I will be gone, but I refuse to miss dinner with my wife, so you may look forward to my riveting company then. And I think you had best reserve the music room for a private concert tonight. I will need the soothing sound of your music to revive me after he has done with me.

Until this evening,
Derek

She could not restrain a smile at his words. She could imagine the grin that lit his face as he penned these words, wondering how she would react to them. Did he think she would smile, as she was? She hoped so.

Unfortunately, if Derek were going to be out of the house for the whole day, it meant that Kate would have nothing to do. She had stopped attempting to plan out her days, as nothing surrounding Derek ever went according to plan, and since she was supposed to be in mourning, she could hardly be expected to take on her usual schedule.

Katherine would have done so.

Kate would not.

She grinned at the distinction, and began to eat her breakfast, feeling rather liberated at having an entire day with no schedule at all.

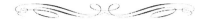

"I will not stand for it, David. Do you hear me?"

"Of course I hear you, Father. I think the whole street can hear you, and perhaps even more, if we would only open the windows a bit."

"Insolence, sir? I will not accept this. I expect better than that from you! What have you to say for yourself?"

"I have been insolent since the day I was born, sir, which you would know if you had paid any attention at all."

"How dare you! Whatever happened to honoring your parents?"

"Oh, Rule Three? Hmm, don't believe that is a Thomas Chambers original. Fairly certain it came from somebody a bit more important, if you can believe it."

Derek groaned and put his head into his hands. The entire day had been a waste of time, words, and breath. His father stood on one side of his desk, his brother on the other, and though they were of a height, they could not, and simply refused to, see eye to eye. The towering rage of their father could not cow David, nor remove the cheeky grin that was fixed on his scruffy face, which was another one of his father's more specific aggravations. It was Rule Twenty-Four, actually. *Always be clean-shaven.*

For most of the morning, and now stretching into the afternoon, the two men had bickered back and forth about various topics, and neither would be moved from their standpoint. Each had tried to bring Derek over to their side, but had not stopped to hear his opinion long enough to get a verdict on whose side he was on. For the life of him, Derek didn't know either. He had lost track of the current thread, but he suspected that while his father had a point, his brother was mostly blameless.

Mostly.

He was certainly doing a fair job of enflaming the situation, and Derek had a sneaking suspicion that it was purely for the sport of it.

He hated when David did that.

"I refuse to be treated in this manner!" his father roared as he brought down his fist on his desk again. That made about twenty times in the last three hours. "Whitlock!"

Derek jerked in his seat, and looked up at his father. "Sir?"

"Fix this."

Derek's brows shot up as his mouth fell open. Was he serious? Fix what? Their non-existent relationship? David's very personality, which seemed to be the thing that their father had the most difficulty with? There was not enough money in the world, nor time enough in existence to fix everything about whatever this was.

"Don't turn to Derek for a resolution," David said, sounding actually angry for the first time today. "Just because he is your favorite son does not make him any more able to fix what you cannot."

"Favorite?" the duke hissed, looking truly malevolent. "How dare you presume to think…"

"I'll presume all I like!" David shouted back, overriding their father, which was something that had never been done in the history of the family. "It is my life that you have problems with, and Derek, being the obedient son that he is, tries to be of some help, but ultimately the trouble, as you see it, lies with me. So deal with me. Not Derek, me." He sneered at his father, and Derek actually feared

for his brother's life. "If you can bear to. I know how you view us."
He gestured sharply to Derek with one hand. "The heir." He jerked
a thumb at his own chest. "The spare." Then he waved his hand in
the general direction of Diana's home. "And the surprise brood mare
in between."

Derek clamped his lips together, and closed his eyes.

"Spare?" the duke bellowed, placing his fists on the desk as if he
were going to spring on top of it. "Did I ever treat you like a spare?"

"No, *sir*," David replied, full of sarcasm. "But you never exactly
made me feel like anything else."

The silence in the room spoke volumes and for what seemed
ages, the men glared at each other. Derek half expected one of them
to toss the desk aside and begin pummeling the other. And he knew
who would instigate the scuffle. His father would never lower himself
to begin such a display, but he would do his best to finish it. David,
however, would start any fight he could and then escape before it got
to be too much.

"I think you had better leave," the duke whispered in such a tone
that the hair on Derek's neck began to stand up. "You may return
when you have gained some decency."

"Then I hope you are prepared to wait for a while," David
returned, his drawling tone back in place, though Derek could see the
anger burning in him, "because what you call decency is a far cry from
what I do, sir. Good day." He spun on his heel, completely turning
his back to their father, then came over to Derek, who rose instantly,
and took his hand. "Sorry, mate," he whispered.

"Just another day with the family, right?" Derek replied in a low
voice that his father had not a hope of hearing.

They shared brief, tense smiles, and Derek clapped him on the
back as David stormed out of the room. The smile faded instantly as
his father looked at him.

"Well?" the duke asked in a rough voice, his chest rising and
falling at an alarming rate.

Derek moved to a closer chair and took a measured breath,
hoping his father would do the same. "I think that he needs some
time, sir."

"We do not have time, Whitlock!" he cried as he threw his hands out. "Do you think that is a luxury our family can afford? People are already talking about the disappointment that he is to the rest of the family, and how he will never measure up to the rest of us."

Derek had no doubt that the only people saying those things were the ones his father deemed worthy of his association, which was a rather short list of the most contemptible members of nobility that Derek had ever met, but that was a moot point here. The rest of Society, who adored David and thought he walked on golden soil, would be of little consequence to the duke.

"I did not even have this much trouble with your sister," his father sighed as he sank into his chair, putting one hand to his brow, "and she was the most headstrong girl I had ever encountered."

And she passed it all down to her younger brother. Derek found it ironic that his father was comparing his siblings, when he had not even flinched at Diana's being called a brood mare by David only moments before. It was very, very telling.

Because it was true.

"You must convince him to change, Whitlock," his father entreated, leaning across the desk. "You must preserve our family's reputation. You are my only hope."

Derek swallowed back the bitter taste forming in his mouth, and nodded slowly. There was no choice but to agree, else he would be on the receiving end of the wrath, same as his brother. And no one would be left to manage the pieces that would fall from their father's ire.

What was he going to do? He had no idea. But one way or another, something had to be if he wanted his family to remain as one.

Or as close as they ever got to the category, at any rate.

Much later that night, after the painfully silent dinner they had shared, Kate found herself playing in the music room while her husband slept on the sofa near her.

She did not mind. It seemed to calm him, which was all she had intended. The lines on his face had worried her, and the disgruntled downturn of his lip had given her cause to think that his day had been a difficult one. With his family, it always seemed to be.

And to think that she had once thought him lazy.

She glanced over at him as she played. He was so still, with his arms folded across his chest, his head resting on a pillow, his lips ever so slightly parted as he breathed silently in his sleep. He finally looked at peace, the tension she had seen in him gone for the time being.

If only his father did not expect so much of him. If only David would attempt to be contrite about anything. If only Derek were not so devoted as to accept whatever responsibilities that were thrust upon him.

But he would not be Derek if he were otherwise.

She smiled softly as he shifted his long legs, stretched out as far as they could be, though still booted. He should have removed them, it would have been far more comfortable. But it seemed he did not care about that.

She was feeling rather keen towards him at the moment. How could she not? He was the chief instigator for the change in her. She was Kate now, in every respect. She was wearing her hair down, she was playing music all the time, she smiled more, she laughed, and she sang.

What had come over her?

What had he done to her?

As she finished the final notes of the song she was playing, she sighed just a touch, letting the notes fade away gently, until only the crackling of the fire could be heard.

"That was a particularly lovely piece, Kate."

She turned on the bench to see Derek staring at her, eyes clear and lucid, a gentle smile on his face. She blushed a bit and offered a smile of her own. "Thank you."

"Was that something I should know or something new?"

Her heart started pounding, and she fought to keep from biting her lip. "It's a new piece."

He gave her an odd look. "How new?"

Her cheeks flamed even further, and she tucked a strand of hair behind her ear. "Very." When he continued to look at her in that manner, she confessed, in a small voice, "I wrote it."

His brows shot up to his hairline. "You wrote that?"

She nodded just once.

He got up from his sofa and went to her side, his eyes wide. "Kate, that was spectacular! I had no idea you could compose!"

"Thank you," she said softly, "but it is really just a hobby, and I'm not very good."

He took her hand and brought it to his lips. "You are very good, Kate, believe me."

She blushed yet again under the power of his gaze and tried to take her hand away, but he held tight. "Derek, you are still affected from sleep, it really was not..."

"I wasn't asleep," he interrupted.

She stopped and looked up at him in confusion. "But I thought..."

He shook his head, his eyes never leaving hers. "I could never sleep while you are playing, Kate. Never."

She wasn't sure whether she ought to smile and accept the extraordinary compliment or protest and be demure again. When he looked at her like that, she could barely think at all.

Derek must have sensed her turmoil, for he only laughed softly and tugged on her hand. "Come on, it is long past bed for both of us. Allow me to escort you to your room."

Relieved that he spoke first so she would not have to, she nodded and stood up. But Derek must not have backed up far enough, and suddenly Kate was so close to him that all of the breath was swept from her lungs in one swift second.

He still held her hand in his, and therein seemed to be the source of the heat now coursing through her. It was the only thing she could feel at the moment.

Derek could feel the change in Kate's breathing, and the shallow puffs of air touched his skin as gently as a breeze. She looked up at him, her eyes wide and luminous in the candlelight, and he saw in them the same confusion that radiated through him. Slowly, he brought his other hand up and touched a ringlet dangling near her ear. Then his fingers brushed her cheek, that beautiful, fragile porcelain that was her skin, and he could not stop himself from stroking it.

She did not breathe, and neither did he. For his part, he could not. His fingers faintly traced a line from her cheek to her chin, just below her lips. "Have I ever kissed you, Kate?" he whispered, unable to find any strength for his voice.

She finally took in a shaky breath, and he felt it down to his toes. "Yes."

"When?" he asked, still stroking her cheek, his thumb tantalizingly close to her bottom lip.

"On... on our wedding day."

"But never since," he murmured, his eyes now following his fingers.

"No," she breathed, her eyes fluttering a bit at his touch.

"I should have kissed you more," he said, finally touching her bottom lip with his thumb. "I should have kissed you every day."

She trembled and shuddered a gasp. "Why... why didn't you?"

"I don't know," he admitted in the barest hint of a whisper. Then, before his brain could catch up with him, he closed the distance between them and softly pressed his lips to hers.

In an instant, Kate's trembling stopped, and so did Derek's heart. So did all other sensation he had ever previously known. All he could feel was the gentle pressure of her lips on his, his on hers, the two of them together. Where he stopped and she started, he did not know and nor did he care. He had never imagined she would be so sweet, that he had ever gone without kissing her after having done so once. He could not have kissed her at their wedding; he would never have been able to stop. He did not know how he would now.

Once, twice, three times he kissed her, though it all blurred together as one long, gentle, searching exploration of his wife's lips.

They molded to his so perfectly it was like something out of a dream, only his dreams could not compare. His hand gently touched the skin of her delicate throat, then he ran his fingers back to the luscious mane of thick, black hair that she blessedly wore down, brought the tips of his fingers back to graze the firm line of her jaw, and finally took the tip of her chin back in hand. He broke off at last, not even able to find the shame he ought for the gasp that escaped him.

But she matched him with one of her own, and for a number of heartbeats, they hovered there, lips only a breath apart. The moment lingered, a faint memory that could be relived with the slightest movement on either side.

Yet neither moved. One breath passed his lips, then two, and then, just as he neared a third, Kate moved.

She took a shaky step away, her eyes wider and more entrancing than before. He wanted her to stay, he wanted her to go, he wanted…

He hadn't the faintest idea what he wanted.

Again, she moved backwards, slowly, almost hesitantly, until only their hands were touching.

"I think…" she started, her voice scarcely above a breath, her lips barely moving. "I think I will see myself to my room tonight."

All he could manage was a nod, his eyes switching between hers and their barely touching hands.

Then, suddenly, the last connection was severed as she stepped back further and turned, unsteadily making her way out of the room. She glanced back at him as she did so, and repeatedly, as if she were afraid he would vanish.

He would not.

He could not.

Only when she had fully left, when he was entirely alone, did he take a deep breath and allow himself to move. He sank onto the sofa he had only just vacated and put his head into his hands as his heart and his head frantically raced in tandem within him.

He moved his hands down to press together in front of his face and stared into the fire before him, now faint and smoldering, but with no less heat than it had before, when it blazed bright and furious.

He could relate.

Chapter Twelve

*T*he days following were some of the most blissful, if confusing, of Kate's entire married life. Derek was so changed, and so was she. Since he had kissed her in the music room that night, which she had gleefully relived over and over again in her mind, he was tender and attentive, and even demonstrative, which she was enjoying more and more.

Now there was not a time they were together when there was not a kiss. Gentle, soft, hesitant though they were, they always came. Now they began to mean more, and she looked forward to them, wondering when and how he would kiss her. He stole more kisses than she would have expected, and their behavior had turned almost playful.

More than just his kisses, she was also reveling in the fact that they were talking every day. Sometimes it was only as she played for him, but he told her everything about his day, about his father and his brother, and even some stories from his childhood. He never demanded that she reciprocate, but she did as much as she was able to. He laughed at her attempts to control things, kept her from ordering around servants more than necessary, and on occasion, still prodded her enough to nearly start a fight.

Only now it was fun.

The only time she'd had any sort of distraction lately had been the day before when Moira, her sister-in-law Caroline, and Caroline's younger sister Gemma, had come for an afternoon of music.

Gemma was a very accomplished violinist, and they had spent the time working on a duet. Derek had come in at one point, his curiosity piqued. He had claimed that he could not approve of such days unless he was privy to a demonstration. Though Gemma was not usually a shy young woman, it had taken a bit of his most charming coaxing to convince her to perform.

It had not been perfect, as they had only begun to practice that day, but it was rather lovely, if she did say so herself. And to confirm her point, Derek had risen from his seat and applauded the both of them. Thankfully, he had not kissed her in front of them, as she would have hated a public display of his affections, but the look he gave her was a kiss in itself, and she found herself blushing all the same.

It had been arranged that they would perform the number together for a small gathering of family and friends in their home in another two days, which placed it tomorrow evening. Kate had practiced quite a bit, feeling excessively nervous about performing before people who were not her husband, but with her new champions, Moira and Caroline, in attendance, she would get through.

She never had discovered just what those two had done in retaliation to Lady Greversham for the words she had uttered about her, but she had heard rumors that Lady Greversham's gown had been quite ruined, and a number of guests had left with soiled slippers. More than that neither would say, but their devious smiles told Kate that it might have been better if she did not know any of the particulars.

Now, as she played through the piece for the duet yet again, she wondered if her life would ever begin to feel normal again. Every day brought a surprise. Every day there was a change, either in her or in Derek. Every day she discovered something new about herself, something new about her husband, or something she had forgotten. She enjoyed the discoveries; she did not enjoy the uncertainty.

"Good morning, Katherine!" called the cheerful voice of Moira, who was suddenly appearing through the door of the music room, looking rather bright and refreshed and excited about something.

Trailing in behind her were Caroline and Gemma, both of whom were grinning.

"Good morning, Moira. Caroline. Gemma." She looked at Gemma with some confusion. "Were we supposed to practice again this morning? I thought we were going to do so tomorrow."

Gemma grinned, her eyes dancing. "Well, I supposed we could have, but no, I did not bring my violin today. I feel comfortable with the piece, if you do."

"Certainly, but what is the meaning of all this, then?" she asked, looking around as the others situated themselves.

"Consider this an intervention, Katherine," Caroline said with a mischievous look.

"Kate," she corrected suddenly, bringing all three pairs of eyes to her. She moistened her lips, then, in a much more calm, composed voice, said, "You may call me Kate."

"Oh, *may* we?" Moira asked with interest, looking at her sisters-in-law.

Kate chose to ignore their meaningful looks. "Intervention?"

Moira gave her a knowing smile. "Yes, Kate. An intervention. On your behalf."

"My behalf?" she asked in surprise, feeling totally bewildered now. "What are you talking about?"

"Your husband, Kate."

"Derek?"

Caroline sighed and put a hand to her brow. "Perhaps you had better start over, Moira. The poor girl is completely lost."

"She's not the only one," Gemma muttered. "I know why were are here, and I still don't understand you."

"Hush," Caroline hissed, rapping her sister on the knee, which made Kate smile. The affection between the sisters was very strong, and Kate had begun to wish that she and her sister had been closer as children. But alas, Aurelia had always been a ridiculous creature with no more sense than a pile of firewood, and that, at least, had a purpose.

"Very well," Moira sighed. "Kate, when we were over here the other day and enjoying the music that you and Gemma were providing, considering that Caroline and I are completely inept at all things musical…"

"Dreadfully so," Caroline commented with a shudder.

"Yes, well, I noticed that your husband, who is secretly a lover of music, and that detail will never leave this room," she broke off to give the other women a severe look, which prompted their immediate nods of acceptance, "was staring at you most intently during the performance."

Kate started to feel her face warm, and she prayed that it would remain a somewhat neutral shade. "Was he?"

"Yes, he was," Moira replied, looking at her carefully. "And you, my dear, were not entirely opposed to it. And I can assure you, the look on his face was hardly one of aversion. I take it your attempts at friendship are going… well?"

Kate almost laughed aloud. Well? That was one way to say it. Things were going so well that she felt as though she were in a dream most of the time. Every time he kissed her, in fact. But that was hardly something one said in front of polite company, no matter how trusted they were. "It is," she said slowly.

"This is worse than sitting for a portrait," Caroline groaned. She sat forward and took Kate's hand. "Kate, we think that your husband might be coming to feel more than friendship for you."

"What?" she asked, her eyes widening. He had kissed her, yes, but he had hardly given her any indication of what his feelings might be. A cordial husband and wife could exchange kisses, and nothing would be said at all about feelings. She had been trying for friendship with Derek, mostly out of necessity; she had never considered the possibility of anything else.

Caroline nodded importantly, and now it was Gemma who took up the charge. "He looked as though he could not decide how to act, but he was enjoying the dilemma."

"I hardly knew his expressions had such detail," Kate said with not a small amount of sarcasm.

"The point is, Kate," Moira broke in before Gemma could retort, "that things are changing between you and Derek, and I suspect most of the changing is on your side? After all, you are Kate now, you are playing now, you are far less formal than you were only last week, and you smile when you say his name."

"I do not!" she protested.

"You do," all three said in unison.

Kate frowned in her disgruntlement and looked at Moira accusingly. "I thought you *wanted* me to be friends with my husband, Moira."

"I did and I do," she said without concern, smiling in spite of Kate's glower. "But I don't want to see you falling at his feet without exacting something from him in return. This should not be so easy for him."

"It is hardly easy," Kate mumbled, folding her arms. "I am not that weak."

At Moira's look, she dropped her arms, and made a face. "All right, so I am not as strong as I think. Is it that way for all women?"

"Yes," said Moira and Caroline as one, while Gemma shook her head. She received a withering look from the others, and then Caroline spoke up again, "These early days are the most important. He knows you are not indifferent to him, but he is not certain how deep the feelings go or how to proceed. We become more simpering and ridiculous as we try to determine how to behave, what to do, what to say…"

"Yes, exactly," Kate murmured, looking down at her hands. "I don't even know if he likes me. I cannot believe that there is more to this than friendship when he is so changeable."

"Oh, I am quite sure he does like you. In fact, I think it is safe to say that more than friendship is on the horizon," Moira said with a devious grin. "The trick is going to be to get there without losing your head. But who is to say we cannot play with Derek a little, hmm?"

"What do you mean?" Kate asked, her brow furrowing in bewilderment.

Moira sighed and took both of Kate's hands in her own. "Darling, we need to have you court your husband."

"Shouldn't that be the other way around?" she said with a small laugh of disbelief.

"Oh, it will turn, don't worry," Moira replied, her grin deepening.

Then she sobered. "But Derek will not act without encouragement. He is too afraid of failure."

Kate swallowed back a touch of fear and apprehension. "What do you have in mind?"

"Don't look so terrified," Gemma laughed. "We're not going to turn you into a debutante."

"No, indeed," Caroline agreed, smiling gently. "We merely think you need to be a little more coy and flirtatious."

"But I am neither coy nor flirtatious."

"Then be whatever you are, Kate, but don't make things so easy for him!" Moira told her, squeezing her hands. "Court him. Encourage him. But don't let him take complete control. You are a strong and independent woman, and you deserve some courting yourself. Now, will you let us help you a bit?"

Kate looked into the eager eyes of her friends, debated for what seemed a very long moment, and then sighed in resignation. "Very well, but I will not do anything ridiculous."

"Would we ask that of you?" Moira asked with an innocent expression.

"Better not answer that," Gemma whispered loudly.

"Noted." She forced a smile on her face. "What must I do first?"

"Well, you are in mourning, so we are not able to play too much with your wardrobe," Caroline said as she looked her over carefully. "But I think we could have a bit more fun with the dark colors. First and foremost, though, is your hair."

Kate reached up to touch her hair uneasily. "What is wrong with it?"

"Do you always wear it back so severely?"

"Yes." She was *not* going to mention that she had been wearing it down at night as Derek suggested, nor that she did so just because she knew he liked it that way. That little detail was going to remain her secret, if nothing else did. "It was how my mother insisted it should be."

Caroline made a small noise of displeasure. "Well, we are going to fix that. You are far too young and too beautiful to wear it that way. I think we can come up with something much more fetching."

"Ladies," Moira said suddenly, a rather amused smile growing on her face, "I have an idea."

"I was afraid of that," Kate murmured, causing Gemma to snicker.

"What if," Moira began slowly, as if gathering her thoughts, "for now, we do nothing but plan? What if we save the moment for revealing the new, and improved, Katherine, Marchioness of Whitlock, for tomorrow evening?"

"Oh, I love it!" Caroline squealed, clapping her hands, as Gemma grinned and nodded excitedly. "Derek won't suspect a thing. It will be splendid. Kate, what do you think?"

Kate looked at all of them, and found herself a trifle touched that these women, whom she had not known for very long, were so intent on helping her, on improving who she already was, on bringing her and her husband closer together. No one had ever wanted to help her this much. And in spite of her worries, doubts, and even fears, she did find herself a little excited about the whole endeavor.

"I think," she managed, blinking back the sudden tears, "that would be perfect. But what will I wear?"

The grins that lit all three faces before her turned her stomach just a bit, and she swallowed hastily.

What had she gotten herself into?

The new chef arrived that afternoon, and it had taken all of their restraint to avoid going down to the kitchens to meet him and see him work, and perhaps taste something. But they were promised a fine meal for his first night, and so they waited.

Nearly three hours later, Derek and Kate eagerly made their way to the dining room, arm in arm. Nothing was on the table when they arrived, save the candlesticks and their place settings, which were in their usual places at the opposite ends of the table.

Derek frowned slightly and turned to the footman nearest him. "Can we move the place settings to the middle seats on this side of the table, please?"

Instantly both footmen in the room sprang into action and adjusted the table to his request.

Kate looked up at him in surprise, and he gave her an innocent look in return. "What? I want to sit by you. How else am I going to sneak food off of your plate when you're not looking?"

She rolled her eyes and smiled at the footmen as they finished. "Thank you, George. Thank you, Richard."

True to the unspoken footmen code, they said nothing, but they did smile at her as they resumed their positions.

Again, Kate felt Derek looking at her, and she met his questioning gaze with an imperious one of her own. "What? I can be pleasant when I wish it."

"You are full of surprises, Kate," he murmured as he took her hand and brought it to his lips.

In spite of the warmth that spread from her hand into her chest, she managed to give him a shadow of the devious smiles her friends had shown earlier. "You have no idea," she said quietly, which made him grin in blatant amusement.

Before he could reply, she sat in the chair before her, and patiently waited for him to do so as well.

He leaned down and whispered, "I could kiss you right now, you know."

"You shouldn't," she hissed back, paling. "There are servants here."

"What if I tell them to shut their eyes?" he replied as his lips grazed her ear.

She jerked her head back as if she had been burned and gave him a severe look. "Derek…"

"Kate," he returned as he met her eyes.

"Not in front of the servants, Derek," she begged through her clenched teeth. "Please."

Sensing this was not a battle worth fighting, he gave in with a longsuffering sigh and took his own seat. "Very well," he grumped. "But only because you said please, and only if you will make up for it double when I escort you to bed."

"Fine," she sighed, even as a smile quirked at one corner of her mouth. "Double. Later."

"And stop smiling like that," he whispered out of the corner of his mouth. "It makes it nearly impossible for me to *not* kiss you when you do that."

"What has you so flirtatious tonight?" she replied, trying not to laugh as she looked at him.

His green eyes clashed with her dark ones, and held her captive, and suddenly, she could not have laughed even if she wanted to. "I'm hungry," he said in a low voice.

Kate lost count of the number of heartbeats that passed, but a good part of her was quickly regretting her rule of not kissing in front of the servants. And Derek knew it, too. He saw it in her eyes. Her lips parted, and his eyes darted to them, then slowly dragged back up to her eyes.

Just then, the doors to the dining room opened and in came the entire kitchen staff, each of whom held a covered platter before them, and Hallstead, the new chef, brought up the rear, with the largest tray in his hands.

Kate inched her chair away from Derek during the commotion, but she knew the short distance would not help. The food would, but it would take a good deal more than that to make him forget. And she had promised him double the usual? She swallowed in spite of herself. She would burn alive.

The platters were placed before them, as one, all of the covers were lifted, and the most intoxicating smells Kate had ever known met her, and her stomach growled at them. The sight that met her was one of exquisite delight. There were potatoes and vegetables and bread that she instantly knew she would take second helpings of, proper or not. The goose on the table looked so tender and moist that her mouth watered. There was a pudding, and a custard, and freshly churned butter, along with some of the fruit preserves she enjoyed so much. And, as if to further her temptation, there was a mountainous plate of strawberry tarts to accompany the rest.

The moment the kitchen staff were gone, the pair of them very nearly dove at the food, taking no care for decorum or propriety as they heaped servings onto their plate. Though they were still well mannered, they could hardly have been called polite. Moaning and sighing and talking before swallowing were all a part of the next few moments as they devoured the best tasting meal they had enjoyed in quite some time.

"Best decision ever," Derek commented as he sliced another piece of meat for himself.

"I agree," Kate sighed as she took another spoonful of pudding. "We are never getting rid of him, I don't care how many sins he may commit."

"Absolutely." He speared one if the potatoes on her plate and shoved it into his mouth, and grinned as Kate rapped his knuckles in displeasure.

A knocking at the door to the dining room halted any retaliation from her as they both stilled and looked at each other in confusion.

"What in the world?" she murmured.

"No clue," he replied. "Come!"

Harville appeared, looking a bit confused himself. "Pardon me, my lord, Lady Whitlock, but there is a woman here who says she's come from Lady Aurelia."

"Did she give a name?" Kate asked, as Derek rose from his chair.

Harville shook his head. "No, my lady, but she does have a note with her. She says she must see one or both of you. I've shown her into the drawing room."

Derek and Kate looked at each other, a feeling of dread welling within them. Derek pulled her seat out and Kate stood, and together they hurried off to see who had come.

The young woman waiting for them had a bundle in her arms, and looked so exhausted that it was a wonder she could stand on her feet. She was moderately well dressed, though obviously a servant. She turned to face them as they entered, her eyes a touch dull.

"Jessie?" Kate said as she entered, taking hold of Derek's arm in fear.

"Lady Whitlock," she said with a tired smile. "I know this is terribly awkward, but when you sent my mistress that note the other day about being willing to watch the baby, she insisted that she take you up on it immediately. So..." she broke off and pulled the blanket away from the bundle in her arms.

They stepped forward, then gasped as one at the face of the sleeping figure she held. "Alice?"

"…here we are," Jessie finished softly with a helpless shrug.

Chapter Thirteen

"*I* cannot believe this. The nerve of that woman!"

"Now, Kate…"

"No! Do not 'now Kate' me, Derek! This is inexcusable!"

Derek sighed and watched his wife pace around the room in agitation. He adjusted the sleeping child in his arms and found himself smiling at the way she snuggled closer to him. He was very grateful they had sent Jessie off to bed immediately, allowing her to leave the child in their care until they had prepared the room for her. Jessie assured them that Alice rarely woke during the night anymore, and she had been fed just before she had fallen asleep, so she would not need to eat again until morning, and so Derek had absolutely no qualms about being left alone with the infant. After all, she was sleeping. For the moment, at least.

"Well, you did write to her, Kate," he brought up, still watching Alice sleep. "We did offer to take her at any time."

"Yes, well, you did not expect Aurelia to simply drop them at our doorstep without any warning at all, did you? No!" She threw her hands up in the air and whirled away with a screech.

"Hush, Kate, you'll wake her."

She turned back and gave him a withering look. He only grinned in response.

That seemed to take some of the tension out of her and she shook her head. "I cannot believe this. Listen; 'Nigel and I would like to spend a day or two with his mother again, and she does so love the boys, but the girl gives her a fearful headache'." She dropped her hand briefly to shake her head in disbelief. "The old crone, she is the reason Nigel is so useless. Imagine Alice giving anybody a headache."

"Ridiculous," Derek agreed softly, amused by his wife's indignation.

"And here; 'As you had so kindly offered to take the infant, I know you will not object to her staying for a few days while we are away. Jessie is a slow and stupid creature, but she seems to get along well with the girl'." Kate dropped the letter completely, letting it fall to the floor, and screeched again, but with more restraint. She placed her hands on her hips, breathing in and out rather shallowly through her nose.

"Kate," Derek said softly, rising from his seat and coming towards her with caution.

"Don't, Derek," she snapped, closing her eyes. "I am so peeved with my sister right now that I am torn between strangling her and screaming my head off, and at the moment both alternatives are rather tempting. I do not want to lash out at you, so you ought to be silent. Don't provoke me."

"Kate," he said again, standing directly in front of her.

Reluctantly, she opened her eyes and looked up at him.

He smiled gently and raised his brows. "It will be all right. Have we been put out? A little, yes. But once Tom and Jackson return with the bassinet, we will be fine. Take a breath, then take Alice in your arms, and see if that removes the stress from your shoulders."

He handed the baby to her, and instantly, the worry in her face left. She looked down at Alice for a long moment, ran a soft finger along her plump cheek, then sighed, holding her closer. "I'm sorry, Derek," she said, looking up at him again with a half-smile. "I shouldn't have reacted that way."

"No apologies necessary," he replied with a shake of his head, laying a hand along her cheek. "It's a hard thing, and we were not prepared for it. But we'll get through, and all will be well, all right?"

She nodded without speaking and he smiled, then leaned forward and pressed his lips to her brow softly.

"No more fretting," he whispered against her skin. "We will

make do." He stepped back and caught her watching him with warm eyes. Unable to help himself, he stroked her cheek, staring into those dark, entrancing eyes of hers for a long moment. It would be so easy to get lost in them, to let them take him captive and hold him until his will was hers, and he knew deep down that he would not have minded it at all.

"I'm sorry that our meal was cut short," he said on a sigh. "It hardly seems fair."

"No, it does not," she replied, looking up at him with a small smile. "But there will be more to come, won't there?"

"Oh, yes," he told her instantly, cupping her cheek with his other hand as well. "Many, many more, I can assure you."

"Good," was all the response she gave, and it was all the response he needed. Heart throbbing in his chest, he brushed his lips against hers, and felt the accompanying shudder rush through her. It pleased him to have such an effect on her, though he was well aware that she had a similar effect on him.

Who would have thought that his little wife, the tyrant of his past, the proverbial noose that always hung over his head, would have such a powerful hold over him? Or that he would enjoy it so much?

They were friends now, and he truly enjoyed that aspect. He loved talking with her. Kate listened with an intensity that made one feel as though one were the most important creature in existence. She never said anything without careful consideration, which he appreciated, as he rarely was so cautious. She was a wise and intelligent woman, and her input was becoming very important to him.

Granted, there were still moments when she was bossy and controlling and a little bit pretentious, but he could accept that. She would not be Kate if she were always agreeable and simple and casual. He would miss the fire in her if she were any other way.

He rested his forehead against hers, exhaling slowly.

"I think I hear them," Kate said softly.

Derek cocked an ear, and, sure enough, he could hear the two men coming down the hall. "I'll go see what I can do to help. I think Alice deserves a proper bed tonight." He stepped around the two of them and started out of the room, but turned back, calling his wife's name softly.

She turned to face him, and his throat closed up just a touch at seeing her with their niece in her arms, looking so natural and easy that it took his breath away. Somehow, he managed a smile. "You look well like this, Kate."

"Like what?" she asked, her brow furrowing just a touch.

"Holding a child."

Her eyes widened and her cheeks tinged with a bit of color.

His smile deepened. "You look very well, indeed." Before she could respond, he left the room to help set up the room for Alice, but he smiled all the while.

Sometime in the middle of the night, Kate woke up with a start, wondering what might have given her cause to do so. There was hardly any sound to be heard, other than the night breeze outside her window. She could not see the clock, but she knew it had to be in the very earliest moments of the morning.

Then she heard a noise, but it was so faint, she could hardly believe it had woken her. A cry, fussy and soft, followed by another whimper of very young distress.

With a firm shake of her head, she tossed off the bedcovers and got out of bed. She fumbled around in the dark for her wrap, giving a small "ah ha!" of pleasure when she found it. Tying it around herself hastily, she hurried from her room and down the hall to the temporary nursery they had set up.

So intent was she on her purpose, and worrying about what Alice might need, that she failed to notice the figure standing outside of the room, where the door stood slightly ajar. She was brought up short with a mostly silent gasp as she finally saw Jessie, who was wrapped in a shawl and smiled kindly at her as she approached.

"Jessie, what are you doing out here?" Kate whispered.

"I'm in the next room, and I heard Alice fuss," the girl replied in a rather hushed voice. "I waited a moment to see if she would continue to sleep, as she usually does, but she didn't, so I came out to get her and I found… well, perhaps you should see this."

Jessie put a finger to her lips and pushed the door open a little more. Kate blessed whoever had made it possible for that door to open silently, for she would not have disturbed the sight that met her eyes for anything.

"Hush now, Miss Alice, do you want to wake everybody up? Come, tell Uncle Derek what ails you." Derek rocked the girl back and forth gently, his face to the window, his back to them. He was dressed only in his nightshirt and dressing gown and his feet were bare, his hair tousled. So he had been roused from sleep as well, and his room was further away than hers was.

"There is no cause for such fussing," he continued to scold in a soft voice. "Just state your complaint clearly and a resolution can be found."

The baby made a slight whimper of discontent, and Derek nodded soberly, then offered his finger to her flailing hands.

"Hmm, yes, that does pose a problem. I'm rather partial to your aunt myself, and I can hardly blame you for wishing she were here and not I, but it's far too early in the morning for me to fetch her for you. Besides, you and I need to have a little discussion, young lady. If I am to appoint myself your guardian unofficially, some ground rules must be set up."

"How long has this been going on?" Kate breathed to the girl next to her.

She shrugged. "He was here when I arrived. He told me he would take care of her, and that I was to go back to bed and leave him to it."

"Did he?" Kate replied softly, turning to look back at her husband, now very nearly dancing with her niece in the moonlight, still murmuring softly to her. She couldn't help the smile that spread across her face, nor the odd squeezing sensation in her chest as she watched him. He would be such a good father; loving, understanding, firm, but fun.

Their children would adore him.

"There now," Derek whispered, pressing his lips to Alice's brow as he rocked her, "that's my girl. That's it." He turned just a touch, and Kate could see the smile on his face as he looked down on the now sleeping infant in his arms.

Unbidden, tears sprang into her eyes, and she had to swallow repeatedly. This was no show for her benefit; he had no idea she was even awake, let alone standing here watching him. This was Derek Chambers, stripped of artifice and disguise, honest and genuine. The man her husband was when nobody was looking. This was something she could believe, something that she could never doubt. Everything else she might be able to question, but not this.

She looked back over at Jessie and smiled. "I think I will go back to bed now. She seems to be in capable hands."

Jessie nodded with a small smile of her own. "Yes, very. Good night, Lady Whitlock."

"Good night, Jessie."

Kate silently made her way back down the hall to her room and settled herself back down under her covers before she allowed herself to sigh in a completely girlish fashion. She might have been hesitant about the slight changes her friends wanted her to make before now, but considering the events of this evening, she was now convinced that it would be a rather enjoyable experiment.

And if Derek's surprise would be half as good as Kate imagined it, the whole endeavor will be worth any pains she had to take.

"Where the devil is she?" Derek growled as he paced the floor of his music room.

"Who?" Colin asked, taking a long drink from the flute of champagne he was holding.

Derek threw him an incredulous look. "Kate."

"Don't be so anxious, Derek," his sister scolded from behind him. "She will be down soon enough."

He turned and glared at her. "What do you know, Diana?"

She offered him a very unconvincing look of innocence. "Why

would I know anything? I have only just arrived."

"Diana."

She rolled her eyes and brushed at her elegant plum colored gown in disgust. "Honestly, Derek, you are the most impatient man on the planet. Did you ever consider that perhaps she is nervous about performing and she and Gemma are practicing?"

That sobered him and his glower turned into a look of concern. "You think she's nervous? I never thought..."

"Obviously I don't know, Derek," she interrupted with a smile. "As I said, I have only just arrived. You are the first person I have spoken with." She gave him a scolding look. "And you have not even greeted me."

He reluctantly smiled and kissed her cheek. "Hello, Diana. Thank you so much for coming. I know it will mean a great deal to Kate."

She smiled brightly at him and looped her hand through his arm. "I would not have missed it. I hope you don't mind, but I've brought Mary Hamilton with me."

"Have you?" he asked in surprise, looking across the room where she indicated. There indeed was Mary, already conversing with Caroline and Geoff, and looking rather well. "I thought she was considered a wallflower."

"She is, but not by intelligent company," Diana retorted hotly, starting to pull away.

"I wasn't saying she is one," he hissed, holding her fast. "You know I think well of her, and certainly that Geoff does. They have been friends for years. I'm glad you brought her."

That seemed to soothe Diana's ire and she smiled conspiratorially. "I would like to introduce her to Katherine, and possibly convince her to sing with them tonight."

"Without practice?"

Diana looked rather mischievous. "Mary does not require much practice where her voice is concerned."

He looked doubtful, but she refused to elaborate.

Just then, the doors to the hall opened and he looked towards them with interest, only to sink back into disappointment when it was

Nathan and Moira. "Where *is* she?" he muttered.

"Stop being so anxious!" Colin told him with irritation. "You are making *me* nervous, and I don't even know your cause."

"I have not seen my wife in hours," Derek ground out. "She has been intentionally evading me and nobody will tell me what it is about."

"I hate not seeing my wife," Edward commented as he came up to Diana's side.

"Spare me," Colin groaned. "I am going to visit with Duncan, as he seems to be the only one not waiting on a woman." He nodded to them all, and then left rather dramatically to join Duncan, who was now chatting with Nathan and his brother Spencer.

Again the doors opened, but this time it was Gemma, and she only stuck her head in. Apparently, it was a cue, for Caroline and Moira stood and grinned. Derek tried to catch the girl's eye, knowing how skilled she was at nonverbal communication, but even she would not meet his gaze.

He huffed in irritation as she pulled her head back out, and growled under his breath.

"Steady, Derek," Diana whispered, sounding amused. "They can hardly hide her from you forever."

"I would not put it past them," he muttered, glaring at Moira and Caroline, who offered him bright smiles in return.

"Remind me to meet them as soon as Kate comes in," Diana whispered to her husband, who bit back a laugh.

The doors opened again, and, almost angrily, Derek turned to face them, wondering which guest that was not his wife would be coming in next. To his relief, it was his wife at last.

But he could not think much beyond that acknowledgement, for all thought and sense was swept away under the wave of astonishment at the appearance of the exquisite creature that was now entering. She was his wife, it was indeed Kate, but never had he dreamed his wife could look as she did now.

Her ebony hair was so elegantly arranged that he had to wonder how many hours it had taken, and if the pins scattered within knew just how fortunate they were. Loose ringlets hung near her ears and face, and one long ringlet in particular hung draped over one shoulder. Immediately he wanted to twirl it around his finger and bring it to his cheek.

He had never seen the gown she was wearing, and suddenly that became his chief regret in life. It was still a gown of dark mourning colors, as was appropriate, but the dark, silvery fabric seemed created for his wife's form and coloring, and instead of looking solemn and somber, she looked majestic, elegant, and breathtakingly beautiful. Her only accouterment besides the subdued pins in her hair was the black ribbon at her throat, and the simplicity supplied her with an air of grace that he had never witnessed before.

In short, Derek was stunned beyond imagination, and the only thing that seemed appropriate was the embarrassingly obvious *whoosh* of air that fled his lungs all at once.

He could not even be upset at Diana's snickering from beside him. Her hand slid from his arm, and where she went, he didn't know, nor did he care. He could not remove his eyes from his wife as she moved about the room greeting guests. Her eyes flicked over to him frequently, but never raised enough to meet his. He was oddly glad. He wanted to enjoy staring blatantly at her without having to endure the power of her eyes at the same time.

"Holy mother of pearl," he heard Colin whisper rather loudly not too far away, followed rather rapidly by a sharp rapping against his chest, courtesy of either Nathan or Duncan, Derek could not be sure which.

He agreed with every word.

"Do close your mouth, Derek," he heard Moira say from his side in a voice that was choked with laughter. "One would think you have never seen your wife before."

"I haven't," he managed hoarsely. "I can't have."

"Well, go and talk to her, you troll, before you lose your tongue," she laughed, pushing him to where Kate was now, speaking with Mary and Geoff.

In a daze, he made his way to her, and as if she could sense him coming, she turned towards him, her eyes finally meeting his. The insecurity was there, but only for him to see, and it was mingled with excitement and pleasure at his reaction. "Good evening, Derek," she said softly, smiling just a bit.

He swallowed and returned her smile, taking her hand in his. "Good evening, Kate." He stepped a bit closer, his eyes flicking to Geoff and Mary, who instantly looked rather interested in the painting behind them. "I haven't seen you all day."

"We had breakfast," she said with a quirk of her brow.

Was she teasing him? The little minx. He loved it. "That was hours ago. What have you done all day?"

Her smile stretched at the edges of her cheeks, and suddenly he noticed a small dimple in her left. It was now officially his favorite thing about her. For the time being. "I spent much of the day with Alice. Then I was forced into my room by my own personal musketeers, and I have not seen the light of day since." She fussed at her dress just a bit, touched her hair self-consciously. "I feel just a little bit ridiculous," she confessed in a whisper, but smiling still.

He shook his head. "Don't." He brought her hand up and placed a soft kiss on the inside of her wrist, his eyes never leaving hers. "You look wonderful."

"Really?" she asked, looking absurdly pleased, if a little breathless.

He nodded, not trusting himself to speak more.

Suddenly noticing how everyone in the room was watching them, they both stepped back. "I should get Gemma," Kate said with a slight toss of her hair, which bounced lightly as she did so. "We ought to perform early before we go in to dinner."

"Yes, of course," Derek said quickly with a nod. "Diana wanted to know if you would allow Mary to sing with the two of you."

Kate looked surprised. "Mary sings?"

"Apparently," he replied, shrugging. "And does not require practice either. The challenge is convincing her to perform."

"Well, if I can, she can," Kate said firmly, looking rather determined. "And if Diana thinks she ought to, then I am inclined to believe it."

"You are quite fearsome when you look that way, you know that?"

She grinned. "I *am* quite fearsome, Lord Whitlock. Haven't you learned that yet?"

She walked away to speak with Mary before he could respond, but his mind did so anyway. He did know it.

She had no idea just how well.

"I cannot believe the change in Katherine, Derek," Diana said, coming back to his side. "And I am not talking about just her appearance. Look at how open she is with the company! Look at how she smiles! It's remarkable!"

"Yes," he said gruffly, shaking off his stupor, "she is coming along rather well, isn't she?"

He could tell the moment he said it that it was the wrong thing to say. Diana went still and silent, and he could feel her coldness. "You are a pompous prig, you know that?"

"Excuse me?" he retorted, turning to meet her furious expression.

She must have seen something in his eyes, for she gave him a bit of a wry smile. "Do you really think she is the only one who needs to change?" With a knowing quirk of her brows, she swept away to rejoin her husband.

Derek watched her go, feeling confused. Change? Couldn't she see that he already had?

He felt different. He *was* different. No longer did he search for things to exploit about Kate. No longer did he want to insult her, or mock her to his friends, or avoid the merest hint of her. He was, in fact, finding that more and more he was searching for a reason to be near her, to compliment her, to think of her.

Did he like her?

Yes. Yes, he did.

"Derek?"

He jerked at the sound of his own name, and Nathan stood there, not three feet from him, looking curious. "What?"

"The music," he said, pointing behind Derek where the pianoforte sat, and where Kate, Gemma, and Mary were situating themselves.

"They convinced Mary to participate," Derek commented

unnecessarily.

"Yes, between your wife, my wife, Gemma, and Geoff, I don't think she stood much of a chance," Nathan laughed, leading the way to some of the open seats. He sat next to Moira, but left space for Derek beside him.

Derek shook his head and chose to stand behind instead, feeling slightly nervous himself all of a sudden. Kate was good; she was very, very good. But as yet, she had only ever performed for him. Could she handle the pressure that was now upon her? Would the other two measure up to her talent, or would they, heaven forbid, overshadow her?

Steady, Derek, Diana's words echoed in his mind, but in his own voice.

Steady. Yes, he could be steady. For Kate.

When everyone was situated, Kate offered a small smile directed at him, and suddenly the butterflies in his stomach intensified, and it was all he could do to smile back in encouragement. Then, with a glance at the other two, who nodded, she began to play.

The sweet notes of the pianoforte lit the room, or so it seemed, and so beautiful was the sound that Derek felt his nerves disappear and he sighed in relief. Gemma joined in with her violin shortly thereafter, and, just as it had the other day, the combination struck him more powerfully than any song he could recall in his entire life. The skill of both women was beyond impressive and, though he had heard them before, it felt as though it was a new experience for him.

When Mary started to sing with the instruments, all time seemed to stop. Never had any persons present imagined that the tall, fairly plain woman would possess a voice so pure, so rich and ethereal. Derek literally felt the hairs on the back of his neck stand on end as the trio continued, each seeming lost in her part, yet they all blended together so perfectly that it became difficult to determine any individual component apart from the others.

The music swelled and faded, flourished and diminished, and each rise and fall took the audience with it. Derek watched his wife in amazement, feeling as though every note somehow came directly from her, as if she were the creator, musician, and artist behind it all.

She looked so alive, so joyous as she played, and so composed and comfortable, as if she had been born to play.

He felt himself choke up as the song finished, and as he looked around, he saw that he was not the only one to do so. Applause broke out from everyone, and the three women stood, took their bows, and looked appropriately embarrassed by the attention. A quick scan of the room told Derek that of all present, only Geoff looked the way he felt; as if he had been kicked in the chest by a particularly swarthy mule, and had been ever so grateful for the injury.

Derek brought his eyes back to his incredible wife, who looked at him earnestly, as if for confirmation of her apparent success. Unable to speak above the applause, and doubting he could have if he wanted to, he nodded once, and then again, and again, and smiled proudly.

She sighed, and he caught just a glimpse of a tear in her eyes. Then she smiled, and the smile that spread across her face was one of profound relief, deep pleasure, and, yes, a little well-deserved pride.

He would never forget that smile as long as he lived.

Chapter Fourteen

*M*uch later that night, after all of their friends had departed, after all of the laughter had ceased, after his sister had given him enough meaningful looks to last him three lifetimes, Derek nearly flung himself onto the sofa in the drawing room with a groan. It had been some time since he had entertained, and he had forgotten how draining it could be. Though everybody that had attended had either been family or close friend, and there were not that many of them to begin with, he was exceptionally thankful to have them gone.

A softer, but no less relieved groan came from across the room, and he opened his eyes to see Kate sinking into a chair as well. She leaned her head back and closed her eyes, then kicked her slippers off and stretched her stockinged toes against the rug.

He grinned at her actions. The old Katherine would never have done anything of the sort. The very idea would have appalled her. He loved the fact that she could not only think it now, but actually do it.

This new wife of his was continually surprising him, some days so much so that he could barely remember the old one. It seemed so strange that they were one and the same, that this version had hibernated beneath the old.

The other surprising notion was just how very much he enjoyed being near her. More and more he wanted to be with her and no one else. His friends, though amusing and supportive and loyal, could not hold a candle to her. And for a man such as him, who had always stood by his friends and valued their company, it was disconcerting.

But pleasantly so.

"What are you doing all the way over there?" he asked with a tired smile.

"Resting," she replied, not even cracking an eyelid in his direction.

"Come and rest over here. There is plenty of room."

"Is it as comfortable as this chair?"

His smile widened. "More so. There is a life sized pillow over here."

A hint of a smile quirked at a corner of Kate's full lips, but she only shrugged her shoulders, then lightly pushed herself out of the chair and, leaving her slippers where they lay on the floor, she sat next to him on the sofa. Derek had a devil of a time keeping his smile in check, and felt like a much younger man, all excitable and anxious.

He was turning into quite the puppy.

"I don't believe this is as comfortable as you indicated," Kate said airily after a moment of silence, frowning just a bit. "I think my chair was far better."

She moved to get off of the sofa, but Derek was lightning quick to seize her arm and hold her fast. "That," he informed her in a would-be serious tone, "is because you have neglected one crucial element."

Kate looked down at his hold on her arm, then gave him a look, raising one brow imperiously. "Have I?"

He nodded sagely. "You forgot about the pillow."

"Ah," she replied with a nod in return. "How very remiss of me."

"But that is easily remedied," he allowed, releasing her arm, and setting his own along the back of the sofa. He then looked at her rather invitingly. "See? Everything is all prepared."

"So it is," she said, giving him a shy smile as she slowly leaned back into his hold, and nestled her head onto his shoulder.

Swallowing back a sudden appearance of nerves, he dropped his arm to encompass her shoulders. When she moved just the tiniest bit closer, he mentally cheered, making him feel even more the giddy fool than he already did.

But honestly, what man on earth did not want to have a beautiful woman in his arms? *Especially* when the beautiful woman in question was his wife?

He felt justified in his stupidity.

"Is it always going to be this exhausting?" Kate asked softly, losing the teasing, confident air of only moments before.

"What are you talking about?" He had long since lost any idea of previous conversations and his focus was entirely elsewhere.

"Hosting events."

He leaned his head against the back of the sofa and sighed. "I don't know. I hope not. We only entertained a small number of people we know and love tonight, and I feel as though I have been dragged behind a carriage. I have no idea what we are going to do when we have to host things for the vast number of people we don't like or couldn't care less about."

Kate found Derek's free hand and almost hesitantly laced her fingers into his, and the jolt that shot up his arm and into his chest left him just a little bit breathless. Gingerly, he began stroking the top of her hand with his thumb. It was an oddly soothing thing to do, and yet again, he found himself whirling.

"I just hope I can do things perfectly," she said quietly, playing with his fingers, not looking at him. "I don't want to let anybody down."

Her admission stunned him. She had been the ideal future duchess their entire marriage, and had only lacked an open personality. Now she had that as well; truly, there was nothing left but for her to be perfect. "Kate, look at me," he murmured, wanting to take her chin in hand, but not willing to let go of her fingers to do so.

She eventually brought her eyes to meet his and he tightened his hold on her shoulders. "You were perfect tonight. I was extremely proud of you."

"You were?"

He nodded slowly. "You played brilliantly, you conversed with grace and ease, you looked every bit the gracious hostess, and quite frankly, you lit up the room."

Kate blushed and dropped her gaze. "Oh, please, Derek, I hardly did any of that."

"You did," he said firmly. "You were in such fine form tonight, Kate, that it brought comment. Everybody was impressed."

"Really?" she asked eagerly, looking back up at him. "Who?"

"Diana, Edward, Nathan, Geoffrey, Colin…"

"Colin?" she interrupted with surprise. "Really?"

Derek grinned. "Really. I'm afraid you have stunned him into complete fealty, Kate. You could knock him over with a blink and he would love it."

A satisfied smirk lit her face and she giggled. "I hardly expected to ever turn him to my side. I shall enjoy this, I think. I have always wanted a minion."

"Poor Colin."

"Who else?" she demanded, poking him just a bit. "Who else did I impress?"

He laughed and batted away her finger. "Everyone, all right? Every single person was complimentary and impressed and thought you did a marvelous job."

She grinned and settled herself against him again, her other hand now joining the first in toying with his. "What about you, Derek?" she asked in a soft voice. "Did I impress you?"

"Yes," he whispered, pulling her in closer. "Yes, Kate, you did."

She looked up at him once more, and it seemed that time stood still. Unable to resist the power that was continually drawing him to her, Derek leaned down and brought his lips to hears, still gentle and light, giving her every opportunity she would need to pull away if she so desired.

He was ready to break away, to cut off this magical connection between them, to regain some semblance of sense and thought, when he both heard and felt a soft sigh escape her.

Then he was lost.

Fingers trembling, he took his hand from her shoulders and threaded his fingers into her hair, scattering a few pins. He ventured to take the kiss a little further, to put a little more of himself into it, to let her feel just how much he was coming to feel for her without voicing the words aloud. He felt her soft, shaking fingers touch his jaw, felt her lips mold to his more perfectly, and his hold in her hair clenched ever so slightly.

"Derek," she breathed, breaking off with a gasp, her hand still on his face.

"What?" he rasped, leaving his lips exactly where they had been at the juncture of her mouth and cheek.

"We have to stop."

He smiled, nuzzling her ever so slightly. "Why? Are there servants in here now?" he teased, pressing a few scattered kisses to her jaw.

"No," she gasped, pushing at him, "it's the door."

He froze momentarily, ears training on the door, and, sure enough, there was a thundering at their front door. How in the blazes had he missed that before?

He pulled back and they stared at each other in confusion, both more than a little breathless. "Who could that possibly be this late at night?" he growled.

"No idea," she said, shaking her head.

"Derek!" bellowed the knocker. "Derek, open up!"

Derek groaned, and touched his forehead to Kate's. "Oh, no."

"What? Who is it?"

"David."

It took Kate's mind a considerable amount of time to process what Derek had said. She was still so pleasantly frazzled by his kisses that coherency was limited and slow.

David? David who? Then she remembered.

"Your brother?" she said at last, trying desperately to hide her frantic panting. "What could he want?"

"Nothing good, I am fairly certain." He sighed, pressed a quick, but no less heated kiss to her lips and pulled back. "This will not take long," he promised as he stood.

"How do you know?" she asked with an amused smile.

"I will make sure it does not." He gave her a look that sent a sort of fiery chill racing up Kate's spine, then turned and headed for the door where Harville was preparing to open it. At Derek's nod, he did so, and though Kate couldn't see him, she could tell that David's appearance was not a pleasant sight.

Derek's brows shot up and a frown formed. "David."

"Derek, it is sooooo good to shee you," came a slurring, drawling voice that sounded very much like David, but at the same time, was so unlike his usual tone and manner that she had a hard time believing it actually *was* David.

Curious, she rose from the sofa and peeked around the corner. The normally so dapper and dashing Lord David Chambers looked more like a peddler who was dressed in fine clothing rather than someone who belonged in them. His hair was rumpled and disorderly, his clothing stained and disheveled, his jaw scruffy, and his eyes bloodshot.

In short, Lord David was exceptionally inebriated.

"Helloooooo there, Katherine," he drawled as he saw her, turning to bow clumsily, and losing his balance. Derek caught his arm before he fell to the floor, but not before Kate got a face full of alcohol laced breath.

"Hello, Lord David," she coughed, taking a measured step back, but smiling with a bit of amusement. She ought to be offended and affronted and appalled, but having never been within fifty meters from someone so drunk before, she found that she was just terribly fascinated and wanted to laugh.

David grunted as his brother shifted him into a more secure hold, and gave Kate a bleary look. "Didjoo know that Derek calls you Kate?" he asked, snickering stupidly.

"Yes, I did, actually," Kate answered, still smiling. "You can too, if you would like."

David looked startled, then squinted up at his brother, who was starting to struggle under the deadweight in his arms. "Waaaaaiiiiiit, she *lets* you call her Kate?"

"Yes, David, she does," Derek sighed, rapidly losing patience, though he was smiling still.

David frowned and tried to stand on his own, but only managed to stumble more fully into his brother's grasp. "Derek, you are a liar," David announced, swaying dangerously as he tried to point a finger up at him. "Sheeee is no devil. She's an annnnnnnngel."

"Yes, thank you, David," Derek said loudly, his cheeks coloring. He looked over at her and mouthed "I am so sorry" with a wince.

Kate grinned at him and his reaction. It no longer bothered her that Derek had once upon a time been critical of her and had called her names behind her back and whatever else he might have done. She had done the same thing with him. They were both different now, and things had changed.

"My lord, what brings you to our humble abode?" Kate asked him, stepping closer.

"So polite, soooooooooo pretty," David crooned as he looked at her. "Did you do something different with your hair, Kate? It's all falling down and pretty and sensual and…"

"Stop trying to flirt with my wife and answer the question, would you, David? I have no trouble dropping you and leaving you on the doorstep," Derek barked, losing his smile.

"You sound like our beloved father did only this afternoon," David remarked, snarling and looking as though he would like to spit.

"Don't spit," Derek warned, and Kate was amused that their thoughts had been so in line. "So all of this was brought on by another lecture from our father?"

David shook his head, which made both him and Derek sway. "A threat."

"A threat?"

He nodded. "'Either you find a wife in the next month or I will find one for you'," he said, taking his voice deeper to attempt to sound like his father, though he failed. "It sheeems I am to be married soon, Derek, whether I like it or not."

Derek groaned and shook his head. "All right, all right, we'll figure something out. We will keep you here tonight," he paused and looked at Kate, who nodded in confirmation, "and then you and I will go see Diana tomorrow when you have sobered up."

"If you don't mind," Kate interrupted gently, "I would like to go check on Alice and then go to bed."

"I can take you up," Derek said immediately.

She shook her head, looking at her husband. "You have your hands quite full. I'll be all right for one night."

"But…" Derek started, then bit back his reply.

Kate knew what he was going to say, somehow. She smiled softly at him, and eventually, he returned it. Her heart warmed and her toes curled at that smile, so full of promise and meaning. She wished they hadn't been interrupted. She wished the night could have gone on forever as it had been. She wished…

"Alish is here?" David broke in, destroying the moment yet again. "I love that sweet baby Alish! Can I see her?"

"Tomorrow," Derek growled, hefting his brother's arm over his shoulder. "Tomorrow you can see her. When you are a better example."

"I am *always* a good egggsample," David slurred defensively as Kate headed up the stairs.

"Of course you are," Derek assured him sarcastically as they awkwardly followed her.

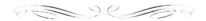

Derek was quite certain the morning sun had never been so bright, and he had never been so delighted about it. David was miserable, fumbling along behind him, muttering oaths and curses against his brother's need to walk everywhere when a perfectly good carriage was at his disposal.

Derek did not feel the need to walk everywhere, really; he merely thought it was a good idea most of the time.

Today was one of those times.

Due to his unnatural ability to only sleep during dark hours, the very grumpy David woke with a raging headache and barged into the breakfast room, where Derek, Kate, Jessie, and Alice already were. He had not said a word, only spoke in grunts, but Derek, having spent a few too many mornings with violent headaches, bloodshot eyes, and limited vocabulary in his wilder youth, was able to provide adequate translation.

The only thing that seemed to brighten David's foul mood was when he caught sight of Alice. Incredibly, a smile crossed his face and he seemed in far less pain than he had been moments before. He changed direction and immediately took the happily chattering girl from her nursemaid's hold. After several rather noisy, slobbering kisses that made Alice squeal, David handed her back to Jessie, who was trying not to laugh herself, and then sat down and silently inhaled his meal.

When Derek had inquired as to whether or not David was ready enough to see their sister, he had merely nodded and left the room. Pressing a light kiss to his wife's hand, Derek followed and smirked at the moaning that reached his ears when the door was opened.

Now they were nearly to Diana's house and soon enough, they would be well on their way to a solution, preferably one that did not involve Derek having to explain to his father why he was not going to marry off his brother to the first available heiress they could find.

"I thought I told you to send a note from now on!" came half irritated, half amused voice from above them.

Peering up, Derek grinned at the form of his sister, leaning rather precariously out of a window.

"Does your husband know you lean out of windows like that?" he called up in response.

"Stop shouting!" David groaned, putting a hand to his head.

"Oh my." Diana winced. "Rule Ten?"

"Among others, I expect," Derek sighed, looking over at David, then back up at his sister. "We have got a serious situation, Di."

"I suspected we might. Come on in, I shall be right down."

Within moments, the three siblings were seated in the front drawing room, and Diana had ordered light refreshment and tea for her and Derek, and a cold compress for David's throbbing head. When the maid brought it in, Diana took the compress and laid it across David's eyes, and sighed. "Honestly, David, are you determined to break every single one of those rules?"

"No," he said stubbornly as he looked at her from under the compress. He grimaced and put his hand on top of the cloth and leaned back. "Just most of them."

"Imagine that," Derek remarked with a smile.

"I have a few that I like," David brought up with a finger. "Rule Eighteen being the primary."

Derek thought back for a moment. "Always dance with a wallflower?"

David nodded, his wild grin the only part of his expression any of them could see. "It's probably the best part of the night, when I do that. They don't care that I'm wealthy or the son of a duke, and they don't ever think that I am going to propose matrimony. I have the best conversations with wallflowers."

"Well, hurrah for you," Diana snorted, sipping her tea. "But what about the rest of the rules?"

"I always carry a handkerchief, I always wear gloves… in public, and I always change for meals." David shrugged, then groaned at the motion. "Other than that, I see no reason to have the rules at all."

The two remaining Chambers siblings looked at each other and shook their heads, both smiling. David had always been the most outspoken of the three of them, and in adulthood he was only growing more so. But one could not help loving him regardless.

Well, maybe one.

Derek sighed and told Diana what David had let slip the night before, with some now sober clarification and elaboration from David himself. The frown that formed on Diana's face was so impressive and imposing that Derek suddenly knew whom she had learned it from. It was the very image of their father, and it had the same effect.

"I do not understand that man," she muttered as they finished the story. "As if David would marry a milkmaid or a courtesan."

"I might," David said with a grin, "if she were pretty enough and had the requisite intellect."

"The point is," Diana overrode loudly, giving her younger brother a look, "that our father should trust David to behave with as much respect as he does the rest of us, especially where his marriage is concerned."

"I agree," Derek sighed as he reached for a biscuit. "But he is immovable. He is determined that David be married soon and that his wife meets all of the necessary criteria," he broke off with a snort and shook his head.

"I don't want to get married now, I am not ready to get married now, and I *will* marry *my* choice, not his," David announced from his semi-recumbent position on the sofa.

"We know," Diana soothed with a slight roll of her eyes. "If we have learned anything from Derek's example, it is that there is great danger in marrying early and to a person of someone else's choosing."

"Yes," Derek murmured, thinking back on his wedding day, on his life up to this point, on the very subject of his wife. "But it turns out I may have been fortunate after all."

"Apparently," Diana agreed with a grin. "But it did take a while. And David is not nearly so open."

"I beg your pardon!" David protested, sitting up slightly.

Diana rolled her eyes again. "Oh, please. Mountains are more movable than you are. At any rate, I think you will need to get out of England for a while. Explore the continent; get all that wicked wildness out of you." She grinned mischievously. "You know, get your priorities aligned."

"I am all for it," David said, returning her grin with one of his own in spite of his headache.

"It will never work," Derek told them both, shaking his head. "The duke will not allow it."

"He will when I tell him that his first grandchild is expected to arrive in about six months," Diana muttered darkly, still smiling. "That should get the old codger to shift his stance."

It took a good half of a minute for either brother to react, and then it took another three minutes or so to calm them down. Even David, with his raging headache, shouted out his jubilation and even went so far as to leave the sofa and race over to give Diana a hug, while Derek merely maintained his position, and grinned broadly.

Diana beamed under their attention, and thanked them, then waved David away like an irritating insect. His headache apparently returned, for he gingerly excused himself from the room, taking his compress with him.

"So help me, Derek, if I find anything resembling regurgitated remains of breakfast in my house, I am marching over to your house and dragging you back here to clean it up."

Derek grinned. "Oh, don't worry about that. He is only going to sleep it off somewhere. Would you mind very much housing him until he is able to take care of himself again? I would, but… I am… that is to say, Kate and I…"

"Yes, Derek, he can stay," Diana interrupted gently, smiling. "You are quite occupied at the moment, aren't you?"

He nodded, not seeing any need to expound further.

"How are things?" she asked quietly, watching him with curious, but kind eyes.

He hesitated for a moment, not because he did not want to share with her, because he did. He and Diana had always had a special bond, and they always told each other everything, things they never shared with other people. It had been suggested that they were actually twins, but given the year's gap between them, it was obviously not true. They were just that close.

No, he hesitated because he had no idea how to respond, how to define what he was feeling.

"I think…" he began slowly, choosing his words with great caution, "I think I might be…" He couldn't say it, he could not define it as such yet. There was too much uncertainty, too much unknown.

"You might be what?"

Of course, Diana would not let things go so easily. There was nothing for it. "I think I might be falling in love with her."

Thankfully, Diana's reaction to his admission was far more reserved than his and David's had been to hers. She said nothing, did not even squeak or shift. More than a little unnerved, and wondering if she were alive and breathing, he looked up, only to find her eyes swimming in tears. Oh dear. That was not good.

"I'm sorry," she whispered, wiping at her eyes, and laughing a little. "Ridiculous, I know, but I have been so emotional lately, and I never expected to hear you say that." She sniffed into her handkerchief.

"Nor did I."

"You need to leave."

"What?" he cried, looking back up at her.

"Sorry, I mean you need to go back home. Go be with her, find out if you really are in love with your wife. Spend time with her, court her, lose yourself in her. You cannot figure this out if you are here, Derek. You need to leave."

"All right," he said hurriedly, getting up, but still watching her with concern as the tears continued to course down her cheeks. His sister rarely lost control of her emotions, and the idea that he was the cause of this sudden break in control was not only disconcerting, but worrisome. If Edward should find out that Derek had made her cry, he would lose the function of his lower half.

"Go. Go now," Diana urged, waving him out as she dabbed at her cheeks.

"Are you going to be…?"

"I am *fine*, Derek," Diana barked. "Go!"

"All right, all right," he replied, holding up his hands in surrender. "I'm leaving."

And he did, but with heavy reservations. The whole walk back to his home, he wondered at her words, at his words, at his own thoughts. Was he in love with Kate? It was possible. It was quite probable, actually. He was certainly growing more and more fond of her as the days wore on. He had promised to stay for two weeks, and now he couldn't even think of leaving. He wanted nothing more than to stay and explore these new emotions; he wanted to understand his wife more clearly; he wanted to understand himself more clearly.

Because never had he been more confused about the man he was than right now.

Before he was aware of it, he was standing in his own entryway, handing his hat and gloves to Harville. "Where is Lady Whitlock?"

"The drawing room, my lord. I am afraid she is a little down at the moment, sir. Lady Aurelia came by this morning and has taken Miss Jessie and little Alice back home. We are all a bit forlorn about it." In truth, the butler did look a little older at the present.

Derek smiled a touch. "I can imagine. Thank you, Harville." He went in to the drawing room, and Kate, though happy to see him, did

171

look sad.

When he asked about it, she hesitated, but thanks to his uncanny ability to prod information out of people, she eventually sighed, and said, "I miss Alice."

He nodded. "So do I. But you may call me a brute when I tell you that part of me is relieved to have her returned to her home."

"What?" she cried. "How can you say that?"

"Because now I have you all to myself again. I love Alice dearly, you know that, but when she was here, you spent most of your time with her, and while I can hardly blame you for that, I was profoundly jealous of my beautiful niece."

"You were?" she asked with a small smile.

"Mmhmm," he said with a nod, shrugging. "I missed you."

"I was right here."

"I missed you."

She opened her mouth, then closed it again. Then she stood and walked over to where he was, still leaning against the fireplace, and wrapped her arms around his waist, laying her head against his chest.

Finding breathing and swallowing a trifle difficult with the sudden lump in his throat, Derek put his arms about her and held her to him. "What is this for?" he asked softly, his voice surprisingly raw.

"That was the nicest thing anyone has ever said to me," she told him, nuzzling against him ever so slightly. "I… I missed you, too."

Derek closed his eyes and restrained the urge to sigh as he touched his head to hers. He had to amend his previous statement; he was most definitely falling in love with Kate. There was no maybe about it. And suddenly, he had to ask the one question that had been eating away at him since he had come back to London.

"Why did you send for me, Kate?" he murmured, loving the feel of her hair against his cheek. "Knowing we didn't like each other, knowing how your mother felt about me, knowing how I felt about her, why did you send for me still? And don't tell me it was for propriety; we caused more of a stir because I *was* there."

She lifted her head and looked up at him. "Is it important?"

He nodded. "It is to me. Please."

She swallowed and he could see the faint shimmer of tears in her eyes. "I didn't want to be alone."

"You had your father and your sister," he reminded her.

"Yes, but… I wanted you."

That hardly seemed likely, and he knew he showed his surprise. "You did?"

"I didn't know who I was without my mother, and the only other person I could identify myself with was you. I wanted you to come and remind me who I was." She smiled up at him. "You did, but not in the way I imagined."

"Well," he said after a moment, once he had swallowed that lump again and managed to smile, "I do aim to please."

She laughed in a low voice, and he could not resist leaning down and capturing her lips in a gentle, teasing kiss that, while designed to render her both speechless and breathless, actually turned *his* thoughts to nothing but a babble of sounds that was rather rapidly fading into a faint humming.

As if she knew this, Kate broke off the kiss and quirked one brow at him, which made him smile, in spite of his sudden state of stupor. He toyed with her still-intact locks of hair, and tilted his head ever so slightly.

"Will you play for me, Kate?"

She leaned back just a touch in surprise. "Now? But it's still early."

"Who says we can only have concerts at night? I love to hear you play any time." He brought one finger to stroke her cheek ever so softly. "Please?"

She shook her head with a smile. "You are incorrigible."

He grinned. "Is that a yes?"

She laughed and stepped out of his hold, but took his hand and led him to the music room. She sat down with a small sigh of mock frustration, and began to play.

Derek propped his elbow on the arm of the sofa and rested his head in it, feeling more than content to sit here forever, watching his wife with an amused smile on his face as she played for him.

He had never known that life could be this sweet.

But he was so grateful it was.

Chapter Fifteen

Kate smiled to herself as she prepared for bed. She had no idea what had gotten into her husband, but ever since Alice had left, he had been attentive and charming and so sweet it was leaving her breathless. Every morning he sat beside her at breakfast, experimenting on how close to her he could get before she would push him away. Every morning he got a little closer.

Half of her thrilled at his attention, reveled in each and every heated look and soft smile. She had never felt more beautiful, more captivating, or more interesting than she did when he was with her. For a woman who had been trained to expect a great deal of herself but to never think much of herself, it was a refreshing change.

It seemed that the plan to court him in order to convince him to court her in return had worked. She toyed with him just enough to keep things interesting, refraining from giving in completely to avoid losing herself in the process. But it was getting more and more difficult to pull back from him when every fiber of her being was screaming to sink further into the swirling depths of temptation and promise that was her husband. No longer was it a test of his affections. It was now a test of her will.

Lately she thought it might be possible that Derek could love her, and this was what held her back. What if he *did* love her? She was so uncertain of herself, of what it all meant; what if she could not fully return the sentiment? She liked him, and on many levels. He was rather quickly becoming the person she wanted to spend all of her time with, and he most certainly was the man who occupied her dreams. He was encouraging, he was affectionate, he was kind; in short, he was everything she had never thought she would have, and especially not from him.

How could she be falling in love with a man she never knew existed?

And she was falling in love with him, she knew enough of herself to know that, and there would be no use trying to deny it.

It terrified her.

She ceased in her preparations for bed and grabbed her cloak and half-kid boots. She needed to think, and there was only one place where her thoughts were clear and pure, regardless of the insanity of her life. She slipped down the hall to the servants' stairs, and used the kitchen door to take her to the back garden. It was only through the back hedge and across two streets before she would reach it, and the secrecy of her journey always left her exhilarated.

But before she could take three steps, she hesitated. While she normally loved this time to herself, to be alone with her thoughts and the night, she suddenly found she did not want to be alone at all. She wanted…

She turned and ran lightly around the corner of the house to the window of Derek's study, and, just as she suspected, the curtains were pulled back. Over the brief course of their improvised courtship, one of the things she had learned was that Derek was fascinated by the stars, and whenever he could, he would stare at them. It was oddly adorable that he had this secret interest in them, and she suspected he had done so ever since he was a boy. As it was turning out, Derek was a man with many secrets, and she suddenly wanted to know each and every one of them.

Moving herself into the light from the window, she waited for him to notice her as he paced around the room. His thoughts must have been rather occupied, for he did not even glance out of the window once. She laughed quietly to herself. Whatever was distracting him, he was doing a very poor job of hiding it. The lines on his face were aging him, and she suddenly saw how Derek would look when they were old and gray, and in the stern line of his jaw, she saw how their son would look when he was not getting his way. She hoped her son looked like his father. She hoped all of her children looked like their father.

She found the very thought of them sent a warm feeling coursing through her. If she kept this up, there would be nothing left of her to pull back.

Shaking herself just a bit, she tossed a small pebble at the window, the sound of which brought Derek's head around in surprise. The shock increased when he saw her standing outside. He tilted his head in question, a curious half smile forming on his remarkably handsome face.

She smiled back and waved him out, inviting him to join her.

He looked confused, but said nothing.

Again she waved, smiling more broadly.

His grin grew and he shook his head, not in refusal, but in amusement.

She took one half step forward, softened her smile and her eyes, and beckoned again with one hand.

Derek's grin faded, but the interest flared in his eyes. She saw him swallow, and then nod. Before she could react, he had turned from the window and almost run from the room.

With a relieved smile, Kate stepped back and waited for him to join her. She did not have to wait long at all.

He came jogging towards her, smiling with a mix of confusion and humor. "Kate, what in the...?"

She shook her head and held out a hand to him, which he took as he reached her. She offered a mischievous grin, and starting to run towards the back hedge, and he obediently tagged along, his hand firmly in hers.

"Where are we going?" Derek laughed as he ran alongside her.

"You'll see," she replied cryptically, unable to resist grinning at him.

"Doubtful. It's pitch black out here." His words were reluctant, though his tone was anything but.

"Oh, come on, Derek. The moon is out, the stars are out, it's a glorious night, and I want to enjoy it with you."

He gripped her hand more tightly but said nothing in response, which she took to be a good thing. They pushed through the hedges with no difficulty, as her repeated trips through had left a small break in them. She could almost feel his anticipation growing with hers as they ran across the streets, the silence of the night adding to the mystery. She hoped she had been right in bringing him along; it felt right to do so.

"Kate!" Derek hissed, a smile in his voice. "Where exactly are you taking me?"

"We're nearly there," she panted, tugging more firmly on his hand as they ran. "This is my favorite place in all the world. I come here whenever I need to think, or to breathe, or gain perspective."

"In the middle of the night?"

"Most of the time, yes. It is on the Mayfield's property, after all, and backs up directly to Hyde Park. Daylight would be highly inappropriate. Not that anybody has paid any attention to it in years, but that adds to the charm of it, I think."

"The charm of what?" Derek asked as he looked at her in exasperation.

She finally stopped as it came into sight, and she sighed. "That."

He turned to look, and Kate was torn between watching him and trying to see this place with new eyes, as he was. She settled for both. Derek's eyes widened as he took in the small gazebo, almost overrun with lilacs, looking like something out of fairytale. The moon reflected brightly off of the nearby pond, casting a faint silvery light across the panorama.

"Oh," Derek breathed softly, moving forward on his own now, though he still held Kate's hand in his own. Only when they reached the gazebo did he speak again. "How did you ever find this place?"

"I don't even recall," Kate said as she gently touched the petals of one lilac within her reach. "But it's been my haven ever since. Lilacs are my favorite flower, you know."

"Are they?"

She nodded absently, still toying with one. "They grow best when wild, they take hold of all around them, and their fragrance is one of the most poignant of all floras. And they are beautiful, particularly in the moonlight, don't you think?"

"I do."

Something in his voice made her shiver and she turned to look at him, only to find him watching her instead of the flowers. "Why are you looking at me like that?" she whispered, feeling very self-conscious.

"Because you are a lilac. You grow best when untamed, you take hold of all about you, your fragrance is rich and inviting, and you have beauty beyond compare, most particularly in the moonlight. A lilac in a world of weeds."

She felt herself blush and released his hand as she began walking along the outside of the gazebo, her fingers trailing amongst the lilacs and the aged wood. "A husband does not flatter his wife, sir."

"Are there rules of husbands now as well?" he asked as he slowly matched her pace from inside.

"As to that, I cannot say," she murmured shyly. "I'm not trained in the rules of husbands."

"Then, as a husband, allow me to enlighten you. A husband with sense enough to marry a capable, wise, and witty wife, who also happens to possess attractive features and accomplishment, is well within his rights to flatter her as he so chooses."

He continued to match her slow and lingering pace, watching her through the gaps in wood, the openings on each side, his eyes seemingly fixed upon her face. She looked up at him on occasion as he spoke, and every time he met her gaze.

"In fact, it is his duty to flatter her, particularly if he is sincere," Derek continued softly. "He is not worthy to bear the title of husband if he does not."

"Sincerity would be important," Kate allowed, flicking her eyes up to his through the opening of the gazebo again. "Vain flattery serves no purpose but to heat the air and puff up the flatterer."

"You think me insincere, Kate?"

"I think you partial and biased."

"Perhaps I am." He stepped forward then, his frame towering over hers, both due to his size and the height of the floor he was standing upon. He stood as close to her as he could while maintaining his position, one hand still gripping the post.

Kate lifted her head to stare into his eyes, her heart pounding frantically. Why did her husband have to be so very attractive? This breathless unsettling of her entire being was rather precarious. She could have moved back, could have stepped away, but something held her captive.

Derek held her captive.

She swallowed hard, but could not find words.

"But being partial and biased doesn't make me less sincere or truthful," he told her in a voice that was almost a breath. "It merely gives me a clearer sight where once I was blind."

"Oh dear," Kate breathed, finding the very attempt at thought rather difficult. "Perhaps I shouldn't have brought you with me after all."

Derek reared back, his eyebrows shooting up nearly to his hairline. "What? Why not?"

"Because I needed to think," she said a little more firmly, taking two small steps away from him, "and it is becoming increasingly difficult to do so with you around."

He grinned rather mischievously at her blunt admission. "Really?"

"As if you didn't know," she scoffed, smiling finally, moving away to continue walking around the gazebo in the moonlight.

"What do you need to think about?"

"You. Me. Us." She shrugged and stopped walking, leaning against one side of an entrance, taking a deep breath and inhaling the calming fragrance of the lilacs. "Who we are, what we are... what it all means..."

There was so much swirling about in her mind. Tomorrow would be the end of the two weeks that Derek had agreed to stay. After tomorrow, he could leave her again, and do whatever he pleased. She didn't dare mention it to him for fear that she would catch in his eyes a flash of relief or victory. If he left, she would not be able to bear the torment. Not from others when it became apparent that she was not carrying his child, but from herself, who had grown so attached to him, so fond of the friendship they enjoyed, and even the breathless moments that were thrust upon her. Life would be bleak without him.

How had she come to this? How had everything in her world become so wrapped up in him that she hardly knew who she was without him?

"It has been a whirlwind time of it lately, hasn't it?" Derek sighed, coming over and leaning on the post opposite her.

She nodded, the very beginning of tears forming at the corners of her eyes.

"We've come so far, you and I," he said softly. "Personally, I find it hard to believe that I ever hated you." He chuckled and shook his head. "It seems so ridiculous."

"I would have agreed with you wholeheartedly back then," Kate replied with a small smile. "But now I have to disagree. I was a shrew. A self-righteous, contentious, cold echo of my mother, hardly fit to be a wife at all, let alone a woman. You were right to hate me."

"And I was an arrogant, cantankerous, pretentious prig, destined to become a doddering codger like his father, no more fit to be a husband than a boulder is." He smiled and shook his head again. "I used to call you a tyrant. I used to say you were spiteful and horrifying and evil. I thought you were the devil incarnate."

"I used to call you lazy," she returned. "I said you were a waste of human form and intellect. I thought you were disrespectful. And ignorant. And annoying."

"Well, I can be very annoying," he allowed with a light smile, which brought one to her face as well. "You had a point there." Then he sobered. "I hardly recognize the man I was, Kate. I despise him. But he was the man that married you, I can't change that."

"And she was the woman you married," Kate whispered, her voice full of regret.

"But we are not married to them now."

She looked up at him, and saw the same regret, hope, and earnestness in his eyes that she was feeling within herself. And again, her breath was stolen from her lungs.

"Are we?" he asked softly, holding her eyes with the power of his own.

"No."

He smiled tenderly, and pushed off of the post, stepping up into the gazebo again. Then he held out a hand to her. "Will you dance with me, Kate?"

Miraculously, she laughed amidst the fluttering of her heart. "Here? Now?"

"Of course, here and now," he said without concern. "Haven't you always wanted to secretly dance with a handsome man in the middle of the night in a lilac covered gazebo on a senile lord's property with the moonlight swirling all about us?"

She wanted to laugh out loud at his impish suggestion, but she couldn't. She couldn't deny that she had wished for exactly that, but she would most certainly not be telling him so. "But there's no music," she protested softly, her lips pursing just a bit as she placed her hand in his and allowed him to help her up.

"Oh, please, Kate," he scolded as he backed up into the center of the gazebo, tugging her along. "Are you telling me you can't hear the songs all about us in that musical mind of yours? There is a symphony playing, Kate, and it comes into my thoughts whenever you are near." As if to prove his point, he started humming a soft tune in his low, melodious voice, and it sent shivers down her spine.

"You are entirely too charming for your own good," Kate muttered with a smile as she moved towards him.

"I know," he quipped, shifting his hold on her hand and pulling her in closer with one hand on her waist, continuing to hum.

"What are you doing?" she half-whispered, her insides aquiver at his touch.

"Teaching you to waltz, Kate. I learned years ago, but it was apparently unfit for the propriety of an English ballroom until very recently." He gave her a look she was far too unsettled by to interpret. "I think it is suited for a husband and wife, though."

Breathe, Kate, breathe, her mind screamed, and it was all she could do to obey as Derek resumed his low humming and guided her in the pattern of the waltz. They continued to dance on and on, just the two of them in the gazebo, slivers of moonlight and stars their only illumination, the stillness of the night their only companion.

Eventually, the proper form melted into something far less, with his head resting alongside hers, and her face turned into his shoulder.

"You waltz perfectly," Derek breathed somewhere near her ear, his voice muffled by her hair. "If I didn't know better, I would say that…" He paused suddenly, though his waltzing never faltered. She felt him shake his head, and bit back a smile when he said, "No, that would be impossible. You are clearly just that gifted."

She snickered softly and lifted her head. "I know how to waltz, Derek."

He pulled back and stared at her, his dance finally faltering, but somehow, he kept them moving in a semblance of the pattern. "You do?"

"I have known how to for years now," she admitted, unable to hold back her smile now. "I overheard some ladies talk about it ages ago, and they were so scandalized by it that I was fascinated. I went home that night and practiced alone in my room. I imagined myself to be quite graceful at it, but never had any opportunity to prove it until now."

Slowly, a disbelieving grin grew on her husband's face until he was beaming. "Wait, I have a secretly improper wife? How delightful!"

"Not improper!" she protested, pushing at his chest a little. "Just… a trifle daring. Secretly."

"Even better," he said with a meaningful waggle of his brows.

She laughed merrily and allowed him to sweep her into a grand waltz movement as he imitated a great swell of the music he had been dancing them to. She sighed and shook her head. "I've never told anybody that before. Just you. And… and I'm glad to have you know my secrets, Derek."

Slowly, he brought them to a stop, and looked down at her with the gentlest, warmest eyes she had yet to see him bear. "I want to know all of them," he confessed, cupping her cheek with one hand.

"So do I," she whispered, wrapping her hand around his wrist and leaning into his touch.

Accepting the unspoken invitation without hesitation, Derek bent his head and captured Kate's lips with his own. Somehow, though he had kissed her often enough, this felt like the first time all over again to her. The same stuttering of her heart, the same trembling of her knees, the same war within herself to both move closer and move away.

Only it was so very different from that first kiss that the two could hardly be related.

There was passion and heat and need in this kiss. Gone was the hesitation, the uncertainty, and the nerves of before. Now there was confidence and delight, and though confusion still swirled around her as it had before, she was not tossed about by it.

Never had anything ever felt so right, confusion or not.

Again and again they kissed, and they were slow, deep, savoring kisses that made Kate feel as though her very bones were melting. In some small, still sentient corner of her mind, she remembered to be grateful Derek was a strong man, as he was all that held her upright. Tight in his embrace, wrapped about him, she had somehow ceased to exist and he and his fire were all that remained.

She felt safe in his arms, in his hold, in his presence. Here was happiness and home and life. Here was where she belonged, where she was always meant to be. And where she yearned to remain. And if that did not scream love, she did not know what else would.

She broke the kiss with a whimpering sigh, feeling that she ought to say something, anything. The moment was too much, too precious to leave things unspoken. "Derek, I think… I think I…" She looked up into his eyes, so full of warmth and understanding, of desire and pleasure, looking at her as if she were the only woman in the world.

She couldn't say it. The words were on the tip of her tongue, were swelling her heart until she felt certain it would burst, but she could not say it. She released a heavy sigh and leaned her head against his chin. "I'm so confused," she whispered in a low, harsh voice as she tightened her hold around his waist.

Derek wrapped his arms around her fully, and tucked her head beneath his chin. "I know," he murmured, pressing his lips into her hair. "I know." He released a slow breath himself, but said nothing further as he held her, comforted her, and waited for their pounding hearts to settle.

Kate nearly cried at such tender attention. She loved him; she *loved* him, and she couldn't even say it. He had to know what she was going to say, what she could not manage to get out. But he had said nothing, had not even looked disappointed or upset. And now he was holding her, knowing that she could not bring herself to say the words that were hanging unspoken between them.

Perhaps somehow, the magic of the night would carry her thoughts to his heart, and he would feel them, would know just how much she meant them, though she could not vocalize it. Someday she would say them; she could not be a coward forever. However, he wasn't saying the words either. Whatever he was feeling, there were no words to enlighten her.

But here and now, in this moment, she thought she felt them. She thought she could hear him saying them to her as well. And if that were true, then she could wait. The words would come in time. So long as she could feel this way, she could wait however long it took.

"Kate, something has been troubling me since last night."

Derek's words brought Kate out of the daze of her thoughts as they ate breakfast together, and she looked at him in confusion. "What was troubling? I thought we had a marvelous time."

He actually blushed a little at the recollection. "We did. Apart from trying to get back through our hedge without bleeding, it was the best night I've had in a long time, and certainly the best dance I have ever had."

Now it was Kate's turn to blush, which she quickly covered by shoving some more eggs into her mouth.

"But besides that point, I tossed and turned all night over one little detail," Derek continued, ignoring Kate's sudden lack of table manners.

"Which was?" she asked when she managed to swallow.

His expression turned very serious. "You said that you go out to that gazebo in the middle of the night alone."

"Yes," she replied promptly. "It's my escape. When I'm there, I can imagine myself as being anywhere but here, anyone but who I am." She smiled softly at him. "But I don't believe I will need to do that anymore."

That deflated him momentarily as he tried to remember how to breathe properly, and he returned her smile. But then he remembered his purpose. "Regardless, you go alone. How often were you doing this, Kate?"

"Oh, I don't know. Once a week? A few times a month? I never sat down and calculated."

Derek felt his blood begin to boil and he clenched his teeth. "That is not going to continue."

Kate stilled and looked at him sharply. "I beg your pardon?"

"It's not safe for you to go gallivanting off in the middle of the night alone, especially in London," he gritted out, trying to remain calm.

"Derek, I have never been caught nor seen," Kate assured him, a small but bewildered smile gracing her lips. "My reputation has not suffered in the least for this."

"Hang your reputation, Kate! I don't care half so much about that as I do for your safety and your person!" He ran a hand through his hair, the panic that kept him awake most of the night coming back to haunt him. "What if you were attacked? What if somebody took you? What if…"

"Oh, don't be ridiculous, Derek," Kate scoffed with a snort. "I always carry a knife on my person whenever I go out."

That brought Derek's tirade up short. She carried… a *knife*… on her person. He ought to say something rather indignant, such as "That makes no difference," or "So do bandits." But all that managed to come galloping out of his senseless mouth was a blurted, "Where?"

Kate gave him a rather devious look, but didn't reply. All she did was take his chin in hand, press a quick, but heated kiss to his unmoving lips, and flit from the room like a bird, saying something about having things to do today, and she would see him later.

He sat at the table for quite some time after she had gone, mulling over their conversation. She obviously saw nothing wrong with her actions, and that worried him just as much as her actions. The very thought of something happening to her made his blood run cold. Yes, she carried that blasted knife, wherever she kept it; and yes, he was rather curious as to location, but that was a quest for another day; but it could hardly matter, no matter how sharp or wicked a blade it was. Assuming she could even wield such a weapon.

With a shudder, he admitted that she probably could, and rather well. If the woman could waltz in secret, who knew what other less than proper things she had knowledge and expertise in.

He couldn't make her stay, he would not. She was like a lilac, in truth; she had fairly blossomed once the pruning and taming had ceased, and he didn't dare subject her to the same any further. But something had to be done, or he would be sitting watch outside of her door the rest of their married life just to be sure that she didn't go alone. If only it were not so far away.

A sudden idea struck him with such force that he sat back in his chair. He thought it through carefully, wondering if the idea were even a realistic one. A fairly scheming grin flashed across his face as he determined that not only was it plausible, it was necessary. It was something she would never in a million years suspect. Today was the two week mark, but this would take far longer than that, which brought a satisfied smirk to his face. Now he absolutely had a concrete reason to tell Kate he was going to stay. And after that… he was quite certain he would have confessed another.

Laughing triumphantly, he jumped to his feet and dashed out of the room, startling the footmen and Harville, and, ignoring them all, he took his jacket and hat and swept from the house, humming his song to her from the night before, and relishing the thought of his task at hand.

Kate would never expect this.

It was just the thing to convince her to love him in return.

For he was no longer falling in love with her. He already did love her. He was very fully already in love with her, loved everything good and bad that was her, and had no doubt he would continue to love her for quite some time after all of this madness was over.

And he would do so quite madly, at that.

Chapter Sixteen

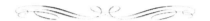

*K*ate absently hummed to herself as she wandered around her home after visiting with Diana and Mary Hamilton, which had been a rather delightful way to spend her morning. They had given her some rather enlightening news concerning her.

During the party at Nathan and Moira's when she and Derek had left so prematurely, the story went around that Colin Gerrard had not only managed to put a great hole into the Marchioness of Whitlock's finest mourning gown, but had also, in the process, accidentally caused her to fall into the fountain nearby. Apparently, Colin was quite mortified about the whole affair, and according to a few of the sympathizing young ladies who had flocked to him in consolation, he had promised to replace it from the money in his own pocket.

She could hardly wait to remind him of his vow.

Diana had also given her all of the details surrounding David's mysterious absence from town, which had caused more than a few tender hearted misses to be desperately forlorn. Rumors had been flying that his angry father the duke had raged with such a fury that David had been thrown from the house and sent off to a monastery in Calais, never again to look upon a woman. Others said that he hopelessly compromised a servant girl and had fled England to escape her seven angry brothers. But the majority of Society merely thought that the dashing Lord David was lying in wait for a new batch of young ladies to fall one by one to his charms.

Obviously, none of the stories were true. Kate didn't even blink at overhearing them. She snickered a little, but other than that, it was just the sort of tosh and bother that one should never pay any mind to. But as David was family to her now, she thought she needed to know the truth. Derek had not been especially forthcoming, but then, the details of anything between himself, his father, and his brother had always been a difficult and private subject in his mind.

Diana had no such restraint.

It didn't take long at all for her to lay out the whole story. The duke had received a letter from the family estate in Scotland. Apparently, someone had been stealing the sheep from the tenants, which was causing a great stir, as it was the main source of income up there. Owing to the fact that something needed to be done about it, and that David was showing no inclination towards marriage at present, and given the fact that Diana had announced her being with child, the duke had decided that, rather than creating a rather violent dissonance between his family right when something so joyous would be occurring, he would send David to investigate the problem.

Kate was surprised by the decision, but saw the wisdom in it immediately. David would be away from his father's overbearing rule and doing something productive in the process. But surely the duke had not come to this rather prudent and uncharacteristically lenient resolution all on his own.

When she had suggested it, Diana had smirked and confessed that she may have had a little bit to do with it, and, had not the letter come on its own, she would have created a scenario to ensure a similar outcome. "David can hardly get into trouble up at the Scotland estate," Diana had assured her. "It is too far from anything to even be remotely tempting."

Kate doubted that David would be without temptation at all, as it seemed to follow him everywhere, but she said nothing.

After he finished in Scotland, Diana went on, David would make trips to each of the other estates to ensure that all was well and see to any needs that ought to be addressed. That would certainly keep him out of London for some time, which was really all he needed. And the duke had sworn not to do anything about a marriage before David returned, and especially not without his consent.

So it seemed that all was settled in that quarter for the time being. David had been so keen to leave that he had done so almost immediately. Kate was profoundly grateful for that. Perhaps now Derek would be able to turn his attention to other matters.

Like their marriage.

She continued humming to herself as she walked along the gallery. Things were looking so promising for them, and she hoped that soon enough she would feel brave enough to confess to Derek just how much he meant to her. She would even ask him to stay with her, to not go back to the country unless she was going with him.

A scant five paces later, she realized what it was she had been humming all morning. It was the song Derek had been singing to her last night. It was the song they had waltzed to in the moonlight.

It was their song.

She would never forget how she had felt in his arms, how she had wished that they could have danced forever in that mystical world they had shared for those few minutes. No more would that gazebo be her spot alone; now it would be theirs. It would always remind her of him.

He had said she could never go alone again, and that suited her just as well, as she didn't think she would ever *want* to go there alone again. But she couldn't tell him that, it was too bold. She had merely laughed it off and kissed him, her first time initiating, however brief it had been.

But it was not enough. She had to prove to him that she loved him by action, as she was unable to by words.

The melody of his song floated through her mind again, and she smiled slowly. She could do something, something that would mean a great deal to him, something that only he would understand.

She would write him a song. But not just any song. She would write *his* song.

And when it, and she, was ready, she would play it for him.

And he would know, at last, that she loved him.

With a firm nod, she whirled and dashed towards the stairs. There was work to be done, and she had no idea how much time she had to do it in.

Kate was lost in her thoughts later that night as she watched the flames dance about the logs in the grate. Something was wrong. Derek was being secretive, standoffish, and distant. Dinner had been so silent and uncomfortable between them, and with things feeling so right of late, it terrified her. Perhaps he did know that tomorrow marked the end of their deal and that he could leave whenever he chose. Perhaps this had all been nothing but a trick, and she was to be left the fool for all to see.

But how could he have designed the moments between them? How could the emotions and heat and sensations been falsehoods, nothing more than cold calculations to entertain him? He was better than that. He would not be cruel, but perhaps in his efforts to be friends, he had led her too far, and now was regretting doing so, and was pulling back to spare her.

Yes, he would do that. But it would not spare her, it would only hurt all the more. Better a cruel design against her than an accidental misleading. One was his fault; the other was hers.

She had spent the better part of the afternoon working on her song for him. It was taking longer than she had planned, as putting into music all that was Derek was quite nearly an impossible task. She was pleased with what she had so far, but she could hardly play him something that she had not completed.

If he stayed, she would finish it. If she found him still here in the morning, then she would know that she had not been mistaken, and that her efforts and emotions had not been in vain.

If tomorrow he were here still, she would know if he might love her.

She swallowed hard as a few tears started to work their way towards the surface. Oh, how she hoped he would stay.

She heard the floor creak behind her then and she hastily blinked back any hint of tears, then, once she was certain her appearance was in all respects normal, she turned. Derek was coming towards her, looking mostly back to his usual self. She felt her shoulders sag just a touch in relief.

She offered a smile, which he returned immediately.

"That was a rather awkward meal we had just now," he remarked as he approached.

She managed to laugh a little, though it was forced. "Rather, yes."

Derek clasped his hands behind his back. "I'm sorry about that. A bit distracted, I'm afraid."

"I understand," she said rapidly, resisting the urge to pull at her gloves or her skirt. Her nerves were rising again, and his collected expression was not doing anything to help that.

He stared at her for a moment, then began rocking on his heels ever so slightly, as if anxious. "What did you do today?" he asked in a polite tone, the calmness of his words sharply contrasting with his actions.

"I visited your sister and Mary." She could have kicked herself for sounding like a schoolgirl. Honestly, it was her husband, not some imposing instructor with a cane to beat her with.

"Ah, and are they well?" he asked, still rocking a little. If he continued to do that, Kate would go mad.

"Rather well, I think. Diana told me of the news."

"What news?" he asked in a harsh, fast tone, his voice rising.

"The baby," she replied in confusion.

"Ah, yes, of course, of course." He nodded swiftly, looking relieved. "Wonderful news."

"Indeed."

They stood there facing each other, looking everywhere but *at* each other, for what felt like an eternity. Finally, Kate could stand it no more. "Would you like me to play?" she asked as she moved to the piano.

"Very much," he responded, again his words coming out rushed. He moved to his usual place on the sofa and looked prepared to listen, but his fingers drummed already on the arm.

Kate struggled to find composure enough to play, but somehow managed. Why was he even here when he so obviously wanted to be gone? But if he wanted to pretend, then she would pretend along with him. If this were the last time she was to play for him, then she would make it count.

She played with feeling, she played with skill, and she played with energy; so much so that when she was finished, she felt exhausted beyond measure. Perhaps the quantity of songs had not been as high as it usually would be, but she dared to believe that the quality was unmatched. She was rather proud of herself.

She chanced a look over at Derek, who was not, for once, watching her. Her heart sank. Had he even been listening?

As if sensing her gaze, his eyes flicked over to hers. "All done, then, are you?"

She nodded, unable to speak.

He stood and offered her a hand, which she took. He pressed a proper kiss to her bare hands, and, though she knew it was imagined, she could feel the heat from it searing all the way to her toes. "Incomparable as always, Kate," he murmured, rubbing a thumb across her knuckles.

Against her will, she blushed at the low timbre of his voice. "Thank you."

He tucked her hand into his arm and led her upstairs, not saying anything further. He didn't even look at her.

He's leaving, she thought. *He's leaving in the morning and he doesn't know how to tell me. He doesn't love me.*

"What was that, Kate?" he asked suddenly, leaning a bit closer.

"What?" she responded quickly, panic rising. "Oh, nothing. I didn't say anything." Had she said something aloud? She couldn't remember. It would have been highly stupid of her to do that. Above all else, she must remain composed. *A duchess always maintains composure.* She closed her eyes with the pain of hearing her mother once more. Would the rules come back to haunt her once he was gone?

When they reached her bedchamber, they stopped and Derek turned to face her, but still he said nothing. He watched her, but not with the warmth and emotion she was used to. This look was more of a study, as if he were trying to read her as he might a book. But he didn't say a word.

This was ridiculous. "Well, good night, then," Kate said softly, placing her hand on the door knob.

Derek stepped forward and pressed a quick, rather emotionless kiss to her lips. "Good night," he replied.

This was frightening. Never before had any kiss between them been so… formal. Kate suddenly felt as if she had lost something rather dear to her, and she would never get it back. The pain that pierced her was swift and sharp, and it very nearly stole the breath from her lungs.

Then Derek came even closer, looking earnest. "Kate…"

"What?" she whispered, wishing he would just leave so she could cry.

He opened his mouth, but nothing came out. He closed his mouth, shook his head, then mumbled another, "Good night," as he turned and headed for his own bedchamber.

This was agony. Kate closed her eyes against the wash of tears and released a soft, shuddering breath. She should never have fallen in love with him.

Trembling, she let herself into her room and changed for bed, ignoring the tears as they rolled down her cheeks.

Tomorrow. She would know all tomorrow.

One way or another.

Groggily, Kate rolled over, placing her face directly into the stream of warm sunshine that had been taunting her for a while. She stretched her arms above her head and groaned at the tension that still resided in them, then tangled her fingers lazily into her hair, finally cracking open her eyes.

Sleep had come very reluctantly last night. She hadn't cried for long. She couldn't when she didn't know how the story would end yet. Once she knew, she could cry. For better or worse.

Lazily, she glanced over at the small clock on her mantle, and gasped, her eyes popping open. It was halfway to lunch already! How had she slept that long? Her entire life, she had always been the first in the house to rise, and often enough, had beaten even the sun. But never, as far back as she could recall, had she slept this late.

She tossed aside all of her bedcovers and ran to the wardrobe. She snatched whichever dark gown her fingers touched first, and scrambled madly at the buttons. There was no time to call for a servant, and she did not need one. Flinging off her nightgown, she clambered her way through the fabric of the dress and somehow managed to get it on properly, and the majority of the buttons done up as well. Some of the higher ones she could not reach, but she would wear a shawl anyway. It was not so warm as to look ridiculous with one, and quite honestly, she was too frantic to care.

Dashing to the wash basin, she splashed some cold water onto her face, hastily patted her cheeks and nose with a towel. Then, using only her fingers, she combed her hair back, taking only a ribbon to pull it away from her face. She looked like a mess, but she was a mess in love and in a frenzy. Looks had little place here.

She seized a dark shawl from her wardrobe and bolted from the room, not even taking time to find slippers. Somehow, she restrained herself from taking more than one stair at a time, though she really would rather have slid down the banister. Once down, she suddenly found herself face to face with Harville, who, miraculously, only quirked a brow at her appearance.

"Where is Lord Whitlock?" she gasped, feeling out of breath, and not at all in the mood to humor even her favorite servant. If Derek had left already, she would turn right back around and shut herself in her room for the next several hours, perhaps days. Surely he would not have left without seeing her. Surely she meant more to him than that.

But suddenly, she was not sure of anything anymore.

Harville grinned rather knowingly. "He is out in the back garden, my lady. He says you can only come out there after you have eaten something."

"Why?" she asked suspiciously, her heart not yet allowing herself to feel calm or relief.

"Because he said, and I quote, 'She's much more receptive to surprises when she has been well fed'." He restrained his grin just a bit. "He's been out there all morning, my lady, and I do not think he will be finished for quite some time."

It took a good twenty seconds for those words to sink in, and then, quite uncharacteristically, she laughed out loud, planted a kiss on Harville's cheek, and fairly skipped to the breakfast room, determined to eat as quickly as she could.

When she had done so, and rather hastily, she made for the door to the back garden, took a deep breath, and pulled it open.

The sight that met her eyes stunned her so thoroughly that she was incapable of thought.

The garden was scattered with workers, men of all shapes and sizes, all of them dirty and sweaty, laboring under the morning sun. The entire landscape of the garden was uprooted and old things, none of which she had been particularly fond of, lay strewn about on one side of the lawn, while fresh and new plants and flowers and shrubs sat waiting for their transposition into the freshly turned soil. In one corner, near the back hedge, a small group of men were hard at work, building a shelter of sorts, though only the base was constructed this far. In the middle of the partially organized chaos, his shirt just as damp, if not more, than the others, was Derek, who was digging a rather large hole with a man she did not recognize.

She looked down at her feet, still bare, and wished she'd had the foresight to grab those blasted slippers.

One of the men noticed her, inclined his head respectfully, then turned and gave a whistle, which brought Derek's head up immediately. He grinned as he saw her and handed his shovel off to the nearest man, who then helped him out of the hole and took over shoveling for him. Looking rather exhilarated, Derek jogged over.

"Good morning, Kate. I trust you've eaten something?"

"I have," she assured him, looking up at his face in confusion. "What's all this?"

He took a breath, looking a touch embarrassed, and glanced down at her feet, then frowned. "Where are your shoes?"

"Derek."

He shook his head. "I'm sorry, Kate, but you really do need shoes for me to explain everything. Go back inside and get some."

Kate huffed and turned to the men working beside her. "Does

anybody have shoes I might borrow for a moment or two?"

"Are you serious, Kate?" Derek laughed from behind her.

"Aye, milady!" called a girl of perhaps thirteen, who was standing next to a lad of maybe ten in the shade with a bucket of water. She darted over and removed her worn and dirty boots. "They ain't much to look at, milady, but they do the trick."

"I shall be grateful to have them," Kate assured her with a smile. "What is your name?"

"Sarah, milady," the girl replied with a bob.

"Well, Sarah, is that your brother over there with you?"

She nodded. "That's Jamie. Pa is working over there and we are tending the water."

Kate looked where she indicated and smiled at Jamie too. "Well, why don't you and Jamie go with Molly, that pretty maid in the door, and have her take you down the kitchens for a bit. We'll call when the men need water."

"Really?" Sarah cried, looking mystified, excited, and relieved.

"Yes, really. There is no need for everybody to be stuck out in this heat. Besides, I need someone to inspect the pies that Hallstead is making."

Sarah grinned. "I can do that."

"I knew you could," Kate laughed, waving Molly over and relaying the instructions to her.

As the children were led off, Sarah turned back, looking worried. "I 'ope my shoes fit, milady."

"I am sure they will, Sarah. I have rather small feet," she whispered loudly, grimacing.

Sarah smiled again and scampered off after her brother into the house.

Kate put the shoes on, felt rather smug that they fit perfectly, and turned back to her husband, who looked positively thunderstruck. "What?" she asked, still smiling. "You said I needed shoes, now I have shoes."

He opened his mouth to speak, then closed it, shaking his head. "You are remarkable, Kate, you know that?"

She blushed and tucked a wry strand of her loosely gathered hair behind her ear. "Derek, what is all this?" she asked, changing the subject. "What are you doing?"

He seemed a little amused by her shift in topic, but went along with it. "I told you that you could never go out to that little park of yours alone again."

"Yes, so I recall," she remarked dryly.

"So unless you are willing to go with me all the time, which I highly encourage…"

She smiled, but said nothing.

"…you would be left without a private spot where you can think and ponder and retreat. So I am giving you your own little sanctuary here where I can keep an eye on you. And where you can still be alone, as it were."

Kate's mouth dropped open, and she looked around more carefully at the changes that were being made. There were stones being put in for a path, bright flowering shrubs replacing cold and formal ones, and the shelter… She could see, now that they had begun to frame it, what it was going to be.

A gazebo. A smaller, simpler echo of the one they had danced in the other night, and one that would fit perfectly in their small garden.

She turned back to Derek, unable to speak.

"Surprise," he said in a soft voice, looking quietly delighted with her response.

Not only had Derek stayed, but in rearranging their entire garden, he had undertaken a project that would keep him here for some time. He was working at it himself, though he hated manual labor. He had organized this whole thing as a surprise to her.

If that was not love, she had no idea what was.

Though he was filthy and damp, though she looked a terrible mess, and though there were servants and workers and men she had never met all around them, Kate could not help herself. She reached up and took Derek's face in her hands and kissed him, in full view of everyone, and without restraint. She felt him stiffen in response, but he quickly recovered and pulled her close, lifting her feet off of the ground. She wrapped her arms around his neck and kissed him with all the love, passion, and energy of her soul, and he responded in kind.

Whistling and cheering and friendly catcalls reached her ears, and she started to giggle, still kissing him. She felt him laugh as well, and then he twirled her, just a bit, and the cheers grew in volume. Unable to hold back the euphoria within her, she broke off the kiss and laughed aloud, her feet still dangling above the ground, Derek's arms firmly latched around her waist.

"I take it this pleases you?" Derek commented wryly, lowering her back to the ground.

She took his face in hand again and rested her forehead against his. "Thank you, Derek," she whispered.

Derek didn't reply, but his throat worked silently. He nodded against her, placing one of his not so clean hands along her cheek, and stroked it softly, and Kate could feel in his touch what he could not find voice to say.

He loved her.

It wouldn't have mattered if the sky had opened up and it began to rain torrentially upon them, Kate would never be happier in her life than she was at this moment.

Sniffling could be heard then, and she looked over at the door to the house where no less than seven servants, including the normally so unruffled Harville, stood, most of whom were crying unashamedly. "We have created quite a scene, I'm afraid, my Lady Whitlock," Derek whispered, finding words at last.

Kate snickered and pulled back, noticing how most everyone was still watching them with broad grins. "I feel as though I should wave to my audience."

"Perhaps you should," he quipped. "But aren't you embarrassed, Kate?"

"Not in the least," she responded, tossing a grin up at him. "I think they may need to get used to it."

Derek smiled in return and took her hand in his own, lacing his fingers through hers and kissing them fervently. "Come, let me show you what we are doing."

He led her around the garden, explaining just what he had envisioned and asking her opinions, and forbidding her to order around anybody, as it was his project, not hers. She had grumped at that, but only in good humor, and she could not keep the smile from her face. He showed her the sight for the fountain he had planned, as a pond in such a small back garden was really not feasible, if they wanted to have any space at all remaining. He took her to the future gazebo, which he promised to shower with lilacs, but as they take time to bloom into the magic that the other held, it would not possess the same splendor for a while.

Kate didn't mind. She only smiled and nodded and squeezed his hand in both of hers, her eyes wide and delighted and taking everything in. Every idea he had planned would suit her to perfection, and she could see in her mind's eye how it would appear when it was finished. It would be the most beautiful of places, but most of all because he had made it for her, and for no other reason than to make her happy.

She didn't deserve such goodness.

"So, what do you think?" he asked when all was done.

"I think it is the most splendid thing in the world," she replied earnestly, looking about her still.

"If you like it, we'll do this at all of the estates," he promised.

Her breath caught and she looked up at him, her smile fading. "You would do that for me?"

Derek's eyes warmed and he took the hand that he held and enclosed it with his other. "I want you to be happy, Kate. Wherever we are."

"We?" she asked timidly, a faint spark of hope flaring in her tone.

He opened his mouth to reply when an interruption in the form of Colin, Duncan, Geoffrey, Nathan, and even Moira, coming around the back of the house prevented him. Without thinking, he and Kate sprang apart, letting go of each other as the intruders came towards them.

Derek stiffened at their appearance, and Kate grinned, knowing his thoughts. She took his hand once more and squeezed it, and only then did he calm. He looked down at her, and she winked up at him. Understanding flared in his eyes.

They could hardly turn their friends away, particularly when they could use the help and Kate could use some entertaining. There would be time for them later. They had all the time in the world. She was not going anywhere. And if the grip on her hand was anything to go by, he was not either.

"What the devil is going on here?" Colin called out as he approached.

"I am getting a new garden, compliments of my husband," Kate chirped with a grin.

Duncan smirked, his eyes twinkling. "So *that's* why we've come, is it, Derek?"

Derek shrugged. "I could use the help, and Nathan owes me. Besides, you could use the exercise."

"True enough," Duncan admitted, shucking off his coat and handing it to a maid.

Without a complaint, except for Colin, who repeatedly announced his hatred of perspiration, the rest of the men did the same and went to work, joining the workers in their tasks as if they were employed to do the same, and it didn't take long for them to become as dirty and sweaty as the rest.

"They just join in, just like that?" Kate asked Derek.

He shrugged. "They are the best of men."

"I can see that," she murmured. Truly, she had misjudged Derek's friends just as she had him. It was a humbling experience.

"I think I should rejoin them."

"Yes, you probably should," she sighed longingly.

He heard her tone and smiled. "I'll see you tonight, Kate. We can talk then."

"If you have not exhausted yourself," she remarked.

"I never exhaust myself," he told her in a low voice, quirking his brows. "I have far more endurance than meets the eye."

She rolled her eyes and pushed him away, though she knew she was blushing furiously. "Get over there, you great oaf."

He laughed and went back to the hole for the fountain.

"Oh, and Colin?" Kate called.

Colin looked up at her with an innocent expression. "Kate?"

"I understand you owe me a new dress." She raised a haughty brow, but was unable to avoid smiling.

He grinned at her. "Yes, I am afraid I do. Terribly clumsy of me. Do forgive me."

"If I must."

He saluted and went back to work, and Kate finally turned to Moira, who was watching her in blatant amusement. "What are you gawking at?" Kate asked her with a grin as she took her arm and led her back towards the house.

"You, dear Kate," Moira replied with a smile. "Your appearance this morning is really quite intriguing."

Kate laughed in embarrassment as she touched her hair. "Yes, I'm afraid I was a bit frantic this morning." They entered the house, and Kate removed Sarah's shoes, then handed them to Jackson. "Take these down to the kitchens, would you, Jackson? And thank Miss Sarah for me, they were most useful."

He nodded obediently and left, and Moira made a sound.

"What now?" Kate laughed.

"You borrowed shoes from a worker's daughter?" she remarked.

"It was a frantic morning," Kate repeated.

"Why so frantic?"

Kate sighed, and gestured down the hall. "Yesterday was the last day of the two weeks," she confessed.

"Oh," Moira said, nodding in understanding.

"Derek could have left this morning. I overslept, and I panicked, wondering if he had done so," Kate told her, removing her shawl and placing it on the table in the hall.

"For heaven's sake, Kate, did you try to get yourself dressed this morning, too?" Moira commented from behind her. "You've got buttons undone!" She stepped forward and finished them off for her.

"I know," she moaned. "I was so rushed, I just threw it on, did the buttons I could reach, pulled my hair back without brushing it, and forgot shoes. I had no thought but coming down to see if he was still here."

Moira's fingers froze at the top button, and she went utterly still.

"Moira?" Kate asked, turning in concern. "Is something wrong?"

Her friend looked as though a ghost had just crossed her path. "You love him. You loved him before he ever showed you that garden he is building for you. That was why you panicked, isn't it? You love Derek."

Kate hesitated for only a moment, and only because she had yet to admit it aloud. But she smiled softly, her eyes starting to prickle with tears. "Yes," she answered, her heart trilling like a melody in her chest. "Yes, I love him."

Moira stared for a long moment, then laughed out loud and pulled Kate into a tight hug, and held her close as both started to cry and laugh at once. Then she dragged her into the nearest room and forced her to tell her everything about the whole affair, sparing no detail. Kate did so, smiling broadly the entire time.

She couldn't help it. She loved Derek, and he was staying. And if the massive amount of work in the garden indicated what she hoped it might, he could be staying for quite some time.

And she simply *had* to smile about that.

Chapter Seventeen

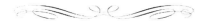

As it happened, Derek did exhaust himself quite effectively working out in the garden all day. He nearly fell asleep at the table over dinner, which was indication enough to Kate that the man was quite plainly fatigued beyond sense. He was rather apologetic as she led him upstairs, shrugging sheepishly at her suggestion that he was not quite as fit as he thought himself. Before he entered his rooms, however, he had paused and looked back at her, his expression the clearest it had been in some hours. "Do you know what my favorite part of the day was, Kate?" he had asked.

She had blushed, imagining what moment had been *her* favorite part, which had made him grin deeply.

"Well, yes, there was *that*, Kate," he had said in a sly tone as he leaned against his doorframe. "That was quite enjoyable. But do you want to know my *other* favorite part?" Before she could answer, he had said, "Your rather small feet in that girl's shoes."

"I didn't mean to prove a point with it," she told him, feeling embarrassed by the pride in his eyes.

"I know, Kate. That was why I loved it." Then, before she could say anything else, he had stepped forward and given her a brief, but rather passionate kiss that had left her gasping for both air and thought. With that wild grin she found so charming, he bid her goodnight and entered his rooms, shutting the door softly behind him.

Kate had found herself standing out in the hallway before his door for some time, simply staring in wonder. What a whirl her life had become! Her own thoughts and emotions tumbling about, she went to her own bedchamber and pretended that she was tired, though sleep would not come for some time as she proceeded to relive certain rather fond memories of the day over and over in her mind, finally drifting to sleep with a smile on her face still.

Now, however, she was just the slightest bit grumpy. It was nearing time for luncheon and Derek was still working out with the men, and she had not seen him since breakfast, and even then, he had only bidden her a good morning and gone out to work. How was she possibly supposed to tell the man she loved him if he were never around for her to do so?

Sitting here in the morning room was not going to solve anything, she decided. She marched down to the kitchens and had a picnic lunch packed for them. Then she sent a footman out to tell Derek that she wanted to see him as soon as was convenient for him in the morning room. He rushed out with a quick nod, and she returned to her previous position on the sofa.

Within two minutes, Derek came rushing into the morning room, boots still caked in dirt. "Kate, what is it? What's wrong?"

She took in the lovely, albeit terribly frantic sight of him. His hair was rather windswept in spite of being sweat dampened, his shirt was clinging to him, and his chest was heaving with his breaths, whether from his work or his running, she couldn't tell. He wore a worried expression on his face, his green eyes wide and scanning over her person as though looking for injury.

Realizing he had said something, she shook her head and met his eyes directly. "What?"

He knelt down before her and took a hand. "Kate, what is it?"

She frowned. "What is what?"

Now he frowned in return, still looking concerned. "You sent for me. Timothy came out and said you wanted me to come to the morning room. I thought that… Kate, is anything the matter?"

"No, not at all," she assured him, not sure if she should smile or not. "I said to ask if you could come as soon as it was convenient."

Derek's face clouded and he stood up, placing his hands on his hips. "Someone needs to explain to Timothy the difference between 'as soon as is convenient' and 'as soon as is possible'."

Kate covered her mouth to hide a helpless giggle or three that escaped. "Is that what he said?" she asked, her voice muffled.

"Yes, he did," Derek replied, clearly not amused. "I thought you were injured or sick or that something terribly wrong had occurred…" He ran a hand through his already mussed hair and then over his face with a groan. Whether of exhaustion, frustration, or relief, she could not tell.

"And you came running in to me?" she asked softly, her own amusement fading as her heart swelled.

He looked at her then, his eyes bearing so much emotion it hurt. "Yes," he said, as if it were the most obvious thing in the world.

Her eyes prickled with tears and she swallowed with difficulty. "Oh," was all she could manage as she fought to keep her chin from quivering.

Derek caught her emotion, and instantly was at her side, pulling her against him, dirt and sweat and all. He released a deep sigh and buried his face in her hair. "I couldn't help it, Kate," he whispered against her ear. "I had no thought but getting to you." He held her closer, and she closed her eyes, reveling in the comfort he gave. *Tell him*, her mind screamed. *Tell him now.*

But she couldn't, not yet. And she hated that she couldn't, knowing she was the worst sort of coward. She gradually pulled away from him, knowing that in her vulnerable state and his overly-attentive one, she was very likely to blurt something out if he continued to hold her. But she smiled up at him, and was delighted to see him return one.

"Well, now that I know there is no disaster brewing," he began, laughing finally, "what did you want?"

"Merely to spend time with my husband," she confessed with a shrug. "You have been so busy of late I have hardly seen you."

"I know," he moaned, taking her hand again. "I'm sorry."

"I thought we could take a picnic today. If you want to, that is."

He grinned, his eyes crinkling adorably at the corners. "I would love to. The men can go on without me, I daresay. I doubt I am of much use."

Kate laughed and patted his chest. "I'm sure you are of much use, but if they can spare you, then I will gladly take you."

"Really?"

She rolled her eyes at his suggestive tone and shoved at his chest. "Idiot. Go change, I can hardly picnic with a man dressed and smelling as you do at the moment."

He looked appropriately hurt. "But Kate, I thought it a rather nice testament to my manliness to look so active and laborious."

"That it is, I'm sure, but Hyde Park might not think so."

His brows raised just a touch. "Hyde Park? We're to picnic publicly?"

Now it was her turn to grin. "Not quite. I know a spot…"

He laughed out loud, throwing his head back just a bit. "Of course you do. I'll be back down momentarily, and then we can be off."

Her smile softened as he turned from the room, then it grew once more as he took the stairs three at a time up to the bedchamber. Life with Derek was never dull, she had to admit. Even when she hadn't liked him, she had known that.

She much preferred liking him.

After enjoying the lovely meal that Hallstead had packed for them, Derek opted to lay down in the grass for a short nap to "recover his strength" so that he might go back to work when the returned. Kate suspected he was merely delaying their return to avoid the labor that awaited him. She didn't mind. She was rather enjoying sitting against her tree, letting the warmth of the sunshine dance through the leaves across her face, feeling the cool breeze tickle her cheeks and sending her hair swaying against the back of her neck. They had managed to reach her secluded spot without much difficulty, though they did have to greet Lady Greversham with tight smiles and bald faced lies in wishing her well. But even the crotchety

Lady Greversham could not spoil Kate's day.

She glanced over at her supposedly dozing husband, who lay stretched out with one arm across his face and the other on his chest. She had mentally smirked when he had skirted the pond where the geese gathered, remembering Diana's remarks on the subject. He had pretended to be avoiding uneven ground for Kate's sake, which she had thanked him appropriately for, though she hid a laugh.

What a puzzling creature he was. A maddening, confusing, delightful puzzle all wrapped up in the form of a ridiculously handsome man. And he was already hers.

It shouldn't be this easy.

She released a sigh and looked up at the sky, where just a few clouds dotted the bright blue color, and she started doing something she had not done since she was a very young girl; she looked for shapes in those clouds, smiling when she found one.

"What has got you so silent, Kate?" Derek asked from his position, his eyes still closed.

"Oh, I'm just looking at shapes in the clouds."

He grinned, but didn't move. "Such a tricky thing, cloud shape identifying. What have you found so far?"

"A rabbit, a butterfly, a flower, and a crème brûlée."

His brows quirked. "Crème brûlée? After those delicious tarts we had just now, you are thinking of crème brûlée?"

"It appeared in the clouds," she protested with a laugh. "I can't help it if my mind jumped to that first."

"No, I supposed not," he sighed. "Crème brûlée does tend to thrust itself wherever it wishes to go. Have you ever noticed the different colors that make up clouds?"

"The what?"

He shrugged. "Think about it. Look above you. No cloud is simply white or gray or black. Some are purple in places, some have no less than five shades of a single color, others have at least three different colors in the same cloud, and some are so thin they could be a veil. Even on cloudy days, the sky is a mass of colors."

Kate had never considered such a thing, but as she took his advice and examined her cloud shapes more closely, she saw what he was talking about. And oddly enough, she found herself wishing for yet another cloudy day so that she could see the sky then with as much wonder as he did.

"You have made a study of the sky, haven't you?" she asked with a fond smile, looking over at him.

"It's not just the night sky that captivates me." He heaved a sigh and shifted just a bit in the grass. "The daytime sky is just as mystifying."

That was not the only captivating and mystifying thing, she thought to herself as she watched him. She was herself entirely captivated and mystified by him. More and more she was finding herself wanting to be with him every moment, and not just the waking ones. What would it feel like to wake in his arms in the morning? Would he wake her with soft, feather kisses that tickled her skin? Or would she wake first and be able to watch him sleep in the morning light, waiting for him to wake?

Suddenly, the prospect of children with this man was not something she feared, but something she craved. She wanted to have sons and daughters who could play with their father and be themselves, whoever they were, and who would not be forced into a childhood of rules and regulations and lectures. She wanted to see Derek rocking their babies in his arms, reading to them in bed, teaching them about the clouds and the stars. She wanted to have children with Derek, not because it was their duty, not for the title, not for the continuation of their family bloodlines. She wanted to have them because she loved him.

Because she could not imagine her life with anyone else.

She thought her heart was going to burst within her, and she restrained herself from clasping a hand to her chest to prevent it. Such a rush of emotion was becoming shockingly frequent, and she didn't know how she was going to contain it if they become regular.

There was only one question remaining in her mind; was Derek going to stay after the garden was completed? And by extension, despite what she had seen, what she had thought, could he actually love her in return?

The fear of his departure sent a chill through her. He was well within his rights to do as he chose, to leave whenever he wanted, and to go wherever he pleased, but he would be leaving behind a wife with a broken heart, and a pile of her broken dreams.

"You know, Kate, I've been thinking..." Derek started slowly, or was it reluctantly?

Her heart sunk to her toes. He *was* leaving. He was leaving the project of her garden into someone else's hands, and he was leaving. She closed her eyes and braced herself for the words, praying that she would be able to retain some sense of composure.

"I was thinking that this has been rather fun, us being friends."

"It has..." she replied carefully, uncertain as to his point.

He rolled to his side and propped his head onto his elbow, peering up at her. "Probably the best time I have had in a long time."

She swallowed down a troublesome lump that had risen. "Thank you."

"I don't want it to end, Kate." He paused. "I'm not leaving."

Her heart, having returned to her chest, now stopped beating. "You're not?" she gasped, feeling as though her mind was working backwards.

"No," he said, as he moved to put his head in her lap. "I'm going to stay and annoy you some more. It's entirely too much fun, and you are far too easy to tease. I have a rather large project to finish, which no doubt makes me seem very pleasant and generous, but when we have done with that, you can be sure I will return to my former state of annoying, troublesome, utterly maddening husband that you so enjoyed before. I shall spend quite a long time driving you to distraction."

She grinned, trying not to cry in relief, and started running her fingers through his hair. "I suppose I shall have to make do," she sighed rather dramatically.

"You don't mind?" he asked, looking up at her, his expression suddenly serious.

She smiled down at him, entwined her fingers with his, then brought their hands up to kiss his. "I don't mind," she whispered happily.

He grinned broadly and reached up to stroke her cheek with his free hand. Then he cupped the back of her head and brought her down for a slow, gentle, lingering kiss. "Now, Kate, how dare you," Derek scolded against her lips. "You have entirely distracted me from napping."

She giggled and touched her nose to his as his thumb brushed her cheek again. "How terribly rude of me."

"Indeed." He dropped his hand and snuggled in more comfortably against her, closing his eyes. "Now stop being so alluring and let a poor man sleep."

"Yes, Derek," she replied dutifully, resuming running her fingers through his hair.

After a moment, his breathing deepened, and he sighed, "You're still alluring, Kate."

"Sorry," she whispered with a smile.

"Don't be. I love it." And with that, he drifted off into sleep, leaving Kate very contentedly alone with the man she loved laying in her lap. She leaned her head back against the tree, and allowed herself a private, unheard sigh of satisfaction.

Derek was staying.

The future was looking bright indeed.

As they reentered their home, fingers entwined, they went by unspoken agreement to the drawing room, exchanging shy smiles and flirtatious glances.

Kate bit her lip and squeezed Derek's hand. "I want to give you something."

He gave her a wry grin. "I would be happy to let you."

She rolled her eyes and sat down on the sofa. "I mean, I want to give you something special. You've given me so much lately."

He toyed with her fingers a little. "Kate, I don't expect anything from you."

She raised a brow. "Nor did I expect anything from you. But I don't know what to give you, Derek. You don't need anything."

He smiled down at her. "I don't particularly think that you needed a whole new garden, Kate. It doesn't matter. Besides, you don't have to give me anything."

"But I want to."

He sighed. "Then you are just going to have to get very creative, Kate. But I warn you, it takes a great deal to surprise me."

"That was what I was afraid of," she grumbled, tugging her hand away.

He snickered and took a seat next to her. "Come on, it cannot be that bad. Surely you can think of something."

"Well," she said slowly, "I have thought of something for you... a rather small thing, really... but it is not ready yet."

"Ah ha!" he cried, rubbing his hands together. "I knew you were a clever girl. Do I get a hint?"

She considered for a moment how to reply, then said, "I have been working at it while you have been out."

He frowned at her. "What sort of a hint is that? How am I to know what you have been doing when I'm out? I am *out!*"

She smirked rather proudly and tossed her hair a little. "Perhaps you ought to come home unexpectedly, then. You would be able to sneak up on me without my having the slightest knowledge of it."

"Are you inviting me to surprise you, Kate?" he asked, looking suspicious. "I smell a trick."

"No trick," she laughed. "Surprise me all you like. I welcome the opportunity."

Derek leaned back a little, his eyes unreadable, but his mouth curved in a warm smile.

Kate tried not to laugh, but really, it was delightful to toy with him. He would have no idea that the surprise would be far more on his side. Another day of work, perhaps, and it would be complete. She could not wait to play it for him and to reveal what she truly felt.

He suddenly laughed in a low voice. "Fair enough, you siren. If you don't mind, I would like to hold my beautiful wife now."

Suddenly shy, she bit her lip and leaned against him, laying her head on his chest. "Your wife will let you hold her any time you want."

He wrapped his arms tightly around her, nuzzling his face into her hair. "Well, then I think she is going to have to adjust her daily routine because I find myself not wanting to do anything else of late."

"That suits me just as well."

Derek tipped her chin back and kissed her, his lips toying with hers in a warm, insistent manner that curled her fingers against his coat. She found herself more comfortably wrapped in his embrace, more open and receiving to his fervent onslaught, and she gave herself up to it. She slid one hand into his hair, sighing at the low growl of approval it elicited.

He suddenly broke off, releasing a sigh and shaking his head against her. "Kate…" he rasped, clamping one hand firmly on the side of her face. He nuzzled her gently and pressed a soft kiss at the very corner of her mouth. "Kate, I should have told you ages ago, but I…"

"Excuse me, my lord, my lady," Harville interrupted.

"Yes, what is it?" Derek nearly barked, holding fast as Kate frantically tried to untangle herself and scoot away. "Stay right where you are," he murmured to her, which she did.

"There is an urgent message from the Duke of Ashcombe, my lord."

Derek sighed and reached for the note. "Thank you, Harville," he said, but the butler had already wisely moved on.

"So help me, if someone hasn't died…" he muttered as he broke the seal.

Kate smiled softly, but said nothing until Derek's face tightened as he read. "What is it?" she asked.

"We are being *requested*," he said, sneering at the word, "to attend the duke and duchess immediately upon receipt of this note."

"Immediately?"

He nodded, frowning deeply. "It appears we have been summoned, my dear." He groaned and touched his forehead to hers. "Do we have to go?"

"I'm afraid so," she said sadly, stroking the back of his neck. "With David gone, it cannot be so bad, can it?"

Again he nodded. "It can, and it will." He winced and kissed her.

"I just want to stay here with you," he whispered.

"I know. Let's go and see what they want, and then it will be over, and we can come back here." She kissed him in return, promising him the prospect of later, then hugged herself close.

"Very well, only if you promise it will be brief."

She pulled back and gave him a look. "We will *make* it brief."

"Oh, yes, we will," he insisted quickly.

Kate offered a dazzling smile and murmured, "Let me go change, and we can be off." She kissed him lightly and disengaged herself from him, taking all of the warmth and pleasure of the moment with her.

Derek released a heaving sigh and leaned back against the sofa, rubbing his eyes with the heels of his hands. Kate was going to be the death of him. A beautiful, glorious, spectacular death that he would enjoy every minute of, but a death all the same. He had been so close to telling her he loved her, to confessing the deepest feelings of his heart.

This meeting with his parents had better be the shortest meeting ever created in the history of meetings.

He had other plans to attend to this evening.

Chapter Eighteen

$\mathcal{H}$and in hand, they entered the grand home of the duke and duchess and they were immediately shown into one of the four drawing rooms to wait for their hosts. When Wooster, who had rather boldly winked at Kate, had left, cackling to himself, Derek had whirled to his wife.

"You would think they could be here already, if they wanted us to come so very quickly!" he hissed.

"Shh!" Kate scolded with a smile. "Perhaps they didn't think we would come as soon as we did."

"I fail to see how anybody might misinterpret the word 'immediately'," he grumbled, sitting down on the sofa next to her. "They wanted us to come, we have come. Where the devil are they?"

"Patience is not your strong suit, is it?" she asked, placing a hand on his knee.

He smiled at last and put his hand over hers. "No, it's not." He leaned over and whispered, "You see, I would much rather be at home with my wife. She is a good deal prettier and far better suited to my personality than either of my parents."

She blushed as he pressed a soft kiss to her cheek and shook her head. "Don't embarrass me before the duke and duchess, Derek."

"I have no intention of embarrassing you. Embarrassing *them*, however…"

"Derek," she scolded with a warning look.

"Oh, very well," he sighed, pulling away from her. "I will be perfectly behaved."

"Thank you."

"For now."

She rolled her eyes and rapped his knee sharply, which made him chuckle. But before he could say anything else, the door opened and the duke and duchess entered. Derek and Kate rose as one and greeted them with a bow and a curtsey, respectively. "Your Grace," they murmured, again in unison.

They received the accompanying nods, and then polite smiles, though the duchess wore one that was a good deal warmer. "Hello, Katherine, how are you?" she asked, coming over to take the seat next to her.

"Very well, thank you, Your Grace," Kate replied, sitting back down after the duchess had done so.

"Whitlock, thank you for coming so promptly," the duke said, taking Derek's hand.

"Your request did say immediately," Derek reminded him as they both sat as well. "Kate and I saw fit to comply."

The duke stiffened ever so slightly at Derek's light use of Kate's name, or perhaps just the version of it, but regardless, Kate caught it. "We hope there is nothing amiss, Your Grace," she said softly, looking over at the stern face of Derek's father.

His dark eyes rested on her, and the tension seemed to abate just a little. "No, my dear Lady Whitlock, nothing is amiss. Not now that David has gone up to Scotland. No, we just felt a little chat was in order."

"And that had to be done immediately?" Derek asked in surprise, though Kate could see his knuckles starting to whiten where his hand rested next to his leg.

Slowly, she slid her hand over and covered his. "Derek," she said softly.

He glanced over and gave her the barest hint of a nod. "Forgive me, Your Grace," he said, turning back to his father. "I meant no offense."

The duke nodded, seeming to regard Kate with a warmer interest now. "We, that is, the duchess and I, wanted to discuss something of the future with you."

"The future," Derek repeated, still tensing.

Kate did her best to soothe him, rubbing his hand, though she really didn't know why he was so upset. It was a viable thing to discuss, though perhaps not in the haste that it was being done. But they could bear with it for a little while, surely.

"Indeed," the duke said with a firm nod, leaning forward just a bit. "Now that your sister is expecting, I think we should look very seriously towards the continuation of the title line."

Now it was Kate who tensed, though she prided herself that only Derek could tell. Instantly, it was his hand on hers. "Indeed?" he asked slowly.

"Yes. It is important that we do not let Diana overshadow the dukedom."

"I hardly think that she's doing that," Derek commented, not bothering to keep the irritation out of his tone.

"Oh, but she is!" the duke protested, ignoring Derek's tone. "You two have been married longer than Lord Beckham and Diana have, and yet you have not produced any children at all, let alone an heir. Do you not wonder that people are beginning to talk?"

Kate felt her cheeks start to warm, and now it would be impossible to say who was holding whose hand, as both were gripping the other so tightly it hardly mattered.

"People will talk," Derek said tightly. "They always do."

"Not about us!" the duke cried, looking far more earnest than Kate had ever seen him. "People are saying that your wife here cannot even *bear* children."

Now Kate new her cheeks were flaming, and she was profoundly grateful when Derek said, "You go too far, sir!"

The duke, apparently unruffled, turned to Kate. "My apologies, Lady Whitlock. That is merely what they are saying, not my own opinion."

Kate nodded, but did not feel any better. This was a side to her father-in-law that she had only heard of, and now she was beginning to understand what his children had been talking about.

"So we must do all that we can to prove them wrong," the duke continued, as if he had not affronted anyone. "Time is of the essence. When can we expect an heir?"

"Kate and I," Derek ground out, his teeth clenched, "will have children when we are ready for them, and not a moment before."

Kate's heart thrilled at how valiantly he was defending her, and she squeezed his hand in gratitude. He returned the pressure, and she resisted the urge to sigh. She loved him for standing up to his father in her behalf; he was the obedient child, who always did as his father thought he should. Now he was his own man, freely expressing his opinions, knowing full well they would be vastly different from what was expected.

The duke, however, was far from pleased. His jaw tightened, his eyes narrowed and he stood quickly. "Whitlock, I would speak to you privately. Now." Without waiting for a reply, he turned from the room and out of sight.

Derek sighed and looked over at his mother, who sat still and unmoving, her eyes locked with his. She tilted her head in the direction of the door ever so slightly, and he groaned. "I will be back soon," he murmured to Kate, kissing her hand as he stood. Then he, too, turned and left, letting go of Kate's hand at the very last possible moment.

"Oh dear," the duchess said softly, still looking after them in apprehension.

"Is it going to be very bad?" Kate asked in a small voice.

She nodded. "I am afraid so. Ashcombe is very determined about the continuation of the title." She turned her green eyes to Kate and offered a smile. "I tried to suggest that now might not be the best time to discuss this, but he refused to listen. You see, I am in frequent correspondence with my daughter, and she indicated that things might be changing between you and my son at this time."

Kate ducked her head shyly. "I think they are, Your Grace."

"You may call me Lydia," the duchess insisted, still smiling. "I think titles are so formal, but Ashcombe does insist upon them. So do you love my son?"

"Yes, ma'am," Kate replied promptly, forgetting about her insistence of given names, not entirely sure she could be comfortable with that.

"Good. I approve of love, though my husband thinks it unnecessary. But I will warn you now, Katherine, if you do anything to jeopardize him, his future, or this family, I will see you ruined."

Kate's mouth dropped open slightly, but she had no reason to doubt the woman's words. Her expression was deadly serious, and there was no hint of humor in her eyes. "I understand," she managed, swallowing.

"Good. Would you care for a biscuit?"

"What is the meaning of this, sir?" came the unmistakable sound of the duke, bellowing from his study.

Lydia froze as she reached for the plate. "Oh dear," she murmured again. "I think we had better go for a walk, my dear." She stood and held out a hand for her.

"I do not appreciate you putting yourself in our bedchamber, sir," came Derek's voice, no less angry or loud.

"Yes, I think you are right," Kate said, standing herself and taking Lydia's hand, allowing her to lead her from the room.

"Someone needs to be in there, as neither of you seem to be!"

"Faster, faster," Lydia muttered to no one in particular as she sped up and took Kate down the hall and towards the back of the house.

"MY bedchamber, MY wife, MY children!"

"MY heirs!"

Kate closed her eyes, wishing she could close her ears as well. She had never meant for Derek to fight with his father, or to put any strain on the relationship that was already so stressful for him. She bit her lip, worrying about the state of affairs in that room, and how either man would come out of it unscathed.

"Here we are," Lydia said with a sigh, stepping out into the garden.

Kate opened her eyes, though tears had begun to form, and tried to appear as relieved as Lydia seemed to be.

But Lydia was far too intuitive, much like her daughter. She looped her arm through Kate's and pulled her close to her side. "Do not let it trouble you so much, Katherine. Ashcombe and Derek have only a few things in common; loyalty to family, knowledge of duty, and temper. Beyond that, they are as different as night and day. This will all blow over soon enough, though it is rather ugly now."

Slowly the two women meandered around the garden, arms linked, though the formal tension was prevalent. Kate felt uneasy about what was occurring within the house, despite the duchess's assurance, and glanced back in apprehension.

"I used to be like you, Katherine," Lydia said rather abruptly. "So young and driven and in love with the idea of being the wife of a powerful and handsome man."

Kate stiffened and chanced a look at the older woman. "That is not why I love Derek."

"I can see that, and I credit you for it. But not all of us are so fortunate." A strange, sad light filled her eyes and Kate found herself suddenly captivated by this woman, whom she knew so very little about. "Ashcombe and I were thrown together by our parents, rather like the two of you were. I never minded, for I never expected to love anybody at all. I am not the romantic sort. I am very practical minded, and it has served me well. But the prospect of being powerful and respected, even as nothing more than a wife, was very alluring. Then I saw Ashcombe, and I was all the more pleased, for attractive people are always well-favored in Society." She tried for a smile, but it faltered. "I soon learned that my husband, though a good man, was blinded by ambition. Nothing else mattered to him but the reputation and respect of the family. I learned that the only way to have a voice was to echo his, and I learned to love this family, this heritage as my own."

Kate was stunned by what Lydia was sharing with her and highly doubted even Derek knew these things about his mother.

"My one regret, Katherine, is that I did not use my own voice," Lydia continued softly, sounding suddenly very weary. "So many times, I merely stood silently by and let him speak for us both. He listens to my counsel now, but very rarely does he accept it. My children could have used a mother who defended them, not one who let others determine their upbringing. I so wish I would have stood up to him once or twice. Now it is far too late to do so."

Wondering how to respond to the sudden emotion, Kate set her free hand on the other woman's arm, and it was quickly covered.

Lydia sniffed a little and offered her a polite smile. "I am so pleased you and Derek are more united now. He could use a good, strong woman at his side."

"I pray I can be both," Kate murmured.

"You already are," Lydia assured her. "We would not have chosen you for him otherwise."

Just then, Derek came storming out of the back of the house, looking murderous and glowering more fiercely than Kate had ever seen him do. And she had been on the receiving end of quite a few of his glowers.

"We are leaving, Kate," he barked, taking her hand. He nodded to Lydia, but said only, "Mother."

"Derek," Lydia replied softly, looking between her son and the house with worry.

Kate could say nothing before Derek was hauling her along behind him, taking them around the house rather than walking through it.

"Derek, what happened?" she gasped, struggling to keep up.

He shook his head, but his grip on her hand tightened.

Their carriage was already waiting for them in front of the house. Wooster must have truly been a wonder of a butler if he could anticipate Derek's storming out of the duke's home. Kate climbed in without much assistance, and Derek was quick to follow, sitting next to her, having still not relinquished his rather crushing hold on her hand.

When they had departed, she looked over at him again. His jaw was so tense she could see a muscle in it ticking. His eyes were fixed straight ahead, and he barely blinked.

"Derek," she murmured softly.

Again, he shook his head, though the movement was very slight, and if possible, his jaw grew even tighter. Any tighter, she thought, and his teeth were likely to crack against each other. But he refused to even look at her, and so she dared not push him. She was simply relieved he was holding onto her so tightly, rather than pushing her away.

They were silent the rest of the journey home, and only when they were back in the house, and ensconced in the music room, of all places, did Derek finally release her hand. She resisted the urge to rub it, feeling that might be the only way to bring back sensation into her fingers. But it was hardly appropriate at the moment.

"Derek, what happened?" she asked softly, watching as he paced before her in agitation.

He said nothing, and only rubbed his hands over his face.

Worry and a bit of panic rising within her, she took a few steps closer. "Derek, tell me what is wrong right now!" she cried. "What did your father say?"

He laughed a short, bitter laugh and finally looked over at her. "What did my father say?" he echoed, a fire starting in his eyes that frightened her. "I will tell you what my father said. He said that I was shaming the family."

"What?" she gasped, feeling her knees give a bit. How could anyone ever think that of Derek?

"Quite," he confirmed, nodding. "I am shaming the family, because I have not bedded my wife, which, apparently, is something that is my father's business."

Kate flushed ever so slightly at his bluntness, but she said nothing.

"I am failing in my duties as a future duke," Derek continued pacing again, "because I refused to let my father control my procreation. I thought that helping him with David would be enough to please him, but no. No, it doesn't matter that David is off in Scotland wrangling up sheep thieves for the dukedom, which I encouraged. No, now it is my turn to receive the sharp end of the iron hot prod my father so keenly wields. I am a failure as a member of the aristocracy because my haste to produce an heir is matched by my haste for a coffin."

"I'm sorry," she whispered.

"Sorry?" he cried, whirling away. "She's sorry!" He threw his hands up and turned back. "Do you even realize what this means, Kate?"

She opened her mouth to reply, but he went on, overriding her.

"I have disappointed my father. I, who have always done everything that he wanted, have failed him. I am the future Duke of Ashcombe; everything that he has and everything that he is lies in my future. A failed marquess is in line to inherit the dukedom. He has *never* raged at me like that before, Kate, not for something that I have done. Do you realize that he could cut me off for this? That he could will everything over to David, purely out of spite?"

"He wouldn't," she breathed in horror.

"Oh, I can assure you, he threatened to." Derek laughed again, though it was forced and sounded rather crazed. "He threatened to turn my inheritance over to *David*! He cannot even bear to look at David, and he threatened to make him the next duke! Have you any idea what that would do to me? I would be left with nothing, Kate. Not a damn thing and no family to speak of. All of this because I have not done my *duty* in securing future bloodlines. Do you want to know what his suggestion was, Kate?"

Again she tried to respond, but he didn't wait.

"He said, 'Take your wife and force her to do her duty to us, however you must.'" He ran a shaking hand through his hair, and shook his head. "Can you believe that, Kate? He wants me to *force* you. For duty. For the family. The title. Our entire lives and the air we breathe for the sake of duty. We are nothing more than a pair of horses, forced to breed for our master's benefit. That is our purpose."

Kate swallowed back a wash of emotions, and tried to come up with the best way to reply to such an outburst. She heard his mother's threat in her mind, and considered what she might be able to do to help, to prevent the ruin they seemed to be on the brink of. "So…" she began softly, "would you like me to prepare for having a child? Is that it?"

"No, that is bloody well not it!" he yelled. "Why do you always think everything has to be just so? No, Kate!"

"No?" she asked in confusion, her stomach starting to tense.

"No."

She licked her bottom lip in apprehension, then slowly asked, "You don't want a child?"

"No, I bloody well do not! I am not my father, Kate. I do not produce a child just for the sake of fulfilling duty, no matter how important." He gave her a disgusted look, and said, "It galls me that you are willing to."

She struggled to maintain calm, especially under so severe an expression. She hated his rage, but she could not refute it. They were helpless, in a way, but it need not be a sort of slavery. If he saw it that way... She took a slow breath, and then carefully spoke, "We do have duties, Derek, and it is naïve to think otherwise."

"Naïve?" he cried, coming towards her. "Naïve, Kate? When have I ever been naïve? I have always done my duty, and to the letter. I lived for duty, I prepared for duty, and I married for duty, and look where that has brought me!"

Her tightening stomach now churned at his words, and for the first time in a long while, her blood began to boil. Her breathing began to quicken, and she met his furious gaze with an equally heated one of her own. "You are not the only one who has spent their whole life focused on duty, Derek. Need I remind you?"

"No, I thank you, I recall quite clearly how arduous your life was before you married me," he replied, holding a hand up. "You did your duty and without too terribly much of a hunt at that. Bravo, Kate."

"I hardly had a choice," she hissed, her fists clenching.

"Oh, and who would you have chosen, hmm? Really, Kate, you snatched the cream of the crop."

"Did I?" she asked with a bitter laugh of her own. "How very smart of me. Well, in that case, forcible marriage might be the best suggestion for a miserable life."

"If you are so miserable, then why remain married to me, hmm?" he asked, standing directly before her, mocking her with his eyes. "It's not as though Society expects it. Why not give in to their doubts and prove them all right? Ask me for an annulment, Kate. Go ahead."

"Well, if you want the shame of getting out of this marriage, then be my guest!" she yelled, flinging a hand out to the side.

"Maybe the shame would be worth it!" he returned, his voice reverberating off of the walls of the music room in an eerie fashion.

Silence rang for a few, heart pounding moments, and when she saw that he would not continue, that he would not take the words back, her heart stuttered and her toes went numb. "If you wish it," she said slowly, feeling rather frozen in place, "then that is what shall be done. I will accept my fate as you so deign it to be, my lord."

Derek stared at her for a long moment, his expression unreadable, his body coiled with tension.

She waited in vain for him to take the words back, to see the matter for what it was. To remember what they had gained these last weeks.

"Perhaps, it would be for the best," he finally said coldly, brushing past her. He paused at the door, then added, "...Katherine." He slammed the door, not caring that it rattled on its hinges, nor how the house seemed to shake with the force of it.

Kate somehow waited until she was positive Derek was out of hearing range before the sobs escaped her. She covered her mouth, but even that could not muffle the frenzy of panicked cries that came tumbling out of her. She collapsed to her knees, then sank fully against the cold marble floor, unable and unwilling to stem the tide of tears that her broken heart threatened to unleash, her sobs echoing against the floors and the walls of the room, and louder still within her heart.

Hours later, feeling drained and worn down, Kate sat in the dining room, waiting for dinner. Eventually, she had picked herself off of the music room floor and taken herself up to her room, where she had restlessly dozed. Waking had been painful, as she realized that it had been no nightmare, but her reality. The tears she had thought long since faded returned, and it had been some time before she felt calm once more.

Now she sat and waited, knowing that her eyes were puffy and that she hardly looked presentable. But she was determined to be here, to eat beside her husband, and perhaps, if he allowed her, to beg for his forgiveness. She dared to hope that something could yet be salvaged from her crumbling marriage.

She glanced at the clock again, knowing that it was only going to be three minutes later than the last time she had looked. She had been sitting here for ages, and she was growing more weary by the second.

"Would your ladyship like to eat now?" asked Molly, her errant blond hair peeking out from under her cap as she poked her head into the room from the kitchen steps.

Kate shook her head stubbornly. "No, I thank you. I will wait for Lord Whitlock."

"Oh, but he ate hours ago, ma'am."

Kate looked over at the girl in shock, her breath simply evaporating within her chest. "He did?"

"Yes, milady."

Though she knew it impossible, Kate could swear she heard her heart crack at the words. He could not even eat with her. Not even in a stony silence or a formal politeness. He would not see her at all. "Then yes, I will eat now," she managed. "But just a little."

As it turned out, it would be a very little that she would eat before she was overcome and had to leave the room, racing back up to the would-be comfort of her bedchamber. She closed the door behind her, and threw herself upon her bed, yet again surrendering to the waves of tears and heartache that were destined to be her companions for some time.

Outside of her bedchamber, leaning against the wall beside her door, Derek listened to the broken cries of his wife, feeling as though his own heart were no longer beating. He shut his eyes as she tried to muffle them, wishing that he had the strength to go in and comfort her.

She continued to cry, the frequency and depth of her sobs growing, and Derek could bear it no longer. He grabbed at the door knob only to find it locked. In his own agony, he rested his head against the door, grimacing. He couldn't bear to knock, to beg for entrance when he could not even meet her for dinner.

He cursed the folly of his pride. What had he gained by fighting with her? Only this growing ache in his heart, and the bleak expanse of his future. She had returned his barbs as expertly as she had ever done, and rather than spar her out of it, he had taken it, and each had felt like a knife in his heart. His Kate was a woman who would not be trampled, and he had attempted to trample her. And for what? To feel that he could win one fight with his wife, when he had lost so stunningly to his father? What sort of victory had he attained? Nothing but a hatred of himself and the sobs of his wife that tore at his soul.

With the only semblance of strength left in him, he pushed away from her door and turned down the hall, away from the direction of his own room. He couldn't sleep now, if he ever would.

She would never forgive him.

He would not blame her.

For he loved her still, and always would.

That stung worst of all.

Chapter Nineteen

The morning dawned cloudy and dismal, which suited Kate just as well. She rose slowly, mutely, forgoing any pride in appearance or manner. She donned her plainest gown, silently allowing Jemima, who was, for once, also silent, to button her up and assemble her hair in the plainest, simplest array possible. But she did refuse to wear it tightly back, as she had before. She was not Katherine any longer, and she would prove it to Derek.

If she ever saw him again.

Her lip quivered ever so slightly and she bit down on it hard. The words he had lashed upon her had been horrible, had wounded and frightened her, but nothing could ever sting like his use of her full name, the name he had only called her when forced to or when out of her hearing. He had called her Katherine, not Kate. Katherine. The name of the woman he hated.

Could one day, a matter of hours, really change everything so completely? From being on the verge of confessing her love and adoration to suddenly having nothing but memories that felt more like dreams; it seemed impossible to comprehend, and yet it was. She might not even have a husband, if he carried through on his threats. Would he? Could he?

She softly thanked Jemima and hesitantly made her way downstairs. Part of her longed for even the merest glimpse of him, just a reassurance that he was here, that he was well, and perhaps, to see if he might miss her too. Another part wanted to hide, refused to see him, wanted to sulk and mourn and become a pathetic shadow of herself, waiting for the misery to overpower her. Still another part rankled at the memory of the fight, was galled that Derek thought so little of her, didn't want to see him at all, for the anger still burned. A last, smaller part felt nothing, was empty, completely numb.

But what did it matter how the many parts of her felt? There was nothing for her to do but go on, attempt to put some semblance of her life back together.

If only she knew how.

Today was cold and dark, and the weather matched the feelings of her heart perfectly.

As she attempted to eat breakfast, alone again, she was able to discern from Harville, who was careful to only leave her enough hints in his morning ramble so as to avoid being impertinent, that Derek had not left and had not requested that anything be packed or readied. He was working outside with the men again, toiling at the garden project he had started for her. Kate had nodded, murmured her thanks, and resumed her small meal, but was unsure if she were pleased by the information or not.

Why was he here, if he could not stand her? Why continue on a project he had begun to please her if that were no longer an objective of his? Why exert such physical efforts for her when he hated doing so, and now had no reason to?

She made an impulsive decision and left the breakfast room, walking rather hastily to the gallery upstairs, which provided an excellent view of the back garden. Since he would not face her, she was left with making her own opportunities to see him. She could not bear to see him face to face, not after the hurt she had caused. But neither could she forgo seeing him altogether, if he were here. She could not go back to pretending he was nothing.

She propped herself in the window seat to one side of the room, hoping to remain out of sight, should he glance up. The work was progressing rather impressively, and it would not take long before all was complete. The gazebo was nearly fully constructed, and now only required painting. The shrubs had all been planted, the stone pathway begun, and off to one side, she could see the fountain, ready to be set in the ground. Everything was in order, and all were busily occupied.

It didn't take her long to find him. He was working the hardest out of any man she could see, digging at the ground where the stone path would go. He seemed obsessed with the work, never once looking around or becoming distracted. He did not converse with any, and there was not a hint of smile to be found in his countenance.

In spite of everything, Kate felt the same pull at her heart when she saw him, and the ache within her grew. His shirt was quickly dampening, though the day was cooler than any they had seen for some time. One of the men tapped him on the back, and only then did his focus move from the ground before him. She saw him nod, then hand off his shovel and proceed over to the gazebo, where men were smoothing out the wood that would become the bench within, and a few were working at the saw on some large pieces for the top. He took over for an older man, who nodded at him gratefully.

In tandem, he worked with the men, over and over again running the saw through the wood, his face a mask of tension. Even from her present position, she could see the muscles in his arms flexing and relaxing as he sawed, and she wished those strong arms would hold her again, would *want* to hold her again. But it seemed improbable at this point.

She would wish all the same.

A large chunk of wood fell off of the end then, and the sawing ceased as the men fetched it and carried it over to the others. Derek wiped at his brow, then, suddenly, he looked up at the window. *Her* window.

Kate's breathing stuttered as her eyes met his, so striking even from this distance. His expression did not change, but she could have sworn his breathing did. He became impossibly still, staring at her without blinking, his entire being fixated along with his eyes. Her heart thudded loudly, pulsing in her ears, drowning out all else in existence.

He was not looking away; did that mean he didn't hate her? He wasn't smiling; had he not forgiven her? Questions poured into her mind, and she could not bear to answer a single one of them. All she could was to gaze upon him, as he did her, longing to see a hint that all was not lost.

But no hint came.

The men returned to his side and he resumed working, never once glancing back up at her window.

Hot tears flooded her eyes, and she turned from the window, clutching at her heart. How would she bear living this way? She didn't know, could not even imagine. In an instant, the world became a darker place, and she could not find a single glimmer of light to cling to.

Mournfully, she descended to the music room, feeling there was the very last connection she had with him. She could finish the song, *his* song, and she determined to do so, but no longer would it be the song she would save for him, to prove her love to him. Now it would become her song about him, her anthem for all that he was and ever had been. It would be the last gift he would ever give her, the painful reminiscence of what had been lost.

Much later, Kate sighed to herself as she finished the rest of her composition, feeling a mixture of pride and loss at the same time. At last she had completed what had begun as a musical declaration of her feelings and had ended as a testament to what had once been. This was something she would always have, and no one could take from her. Perhaps one day it would bring back happy memories instead of the pain she was feeling now.

She had been working at it for hours today, forgoing luncheon, as she was not the slightest bit hungry. Now she had no idea what time it was, and nor did she care.

A soft knock came at the door, and her heart leapt within her. Had he heard after all? Had he come to see her at last?

"Come," she managed, brushing strands of hair out of her face.

Harville entered, sending her a sad smile as if he could sense how keenly she would be disappointed. "Begging your pardon, milady. Lady Beverton is here to see you."

Kate swallowed and wished she had been able to see him and hear the words he had spoken without tears forming again.

Harville shuffled anxiously at the door. "Shall I tell her you are not receiving, milady?" he asked softly, his eyes full of concern.

"No," she sniffled, trying for a smile. "No, thank you, Harville. She wouldn't listen anyway."

He nodded, smiling. "That is what I figured as well, milady. Shall I show her in?"

"Please."

He bowed and left, giving Kate a little time to prepare herself. Moira was far too intuitive to not notice that something was very much amiss, but perhaps she could hold her off for a while.

"Good afternoon, Kate," Moira called cheerfully as she entered, Harville closing the door behind her. "I have come to see if you… oh my, are you all right?"

So much for that idea.

Kate shook her head at her friend, hoping against hope that she would not ask.

But that was not Moira. She immediately came over and pulled Kate to the sofa, then sat beside her, holding her hands tightly. "Kate, what is it?"

She opened her mouth, but hesitated. What was there to say?

"Kate, please trust me," Moira begged, her bright sapphire eyes earnest and worried. "What's wrong?"

"Everything," Kate whispered, feeling those blasted tears rising within her again.

"Could you elaborate just a little bit?" Moira requested, a hint of a smile at her lips. "Everything is a bit much to take in."

"I have lost him, Moira."

"Lost whom?" she asked, stroking her hands. "Derek?"

She nodded frantically.

"Not possible," Moira said firmly with a shake of her head. "That man is so head over heels for you it is remarkable his feet ever touch the ground."

Kate's face crumpled and she turned her face into the back of the sofa. "Not anymore." She could not say anything else as the tears erupted once more, her entire frame shaking.

Moira's hand rubbed soothingly up and down her back and she scooted closer. "Oh, Kate," she said softly. "What happened?"

In broken sobs, Kate managed to pour the whole story out,

leaving nothing unsaid. Her grief overwhelmed her, and Moira held her fast, listening all the while.

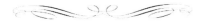

Sleep was impossible. She had tossed and turned for the longest time, surely hours by now, and she was no less able to sleep than she had been at the beginning. She lay still for a moment, the darkness of her room oddly comforting.

She knew the trouble.

She missed Derek.

Where was he? What was he doing? Was he able to sleep tonight? Did he miss her?

Moira had stayed for most of the afternoon, letting Kate play as she wished, only lecturing a little on their behavior. She had cried with her as she played Derek's song over and over, and only softly said her name when she thought it was enough. Kate knew she was worried about her, but she could not help but play it. She could play it brightly and remember Derek's smile, or she could play it slowly and remember the warmth in his eyes. She could play the same song in so many different ways, but Derek was always there.

That was the point of the song.

She could not cry anymore. Her eyes were swollen and red; there were hardly tears to cry any longer. At some point, she would lose the desire to cry, and then the need to.

Shaking her head at her own black thoughts, Kate pushed herself out of bed and pulled on her wrap, opting to drift through the house like a ghost rather than lay here and give in to dark thoughts. She wandered up and down the hall, silently treading along the carpet, without light or candle.

She needed to get Derek alone with her tomorrow. She needed to talk with him, regardless of how he felt about her now. She could not continue on like this, as if they were two strangers inhabiting the same space. He could not avoid her forever, and she refused to let him.

But how could she? He was not exactly being made available to her. Again she was alone at dinner, and when she had softly asked Harville where he was, he had merely shaken his head and said he was out.

Enough was enough. No matter how angry Derek might be with her, she deserved to be heard, to explain everything to him. She loved him enough to fight for this marriage, and for their love. He had loved her once, she had felt it, and he could not deny it, try as he might.

She walked through the gallery, faint moonlight streaming through the window panes, the clouds having vanished some time during the day. She looked up at the faces of the men and women who had lived here before, who had gone on to be dukes and duchesses and other important members of Society. All looked so formal and solemn, no hint of joy in their countenances.

Kate had been one of them. Day to day duties were all that she had, and a future of more duties. Derek had been one of them. Going on with what was expected, valuing title and heritage and duty above all else. Then they had miraculously found each other, the true self on the inside that no other person knew so intimately, and suddenly, duty had vanished.

There was nothing wrong with how they had been.

But there was so much more to be had.

With a sigh of longing, Kate found herself looking up into the face of her husband, the portrait that had been painted shortly before their marriage five years ago. He looked so handsome and proud, but not haughty like his predecessors had. There was a glint in his eye that spoke of an adventurous mind, of a sparkling wit, of a heart that was far warmer than anybody could expect. He would make a fine duke when the time came.

She hoped she could be his equal in that respect.

She moved on to the window where she had seen him this morning, where their eyes had met again after what had felt like years apart, though it had only been a day. The distance between them was far longer. It might as well be miles of ocean and she was in a boat with no paddle.

This was the time, she supposed, to get out of the boat and swim.

A movement outside caught her attention and she hid herself slightly behind the thick curtains, but kept her view. A man was pacing around in the tiny gazebo, now entirely finished but for the paint. Her heart stuttered with fear, wondering who would disturb their unfinished garden in the dead of night.

The fear vanished when the man turned his face into the moonlight.

It was Derek.

His eyes were closed and he leaned against one post, his shoulders slumped. His face was drawn, his expression in every respect pained. Even from her vantage point, she could see him swallow hard, and suddenly, she had to do the same.

He sat on one of the benches, the one next to the lilacs that waited to be planted along the outside. He breathed in deeply, then exhaled slowly, and Kate felt tears sting the corners of her eyes once more. Apparently, she was not out of tears. He had found a way to draw forth more.

She covered her mouth as she watched him, as he leaned forward and put his head into his hands. His behavior was, in every respect, that of a man tormented. And she had been the cause of it.

She yearned to go to him, to comfort him in his hour of despair, to hold him in her arms and let him do the same. She wanted to kiss that strong jaw, whisper words of encouragement that might lift the heavy burdens he had placed upon himself. She wanted to be whatever he needed her to be.

Suddenly, she couldn't watch him anymore. It was too much, too painful, too poignant to bear. She turned from the window and softly returned to her bedchamber, her heart full to bursting. She slid beneath the bedcovers, now content to lay here until sleep found her, if it ever did.

She would find a way to make him love her again.

And when she did, she would never let him go.

Chapter Twenty

$\mathcal{T}$he sun had not even risen before he decided that he could not take it anymore. He dressed quietly, taking only the bare essentials; trousers, shirt, coat, and boots. Everything else was superfluous. Besides, he did not care if he looked wild and ridiculous and shockingly lapsing in fashion sense. He had no intention of seeing anybody anyway.

He was not so foolish as to think that he could avoid everybody in London, but as the majority of the city would still be sleeping, he felt quite confident that he could enjoy the peace of the morning without too much disturbance. He left his bedchamber, dutifully avoiding looking at Kate's door, for fear that he would be drawn to it as he had so many times before. Silently he crept along the corridor, the stairs, and the entryway, not even glimpsing a hint of a servant. The great front door let out a low creek, but it too was soft, as if everything in his possession was aiding him in his escape.

But where could he go?

Standing on his front step, the eastern sky only just beginning to lighten, Derek thrust his hands into his greatcoat pockets and sighed. He could not go to Hyde Park; it would remind him of picnicking with Kate. He could not go to the little gazebo hidden away on the Mayfield's property; it would remind him of dancing with Kate. He could not go to Nathan's; it would remind him of laughing with Kate.

He dared not disturb his friends this early, especially if he wanted them to remain friends after this morning. And they would ask about

Kate. There was nothing left for him but to either remain here or wander the streets aimlessly until a solution or alternative presented itself.

He could not remain, not with Kate in the house, not if he wanted to retain any semblance of his sanity. He therefore chose the latter, to wander the London streets in the hours before dawn, hoping against hope that he would feel different upon his return.

Head bowed, he walked, taking no notice of his surroundings, save the occasional patch of fog that was so prevalent in London mornings. He had slept for only a few hours last night, and it had been a troubled sleep at that. Sometime in the night he had come to realize that he was not angry with Kate any longer, and perhaps had never been. His anger had been directed towards himself, at his inability to stand up to his father when it had mattered. If he had done so, there would have been no argument. He would never have lashed out at Kate, unleashing a torrent of misdirected frustration upon the one person who he should have held onto.

What he was feeling towards her at the moment was fear. Fear that she did not want to remain his wife. Fear that he had gone too far, said too much. Fear that the woman he had fallen in love with had been a mere fantasy.

It had to be real. He felt too much for it to be all imagined, for *her* to be all imagined.

He loved her, and with an ache that would never quite dissipate. These past weeks had opened his heart to emotions that he never thought he would feel, and he felt more alive than he ever had. It was a bizarre sensation, having never known anything had been lacking in his life. He had been content and satisfied with his lot, and there had never been a moment that he wished for something different.

Well, maybe one or two moments, particularly when he had thought about Katherine.

But now… now the very thought of Kate sent a fire into his heart, and it raced along his limbs and filled his being until there was nothing in him but her. Now he had dreams for the future, not just ambitions. He saw the future could be bright and happy, not just an endless monotony of days and responsibilities. He could revel in each sunrise that greeted him and take pride in the sunsets.

How could he go back to that former life of ignorance and blindness? Having tasted the sweetness of this life, how he could he abandon it for the paltry, tasteless existence of before? Having seen the beauty of the light, how could he return to darkness?

The notion pained him, and he shook his head as he rubbed at his chest. He couldn't do it. There was nothing to go back to, no life for him there. He was too changed for that, and too far gone to try.

Duty. That was what it had come down to. He balked at duty for the first time in his life, and she, ever the practical and pragmatic one, had reminded him of it. She was right; it was naïve to ignore duty. Yes, they had the right to their own time of fulfillment, but there was duty still. He had known that all along, and he had never thought of refusing to fulfill it. But Kate was no duty, and she had no duty to him or to his father, regardless of what the duke had said. She was not just a woman he had married to provide heirs and a continuation of bloodlines, not any more. She was his wife, his better half, and he wanted no other. He could honestly say he had never thought of any other.

All his life there had only been Kate.

There only ever would be.

In short, Derek was the biggest fool that had ever walked God's good earth.

The first light of the morning crept over the trees then, and slowly Derek turned to watch it, finding himself on a bench somewhere in the vicinity of Hyde Park, in spite of his attempts to avoid it. Another morning, another day dawning without the brightness of Kate's smile to accompany it.

He could go back, he could go home and wake her. He could sit on the edge of her bed and wait for the sunlight to peek through her curtains and dance across the perfect skin of her face, wait for those long eyelashes to flutter in protest of waking, wait for those dark, entrancing eyes to open with the deep, slumberous look that filled them in the mornings. He need not say anything; he would not be able to. He knew he would never be able to restrain his expression, not when he was fairly bursting with emotion now, so far from her.

She would know immediately how ardently he loved her, and perhaps, if her heart were as large and warm as he thought it was, she would forgive him, and they could start over.

He longed to begin their marriage again, to pretend the past had not existed. There were so many wrongs to make right, so many mistakes to atone for. If they could begin anew, he could be better than he had been. He could become the man Kate deserved to be married to. Neither of them had had a choice in this marriage, but they could choose how to live it now.

If she would let him make amends, he would spend the rest of his life proving his worth.

Yet here he sat still, elbows on his knees, hands folded before him, head bowed as the morning rays crept closer to him. Unable to move, unable to do anything but mourn. Never had he been so helpless. Or hopeless.

"Derek?"

His head jerked up at the soft, feminine voice and blearily he met the eyes of his concerned and startlingly close sister. Where had she come from? How long had she been there?

"You look terrible," she remarked rather bluntly as she took in the state of him.

"Diana?" His voice was slow and rough, unaccustomed to being used after so many hours of neglect.

"What are you doing?" she asked softly, pulling her shawl more tightly around her.

He shrugged, and said, "Couldn't sleep."

She made a small noise of understanding, though her expression never changed. "It's early," she commented.

"Not really."

Now she frowned, and Derek knew he was in for it. "How long have you been out here, Derek?"

"I don't know," he said with real honesty, his voice cracking rather shamefully.

Diana took his arm and, with surprising strength, pulled him off of the bench. "Come on, you are coming home with me. Have you eaten?"

He shook his head. "I'm not hungry, Diana."

She sighed in frustration. "Now I know this is serious. Well, I am hungry, and I hate eating alone, and since Edward is gone, I am forcing you to eat with me."

Derek managed a wan smile and allowed her to loop her arm through his. "You aren't walking alone, are you? If Edward is gone…"

"No, no," she interrupted, waving him off, "I know better than that. Charles is about twenty paces back. He is not very happy with me for going out so early, but I don't sleep well when Edward is gone, and a morning walk does wonders for my… condition." She made a face of disgust. "Mornings are always so unpleasant. But the fresh air helps a great deal."

"Are you well?"

She shrugged lightly. "Well enough, all things considered. I daresay the unpleasantness will pass soon enough." She looked up at him knowingly. "What about you?"

He opened his mouth, then closed it again. What was there to say? No, he was not well. He was so very far from well.

"I see," she murmured, rubbing at his arm soothingly. "All right, then, Derek Chambers, the moment after I have eaten, and you have as well, we are going to have a discussion. A very long, very detailed, very intense discussion about what is plaguing you."

"I don't want to talk about it," he said roughly, stiffening in her hold.

"That is just too bad," she snapped, her green eyes flashing up at him. "You know perfectly well that you never keep secrets from me, nor I from you. You are not about to start now when you need somebody to talk to, no matter how you bristle about it."

"Tyrant," he muttered, though he felt the tension leaving him. What would it hurt to tell Diana? She was right, he always told her everything. She knew him well, as well as any sister had ever known a brother. She had grown wise and he valued her opinions and advice. And she liked and respected Kate. Yes, he could tell Diana. He might get beaten over the head with the nearest blunt object, but at least he would know it was well deserved.

"All right, Derek, tell me everything."

Derek quirked a brow at his sister, who was now sitting on the sofa in her morning room, and staring rather expectantly at him. True to her word, she had forced him to eat breakfast with her, and grudgingly he had done so, his nonexistent hunger flaring up once he had begun, which had made Diana smirk in satisfaction. Now that he sat in the chair next to her, he found himself even more reluctant than before to share what had happened.

As if she could sense his turmoil, Diana reached over and took his hand. "Derek," she said softly. "Tell me. Please."

He sighed heavily and settled himself more completely in his chair. This was going to take a while. Then, slowly, he began to tell her what had been happening, how he had struggled to find a way to show Kate what she meant to him, how he had promised to stay, how close they were becoming. All the while Diana smiled, still holding his hand tightly.

When he reached the part about the fight with the duke, about forcing Kate to do her duty, Diana's face became a mask of horror and revulsion and her hold on his hand became clenching. But, much to her credit, she said nothing, which Derek appreciated.

He tried to rush through the part about his fight with Kate, but Diana forced him to recount everything in detail, slowly, reliving the terrible moments over again. Again her face had transformed, this time into a vacant expression, without any single emotion to be identified. Some small corner of his mind warned him about the danger in that, but it was too late to retreat now.

His tale finally told, he sat back fully and slid his hand from Diana's grasp and met her eyes fully.

"So, what do you think?"

Diana swallowed, seemed to gather her thoughts, then said, "First, I think our father showed a deplorable lack of intelligence, tact, and good behavior with respect to your wife, and in his treatment of you. His words were barbaric and callous, not to mention very poorly thought out. There is no excuse for that. It's no wonder you were so agitated, I would have been spitting fire. Poor Kate, what a burden to have to bear!"

Derek gave her a faint smile of acknowledgement, but said nothing.

"Second, I think both you and her are behaving like a couple of spoiled children."

"I beg your pardon?" he coughed, sitting up.

Diana gave him a hard look. "Honestly, Derek, I cannot believe you. Threatening to go through with annulment all because she said the word duty? What nonsense! We all have duties, you know that. No, no," she said, throwing up a hand at his stammering protests, "I have already said that Father was a bullheaded monstrosity with no sense. We are agreed that he was in bad form. But you! And she! Fighting with each other over something so trite when you ought to be standing together as a united front! Don't you *want* to have children, Derek?"

"Yes, but…"

"And you *do* want Kate to be the mother, don't you?"

"Of course, I do, but…"

"Then how *dare* you insinuate otherwise! She asked you a plain and simple question, one which you should have been more than delighted to respond to, and instead, you made it seem as though you never wanted children merely because our father thinks you should! Really, Derek, where was your head?"

"I don't know," he whispered, leaning forward and putting his head in his hands. "I never meant to say I didn't want children, I just didn't want to start our family in response to the duke's demands."

"Then you should have said *that*," Diana said, her voice growing kinder. "I know you were worked up and in a rage, but consider; Kate was willing to do whatever it was you wanted. If you wanted to start a family, she was willing. It was *her* suggestion to prepare for a child. In spite of Father's cruel words, in spite of her apparent doubt in your affections, she offered to bear you a child. What does that tell you, Derek?"

He shuddered and gripped at his hair, groaning softly. "I didn't mean to fight with her, Diana. I don't know who I became in there, but it couldn't have been me. What if I have ruined everything?"

Diana took his hands and forced him to look at her. "Derek, you are one of the very best men that I know. You may have behaved badly, but when the heart is in the middle of things, everybody thinks a little more stupidly."

Derek shook his head, unwilling to brush off his behavior so lightly. "I should have thought better, I should have seen... No wonder she fought back, I was hardly reasonable."

"I wasn't going to say anything, but..." Diana said nonchalantly, giving him a half smile.

He allowed himself a brief roll of his eyes, then sighed. "I just became afraid when she didn't say anything after my outburst. I wanted her to be shocked, scared, even defiant. I never expected her to be resigned to my decision. I wanted to take it all back and tell her I didn't mean a word, but I couldn't. What if she really wants to be rid of me?"

"Can you really believe that?" Diana asked sadly. "After all that you have been through, after all she has become, all *you* have become, you really think she doesn't care about you? You still doubt her?"

"I don't want to," he rasped, shaking his head, a lump forming in his throat. "I don't want to, but I can't help it."

"Derek?"

Both Derek and Diana turned at the new voice, and it would have been impossible to say who was more shocked at the sight of the Duchess of Ashcombe standing in the doorway to the drawing room, looking worried. "Mother?" Diana gasped, her cheeks paling a bit. "What are you...? Is Father...?"

"Oh, no, I am here on my own," she reassured them hastily, her eyes nervously flicking over to Derek, who had gone still, his jaw tensing. "I... I came to speak with you, Diana, and then I heard Derek, and I..."

"You heard," Diana sighed in realization, closing her eyes. "Of course."

Derek stood and turned. "Thank you for listening, Diana," he said curtly, not addressing his mother at all.

She smiled up at him faintly, her eyes apologetic, and nodded.

"If you do not mind, Derek, I have a few things to say to you," their mother said softly.

"Say them, then," he snapped, barely glancing in her direction. He knew his mother, and though she was kind, she was also loyal to his father. Every decision of his she had stood by without comment. Derek was in no humor to be reminded of his apparent failure, even by his mother.

"I… I told your father he had gone too far," Lydia said softly, wringing her hands in an uncharacteristically nervous fashion.

"Oh, thank you so much, Mother," Derek drawled sarcastically. "That helps the situation a good deal."

Her brows drew together and her mouth became a thin line. "Derek, I have never taken that tone from you and I will not do so now. I am telling you that I disagree with your father emphatically, when have you ever known me to do that?"

She had a point; his mother had only ever gone along with his father's words, orders, and wishes, and never in his life had he heard her say anything against him. He sighed and turned to face her. "You're right, Mother. I apologize." He shrugged, and said, "As you can see, I have been a bit on edge lately."

She smiled sadly and nodded. "I do see that. You have had a difficult couple of days." Her smile faded, and she began working at her hands again. "But I fear I may have to share some of the blame." She gestured for him to sit back down and she took the seat next to Diana on the sofa. "As you may remember, I took Katherine…"

"Kate," both Derek and Diana interrupted, which was simply not done in their family.

Lydia looked at them both in bewilderment.

"It's important," Diana murmured, looking over at Derek's tormented expression.

"Very well, then," Lydia said slowly, her mouth twisting as if her tongue were testing out the abbreviation, and she was not certain if she liked it. "I took Kate out to the back garden to avoid overhearing you and your father."

"I recall," Derek replied, waving for her to go on. "Thank you for that." It would have been horrifying to have Kate hear everything that had been said. He had not told her everything that had been said and he never would.

She nodded briefly. "Before we went out there, I said… well, I may have said something that affected her response to you."

Derek felt his insides freeze. "What did you say, Mother?"

"Well, if I can recollect clearly," she said hesitantly, looking away.

"You can," her children insisted firmly, both fully aware that she had always had perfect recollection of everything she had said.

"I believe I said, 'If you do anything to jeopardize him, his reputation, or this family, I will see you ruined'."

For a long moment, the room was silent. And then Diana breathed, "Mother!"

Lydia dropped her head, grimacing.

"Why would you say something like that?" Derek managed, his voice weak.

"Because it is true," she told him, her eyes bright with unshed tears and filled with earnestness. "You and your sister and your brother, this family means everything to me. And to your father. She had a right to know where we stand."

"But Kate is already *part* of the family!" Derek cried, his voice stronger. "She has been a part of this family for five years, Mother! You have known nothing but prosperity and respect and dignity from our part, and it is mostly because of her! I have had very little to do with any of it, believe me. If anybody is going to jeopardize this family, it is more likely to be me than it ever would be her. Leave my wife out of it!"

"So you do love her, then," Lydia said softly, her eyes warm in spite of her sorrowful expression.

"Of course, I love her!" He shot to his feet and rubbed a hand through his hair. "I love her so much I am fairly sick with it!"

"Then do not let her go, Derek," she urged. "You need her."

"I know, Mother," he said as he turned from the room. "Believe me, I know."

"I am sorry, Derek," she called, her voice shaking.

He stopped, glancing back at her. His mother had never

apologized to him either. The woman who was normally so proud and regal and refined now was humble and penitent and... motherly. She had always been kind, but never open. Now here she was urging him to go back to Kate, to hold on to her, to become a family with her. He had never known his mother to be like this.

Perhaps there was hope for his family after all.

"I am so sorry," she said again. "For all of it."

He nodded, swallowing back yet another lump. "Thank you. Good day, Mother. Diana." He walked out the door without responses, and headed for home. He had business to take care of today, which could not wait, and it would take some time. But after that, he was going to get his wife back.

No matter what it took.

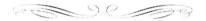

As quietly as he could, he reentered the house, now wide awake and bustling as usual. While he desperately wanted to mend his situation with Kate, he could not do so now. He needed time to think, to collect himself, to find exactly the right words to say to her. And time to be with her, which he did not have now. He had to meet with solicitors on important estate matters he had put off for far too long, and then his friends later in the day, and all of that would undoubtedly last well into the evening.

Thankfully, nobody said anything as he quietly and quickly made his way up to his bedchamber. He changed into more proper attire, then came down again a few moments later and moved to his study, needing to gather the necessary information.

Kate would no doubt think him out with the other men in the garden this morning, so she would not be looking for him within the house. He had urged the men to continue with their plans, under the watchful eye of Mr. Tanner, the man he had consulted as to the design. He had no doubt things would move along smoothly without him present.

At last, he had all that he needed for his meetings, and he walked out of his office towards the entryway. But as he walked by the music room, its door shut as usual, he heard music coming from within and he was powerless to resist the pull of it. He stopped and stood like a fool outside of the door, listening intently to the mournful music his wife was playing.

His heart caught as he recognized the melody. It was the song he had been humming ever since they had danced in the gazebo, the song he had hummed as he danced with her. She had turned it into a real song, had added harmonies and life to what he had so sporadically created.

Her words to him echoed in his mind then. *Perhaps you ought to come home unexpectedly, then.* Was this what she had been working on while he was out? Had she turned his random humming into a composition?

Moaning softly in his own tormented agony, Derek leaned his head against the door, listening with more intensity than he had anything in his life. He wished he had the strength to go in and listen fully, to be there with her as she played, to watch her face as she did so. It was his favorite thing to do; not that he didn't love the music, but he adored watching her face as she played. She became transformed, moved by the music, put everything of herself into each and every note, and it was beautiful and captivating. He missed that.

He missed her.

"That is your song, Derek."

He turned his head at the soft, barely audible voice and saw Moira, obviously just arrived, watching him with a pitying look in her eyes. "What?" he mouthed more than said, though some sound escaped.

"She wrote that for you. She has been playing it ever since she finished." She looked at the door sadly. "It's all she plays anymore."

He grimaced as if struck and shut his eyes tightly, returning his head to his previous position. "I had no idea," he breathed. "I couldn't have…"

Against her nature, Moira did not respond.

Derek longed to stay, to take Kate into his arms and beg for forgiveness. But he could not, not yet. "I have to go," he said softly.

"Don't tell Kate I was here. Don't tell her I heard."

"But…"

"Ask her to wait up for me tonight," he overrode, pushing his head away from the door, but keeping his hand firmly against it. "Tell her I want to talk with her. Tell her… ask her to wait for me. Please."

Moira looked at him for a long moment, then nodded once.

"Thank you," he murmured. He looked back at the door, heard the faint strains of music die away, and sighed. Then he dropped his hand and walked on towards the entryway, head down, brushing past Moira without acknowledgement.

Tonight he would tell Kate everything, try to mend what had been broken, and beg her to start again with him. He needed her, and he could only pray she needed him, too. There was no hope for them apart.

Chapter Twenty One

"*He*'s not listening to a word we're saying."

"He's not drunk, he hasn't touched a thing."

"Is he breathing?"

"He looks ill. Maybe he's ill."

"He is not ill. He's in love."

"…So he's ill."

"No, Colin, he is *not.*"

"Shut up, Nate. Derek's all peaky and sighing and hasn't said a word in two hours, and my late Aunt Agatha would be able to see the dark circles around his eyes. The man is deathly ill, I tell you."

"I am fine," Derek murmured, shaking his head, his eyes not seeing anything, least of all his friends at the table with him.

"He speaks!" Duncan cried, slapping him on the back. "We were afraid you had drifted off into some other realm and we had lost you forever."

He tried for a smile, but it was hard to come by.

The last several hours he had been occupied with business, but sitting here now, as he should have been listening to details of some ridiculous venture Colin had heard about, he could not remember a single facet of anything he had discussed with anyone today. He felt as though his entire day had been nothing but a fog, with one bright, shining moment of glory that came in the form of a song written for him by the woman he adored.

And he was sitting here with his friends while she waited for him at home. What had been so pressing today that he could not have done tomorrow or the next day? Why had duty come before his wife again? Before his heart? That was quite enough of that.

He didn't want to be here. He wanted to be there. His heart started pounding, and his fingers tingled. There was so much to do, and none of it would be done here. All he needed was Kate.

And he needed her now.

"I have to go," he mumbled, starting to get out of his chair.

"What?"

"Where?"

"Why?"

"All right."

"Nathan!" Colin protested, giving him a disgusted look.

"What?" Nathan replied, standing as well. "If Derek feels he needs to leave, then by all accounts, we should let him. Particularly when he looks like this. Don't you think he probably has somewhere better to be?"

Colin opened his mouth, then closed it and grumbled, "There is no fair response to that question."

"Derek, what is going on?" Geoff asked softly, his blue eyes cloudy with concern.

"I have to go to Kate," he said, taking his jacket from the back of his chair and putting it over his arm. "We... I..." He shook his head. There was no time to explain everything, and he had no desire to relive it again. "I have to go," he repeated.

"Very well," Nathan said, a bemused smile on his lips. "We can finish this at another time."

Derek nodded, meeting his eyes. Perhaps Nathan sensed what lay beneath Derek's words. Besides having a keen intuition about people, Nathan also had a wife. He would understand how tossed about a man could be when he was in love with a woman.

"Tell Kate hello from us," Duncan told him as he rose to shake his hand in farewell.

"Oh, I hardly think he needs to tell her that *now*," Nathan disagreed, his smile growing. "Surely that can wait until later."

Derek grinned in response, feeling his heart lighten a touch. "It just might." He nodded at them all and turned from the room, walking rather briskly.

"I don't understand any of this," he heard Colin say as he left.

"You will when you're older."

"Oh, shut up, Geoff."

Derek didn't even call for a carriage to take him home. He could be halfway there before one was readied, and besides, he wanted the exhilaration of walking, knowing he was going to see his wife, that he was going to tell her that he loved her. He should have done so ages ago.

He didn't care if she might not be able to return the words, though he hoped she would. He would wait forever if she could give him the faintest hope of a return of affection in the future. He would rather be with Kate and waiting than without her and never know.

Feeling more excitement, Derek started to jog. Walking was not fast enough. He wanted to tell Kate now. He wanted to give her everything he was and let her do with him as he wished. What use was pride when he was without the woman he loved?

The jog turned to a run and a few strolling Londoners gave him questioning looks as he passed them and he knew they would whisper and gossip.

He did not care.

Let them say that the Marquess of Whitlock was seen running towards his house, looking like a madman as his jacket lay over an arm and his cravat was rapidly loosening, soon to unravel, no doubt. Let them call his behavior shocking, his appearance disgraceful, and whatever else they wanted. He was a man in love, and he was not going to patiently ride in a carriage or walk calmly when so much was at stake.

Suddenly he became aware of his surroundings as all of his senses became alert at once. There was light in the distance, in the direction of his house, far more than would have come from the street lamps. It almost looked as though dawn were approaching, though the light was to the west. Faintly he heard a great many voices yelling in the distance, and he slowed his pace in confusion. A carriage raced passed him, a bell upon it clanging loudly, the horses pulling against their restraints as they sprinted, the coachman's whip lashing rapidly against their flanks.

Then the smell reached him; the burning, heavy scent of ash that suddenly pervaded everything around him. His eyes darted back in the direction of the light, and he saw the thick, billowing clouds of smoke rising from it.

"No," he breathed, his heart stopping in his chest. His legs began to move again frantically, his mind racing ahead of him.

It could not be… It *could* not be…

But the nearer he got, the more it became apparent that it could.

He made the last turn and saw, to his eternal horror, his home encased in fire. Bright orange and yellow and white flames raged up the sides of the house and reached towards the sky. Through windows he could see the same blaze from within, only the barest hint of furniture to be seen. The bottom floor was not yet consumed, but everything above was rapidly becoming an inferno.

The only figures he could see were those of the gathered crowd and the brigade fighting the flames.

"No!" he screamed, racing towards it, dropping his jacket somewhere in his haste. The windows on the second story broke with a deafening crash as more flames battered about and within the rooms. The roar of the fire sent a chill coursing through him, even as the heat became more and more apparent.

A man suddenly restrained him, throwing an arm across his chest. "I'm sorry, sir, but you cannot go past this point. The house is too…"

"No!" Derek raged, thrashing against him. "That is my house, let me pass!"

"I am sorry, sir, but you cannot…"

"Oye!" someone who sounded a lot like Colin called from behind them, and suddenly, the restraints were gone and Derek stumbled frantically towards the men trying to contain the fire.

"Don't you know that's the Marquess of Whitlock?"

"Idiot, that is his house!"

Derek heard his friends with the man, but he could not comprehend the words, not now. He couldn't breathe, he couldn't think, he could barely speak, and nobody was listening. "Where is she?" he panted, looking around. "Where is she?"

But he saw no one but the fire brigade, and they were too occupied to reply.

He struggled to get by them, but they were unyielding. "I have to get in there!" he bellowed, shoving at two of them. "Let me through! This is my home, let me in there!"

"Sir, you will have to stand back or we cannot..."

He let out an animalistic roar of protest and reached for the house, as if he could somehow pull it closer. He thrashed against the men, kicking and punching whomever he could, but two rather burly ones pulled him back and held him firm.

"Sir, we need you to remain here," one of them grunted.

He tested their grip, only to have it tighten perceptibly. "That's my..." he gasped, unable to tear his gaze away from the flame-consumed building.

"Gents, we'll take it from here," came the rough voice of Duncan, who somehow managed to put enough authority into his tone to convince the men of it.

"Derek," Nathan said softly, taking his arm when his captors had gone.

"She's in there," Derek whispered, his throat closing up even as his eyes watered. "She's..." He shook his head. "She's in there!" he cried, straining for the house again, only to have Duncan's arms fasten around both of his from behind.

"Derek, you can't go in there," he murmured in a surprisingly gentle voice for one who could hold him so immovable.

"I have to!" he cried, struggling still.

"Derek," Nathan said again from somewhere in his vicinity. "Derek, it's too late. There is nothing we can do."

"No," he protested weakly, even as his heart sunk. There had to be a way in. There had to be some way to...

A loud crashing came from within the building, and more flames came pouring out of another window, even as a groaning and creaking of burning wood filled the air. Derek could not help the whimpering moan that escaped him as his knees buckled beneath him. Duncan released his arms, and Derek sank to the ground, watching helplessly as his dreams turned to ash with all else that was his.

Too late. He was too late. There was no more reason to hope. No one could survive so powerful a destruction. It didn't matter that he had been about to tell her everything. It didn't even matter what had been said or not said. The fire did not care. It was too late.

It was too late for everything.

His friends stood around him, saying nothing, someone's hand resting on his shoulder, and they all watched as the fire brigade frantically try to save something of the house. He wondered why they bothered. It was just a house. There was nothing to it anymore, not for him. He dropped his head into his hands and pressed his palms deep into his eyes, wishing he could blot out the hellish vision before him and never see it again.

"So help me, Harville, if you don't stop trying to help, I will tie you to all of the footmen."

Derek froze as somehow he heard the voice he loved so dearly over the sound of the brigade and the blaze, authoritative and firm, and the most beautiful sound he had ever heard. But he couldn't have, it was impossible… Even so he looked up, looked around, but no one else seemed to have heard it.

"Excuse me, I am sorry, but are you actually good at this?" the voice continued, sounding so much like the old Katherine that it made Derek want to laugh. "Because the fire is clearly *not* getting any better, and if you cannot do this properly, then I suggest you go and do something else."

Now he couldn't be imagining it. Not even his imagination could conjure up a repartee as what he was hearing. He scrambled to his feet, still looking around, but not seeing anything. His heart raced as the voice became louder and clearer, and, though he could hear his friends curiously calling his name, he would not heed them.

"Proper insurance? What do I care if I have the proper insurance to have you put out this fire? It *is* your job to do so, is it not? Personally, I have my doubts, so if you might direct me to some *capable* fire brigade members, I would appreciate it."

"KATE!" he bellowed, running along the line of brigade members and onlookers, unable to see the source of that beautiful voice.

The words stopped and he heard a disbelieving cry of "Derek?" from somewhere before him.

"Kate!" he called again, aching with hope.

Suddenly, there was a break in the group and there, looking a little rumpled, a little sooty, but altogether well and whole in her nightgown and wrap, hair down and slightly mussed, was the glorious sight of his wife. His chest threatened to explode with the burst of emotion that surged through him as he saw her, and his throat became so constricted that all he could do was swallow. He opened his mouth, but found no words to be had, and only a weak, guttural burst of sound erupted as he surged forward and snatched Kate up, unable to believe she was well and whole.

Derek could not restrain the tears that poured from his eyes as he buried his face into her neck, his arms tightening around her and holding her as close as he could. He shook with emotion, and stroked her hair again and again, reassuring himself that she was here in his arms. "Oh, thank God, thank God," he rasped, shuddering as he clung to her.

He pulled back and took her face in his hands, and pressed a hot, searing kiss to her trembling lips, tasting the saltiness of her tears as she returned it fully, whimpering softly at the passion. He broke off and stroked her cheeks, one hand clutching the back of her head. "You're alive," he said on a breathless chuckle. "You're alive."

"Derek," she gasped, her tears streaming as she gripped the back of his neck tightly. "I'm sorry. The house… your family's house, I'm so sorry."

"I don't care about the house," he said quickly, kissing her again and again, raining kisses across her face. "I don't care about the house. I love you, Kate. I love you and I'm so sorry for everything, I just…"

Now she kissed him, silencing his apology and sending his senses reeling again. "I love you, too, Derek," she whispered against his skin. "I'm so sorry. I could never leave you, you must know I couldn't. I love you too much to ever consider it."

"Thank God," he said again, pulling her to him and sighing with relief into her hair. "I thought I had lost you then, and then I almost lost you now…" He shook his head as his emotions rose within him again. "I love you," he whispered. "I loved you a long time ago and I never said it."

"I know," she replied, her slender arms fixed around his neck. "I know. Me too." Then her body shuddered and frantic but silent cries burst forth.

"Shh," he soothed, rubbing her back. "Kate, I'm here, it's all right."

"I've never been so scared in my entire life," Kate sobbed as she clung to him. "I was waiting for you in my room, like you asked, and I was going to tell you that I was sorry and I loved you and I wanted to forget all about duty and just be with you always, just us, and I wanted to have children because I loved you and not because we're supposed to."

"Kate, you don't have to explain anything," Derek said softly, running a hand over her hair again.

She shook her head against him, and went on. "And then Molly fell and dropped a tray, and I raced out to check on her, and when I came back into the room, my bed curtains had caught fire. I suppose my candle was knocked over and it was already too hot for me to do anything about. I called for the footmen, and they tried, they really did, Derek, but everything caught so fast, and it was too dangerous. I called them back and we ran to fetch all the others, and we got everyone out, Derek, but I was so scared. I couldn't show it, but I was terrified."

"I know, love, I know," he told her, his voice choked with his own emotion. "I know, me too. But you got everyone out, Kate. Everyone is safe, and that is all that matters. You're safe now. Everything is all right."

Eventually, her tears quieted, and then she turned in Derek's arms to watch the brigade fight the fire. She pulled his arms more securely around her, and leaned back against his chest, and though their home was engulfed in flames, though he was standing here watching their possessions burn, Derek was more content than he had been in days.

"I love you," he murmured, pulling her closer still and pressing a soft kiss to her cheek.

She echoed his words back to him, laying her head back against his shoulder, a hint of a smile on her face even as she watched the fire.

Long into the night and into the morning, they stood there, occasionally murmuring words of love and apology and comfort to each other. When the fire was no more than ashes and smoke, the brigade mostly gone, and their home a shell of what it had been, now black with soot and a near complete ruin, they ventured closer and hand in hand they examined the damage.

Derek could hardly believe the sight. Where once there had been luxury, there was now waste. No room had been spared, though some might be salvageable. But most things were destroyed, and Kate could have been trapped in this, could have perished along with their possessions. He could have lost her with everything else, and she would have been the only thing he could not bear to lose. Possessions could be replaced. She never could be.

"The kitchens are in fair condition, being beneath much of the rest of the house," Hallstead announced as he entered what was once the music room, where the pianoforte now lay in pieces. He and some of the footmen had explored other areas of the house, looking for anything that could be saved.

"The back garden is entirely unaffected, my lord," said Jackson, who had lost his wig at some point.

"But the bed chambers are all a complete loss," reported Jeremy.

"All of the third floor is," said George.

"All of it?" Kate asked softly. "The gallery, too?"

"Yes, my lady," he mourned in a low voice. "The gallery too."

"Thank you," she replied, swallowing with difficulty. "You may all proceed to the home of the Earl of Beverton. The earl and countess have offered to employ you all until we decide what to do. If you wish to go elsewhere, we understand."

But all of them nodded and proceeded out together, headed with the rest of the servants to Nathan and Moira's. Kate turned back to Derek, who had not looked up from the rubble of the piano yet.

"I am so sorry, Derek," she whispered, looking around. "This is… it's just so…"

"I told you," he said in a low voice, not moving. "I don't care about the house." He slowly turned to her, his face anguished. "I almost lost you. I could have lost you so easily."

"But you didn't," she reassured him, stepping closer and laying a hand alongside his cheek. "I'm right here."

He covered that hand with his own and pressed a kiss into her palm. "I love you. That was what tormented me the most. I love you so much, Kate, and I never told you. You never knew."

She smiled up at him. "I knew."

He returned her smile, but in confusion. "How could you know? We fought all the time. How could you…?"

"Every day that you stayed after our agreement, I wondered, I hoped. When you told me you weren't leaving, I knew. I doubted once or twice, but in my heart, I knew."

He grinned fully. "I hadn't planned on staying, you know. I was just too afraid to remind you of our agreement."

She matched his grin. "I was too nervous to bring it up. I didn't want you to leave. I loved you, and I didn't want you to go."

He sighed and kissed her hand again, then carefully led her around the rubble and ruin and out to the back garden, where everything lay as pristine as it had been the day before. "Did you know that the lilac symbolizes first love?" he asked as he took her over to the gazebo, where the lilacs had been planted.

"No, I didn't," she replied, bemused.

"I find it oddly appropriate."

"How so?"

He shrugged. "You were my first love."

Kate laughed as they entered the gazebo. "Oh, I doubt that, Derek."

"It's true," he promised, turning to face her. "I never loved any woman before you."

She looked puzzled and peered up at him in wonder. "But you

only loved me recently. How could you...?"

"I was engaged most of my life," he interrupted gently. "I never looked for anything else, I saw no need to. So it's true that I have only ever loved you. You were my first love, and you are my last love." He took a deep breath, and then said, "And I am choosing you, Kate, if you will have me."

She opened her mouth in shock, and he rushed on.

"I know we are already married. But now I *want* to be married to you. I want to spend every day with you. I want to raise a family with you. I want you to fill our house with daughters that look exactly like you, and I don't even care if we have any boys at all."

Kate laughed and wiped at a tear that had begun a course down her cheek.

He smiled briefly at her laughter and took a hand in his. "I want to spend every day of the rest of my life making you happy. I can't do all that I must do and be all that I must be without you. I need you, Kate. I've needed you for years."

Fighting for control of her emotions, Kate gave him a watery smile. "I need you, too, Derek. And I choose you. Every day."

Derek broke out into a relieved grin and pulled her into his embrace, kissing her softly. "I love you."

"I love you," she whispered, holding him tightly.

"Now that brings to mind another question," he said in a gruff voice, pulling back a little to look at her.

"It does?" she asked with a laugh. "What?"

"When exactly did you decide you loved me? I was hardly easy to love."

"On the contrary, I found myself quite unable to resist you," she teased, lacing her arms around his neck. "I tried very hard, believe me, but alas..." She shrugged and sighed in defeat.

"While I am delighted to hear that you fell in love with me against your will, that fails to answer the question," he scolded, trying not to look too pleased with himself. "When?"

"Oh," Kate sighed, thinking back and touching her forehead to his, "probably somewhere between the strawberry tarts and the dancing in the moonlight."

"Not this garden?" he asked in surprise.

She shook her head against him. "No, no, I already loved you before then. That merely put an exclamation point on the end."

Derek burst out laughing and pulled his wife even closer. "Oh, Kate, Kate, Kate... we may have had a rough start to our marriage, but from here on out, it is going to be the stuff of legends."

She chuckled softly. "With battles and dragons and damsels in distress and knights in shining armor?"

"Yes, yes, all of that," he agreed with a nod. "And bright, fantastic, victorious happily ever afters."

Epilogue

"Remind me to never answer a summons from Derek ever again."

"You are his brother. I think you have to."

"You would be surprised, Duncan."

"I, on the other hand, have every right to refuse him. Don't you have footmen, Derek?"

"Of course, I do, Colin. I just thought you would appreciate the opportunity to put your exceptional physical strength on display."

Colin sniffed and folded his arms. "Well, who is looking?"

"Kate."

He shook his head immediately. "Doesn't count."

David went up on tiptoe and shaded his eyes as he looked down the street. "I think I see Elinor Milton over there, who looks very interested in what we are doing."

"Right then, shall we lift on three?" Colin asked as he rubbed his hands together.

The others rolled their eyes, but took position.

Kate snickered as she moved out of the way, shifting the husky toddler on her hip. "Alice," she called, "be careful, they are coming through now. Do not get in their way, all right?"

"Yes, Aunt Kate," the little blond girl playing in the corner of the room replied with a smile.

The four men lifted the massive instrument and awkwardly made their way into the house, barely fitting through the door. Still the cover lay atop it, hiding it from her view. All that Derek had told her was that the new instrument was being delivered today, and she was curious. They had already purchased a new pianoforte to take the place of the one that had been lost in the fire. It had been the first piece of furniture that Derek had placed in the London house when they had rebuilt. It was a fine instrument, but hardly the quality of the one they had before. Not that she minded, for any instrument was better than none at all, but really, they didn't need another.

"Easy, easy," Derek said as the men turned the corner and made their way towards the music room.

"You go easy," David huffed, his arms straining under the weight. "I'm trying to avoid losing my arms over here."

"What do you think, Harry?" she asked the little boy perched on her hip. "Does Papa need to watch his words around Uncle David?"

"Dave!" the little boy called happily, waving.

"Favorite," David declared proudly, unable to resist grinning at his nephew.

"Less talk, more work," Derek returned, frowning in Kate's direction, which made her smile.

The instrument tilted precariously, and all four halted and shifted their grip to secure it once more. In the process, the cover slid off and Kate gasped as she suddenly beheld the most beautiful, not to mention elaborate and blatantly expensive, instrument she had ever beheld.

"Derek, we do *not* need that," she scolded, placing her hand on the hip her son was not inhabiting.

"We do, too," he panted as they continued to move towards the music room.

"Whatever for?" she asked as she followed them.

"Because, my love," he managed to force out, his teeth clenched in his effort to maintain his grip, "you are the most beautiful, most gifted, most accomplished musician in all of London, and you deserve an instrument to match."

"Less talk, more work," the other three chimed together, bringing back Derek's glower.

Kate clamped her lips together and tried to avoid laughing. "I do not need two instruments, Derek," she protested as they moved to set the piano near the other.

"The other is going to your sister's for Alice to learn on."

She grinned. "Really?"

"Really."

"Does Aurelia know this?"

"Of course not."

Now Kate had to giggle as she looked over at Alice, who watched the men curiously, her dolls forgotten. "She will hate you forever."

"I know." In spite of the heavy burden he was holding, Derek managed a jaunty grin.

"I would love for Alice to learn," she mused aloud. "It would be so good for her."

"Kate, I am begging you," Colin groaned from his position on one end. "Stop talking. He will always respond, and he always slackens his grip when he does."

"Sorry, Colin," she apologized, smiling.

"Maybe if you *had* a wife, Colin, you would understand," Derek snapped, sidestepping his end into position.

"What, that marriage makes a man go soft?" he asked innocently, which made Duncan and David snicker.

"No, that a man gets into trouble if he does not respond to his wife."

Colin seemed to consider that for a moment as he moved his own end, looking remarkably unruffled by the exertion required of him. Then he shook his head. "No, I am still going to have to insist that the first is true. Particularly with you. It's very sad."

"Colin, do you *like* having friends?" Derek asked, tilting his head. "Because we can change that."

"And let's set down on three," Duncan said loudly, offering a rare grin.

On the count, the men set down the instrument, each releasing a rather heavy breath of relief when they had done so. Then they turned to look at the other, which was much smaller and would be a great deal easier to move.

"Shall we go on with this one, then?" Duncan asked, hands on his hips.

Derek shrugged. "Might as well." He turned to look at Alice, who grinned the moment he did so. "What say you, little miss? Would you like us to take this over to your house right now?"

She gasped and darted over to him. "For me? For me, Uncle Dewek?"

He grinned and squatted down to be at her eye level. "For you, indeed. Do you want to learn to play pretty songs like your aunt does?"

"Yes! Yes, pwease, Uncle Dewek!" she cried tugging at his arm.

Chuckling, Derek placed a quick kiss to the little girl's cheek, then stood and faced the others. "Well, gents, you heard the lady. Let's move this one out to the wagon."

Without a single word of complaint or protest, and not a groan to be heard, they did so, and far more easily and quickly than they had previously. When the instrument was loaded, Colin and Duncan leapt aboard to help the driver secure it.

"I so wish I could see Aurelia's face when that arrives," Kate said as Derek came over to her.

"As do I, but Colin is going to ride over with the driver, and has promised to return with a full report. You know how detailed Colin's reports are."

Kate grinned mischievously. "That will be vastly entertaining."

"You shouldn't be up on your feet," he scolded gently as he reached her. "Especially not with this fellow weighing you down." He reached for his son, who went to him happily, jabbering away in his mix of nonsense and words that entertained his parents to no end.

"I am *fine*, Derek," she told him, putting a hand to her swollen abdomen. "I have at least two more months, and I feel perfectly well."

"Even so," he began, only to be cut off by his son squealing in excitement as David started towards them, Alice having latched on to one of his hands already.

"Do you want to come and play with Uncle David, too, little man?" David crooned as he approached, which sent Harry giggling.

"Why am I so unloved?" Derek moaned as Harry practically climbed over his shoulder to reach David.

David shrugged as he took Harry. "I could say something about looks, but Kate has a very mean, very fast punch, and I don't want to injure myself any further today."

"Wise man," Kate said, nodding in approval.

Derek grumbled as David ran off with the children, already making them laugh and cheer and screech in delight.

"Derek," Kate said softly, taking his hand, "really, why this new instrument? I don't play nearly as often as I used to, and with the new baby coming, I will barely have time to sit down, let alone perform."

"Because I can," he replied simply. "I will hear no more about the expense, Kate. It was well worth it."

"But if you…"

"Shut up, darling, and let me spoil you," he ordered, clamping his hand over her mouth.

She tried to glare at him over his hand, but at his severe look of warning, she had to smile.

"Papa!"

Derek turned and grinned as Harry came toddling towards him. He scooped the boy up in his arms, and tossed him into the air, making him squeal in delight, then set him down again as he saw David and Alice running towards them, in some sort of game of chase, with David growling like a monster.

"Go save Alice from the monster, Harry," Derek urged, giving him a little push. "A proper gentleman always rescues a damsel in distress."

Harry looked up at him with a frown that was exactly like his father's, his green eyes curious. At Derek's nod, the look became determined, and he raced towards David.

Derek shook his head in amusement, then turned back to Kate, who was watching him with a smile.

"What?" he asked.

She closed the distance between them and took his face in her hands, then pressed a very sound kiss to his lips.

"What was that for?" he asked when she broke off, wrapping his arms around her.

She shrugged and slid her arms about his neck. "Because I love you. Because you are so good to me. Because you gave me a beautiful son. Take your pick."

"Hmm," he mused aloud. "Well, I do like all of those. But I told you I wanted daughters. Ones that look just like you."

"I am trying," she protested, giving him a rather wry look, "but I cannot help it if they come out boys instead. Surely you want sons as well."

"Oh, of course," he assured her lightly. "Harry is the finest son that was ever born. I wish he looked more like you, but that is neither here nor there. But please tell me I get a daughter."

"I promise, as much as I am able to," she said solemnly as her eyes danced, "that you will have at least one daughter. I don't know that it will be this one, but someday, you'll have one."

"You think it's a boy?" he asked, a smile forming as his eyes flicked to her growing bulge.

"I can't be sure," she said with a laugh. "I thought Harry would be a girl, remember?"

"I do. What a surprise he turned out to be." Derek smiled fondly at the memory.

"Were you disappointed?"

He looked back down at her immediately. "Disappointed? No, never! I was delighted that we had any child, boy or girl. I was so relieved you were well, and he was well, that I had no room for any other emotions."

"Good," she sighed, tightening her hold around his neck. "I love you, you know."

He smiled and touched his nose to hers. "I know. You said that already today."

"How very excessive of me."

"I don't mind," he whispered conspiratorially. "You see, I love you too. I was thinking it all morning, but I think I said it already before we got out of bed."

"We are just squandering those words away, aren't we?"

"Scandalously." He pressed his lips to hers, lingering.

A loud snarl followed by uproarious laughter broke the moment, and Derek groaned as he pulled back. "Please, darling, if we do have a son next, don't name him David. I couldn't bear it."

Kate snickered and shook her head. "I will not name our next child David. Perhaps a later one, as I really am terribly fond of David, but not the next. I was thinking of the name Colin, what do you think?"

"You wouldn't," he gasped, paling ever so slightly.

She shrugged again. "I just might, you never know."

Derek growled and swept Kate up into his arms, making her screech in surprise.

"Derek, what are you doing?" she asked, giggling helplessly.

"We are going to play with our son and our niece and my ridiculous brother, Lady Whitlock. It is time we prove just how fun we are."

"I see," she replied with a nod. "And what role will I play?"

"Why, the damsel in distress, of course!"

"Ah. And would you be the villain carting me off or the knight saving me?"

He snorted in derision. "The knight, naturally. Don't you see the shining armor?"

Kate brushed back his hair fondly and smiled. "Why, yes, I do. Forgive me, sir knight, for doubting."

"Never fear, fair damsel. It is a great fool who would be offended by so beautiful a maiden he is fortunate to hold in his arms."

Kate smiled softly at his jest, but couldn't help looking at her husband as he carried her towards the game. Their marriage had not been perfect, but she would not want it any other way. Happily ever after took some effort, after all, and how happy was the effort!

A swift kick from her unborn child brought a smile to her face, and she admitted silently that the child would probably be a girl after all. Derek would get his wish, and he would slay dragons for them all. What an ending they had managed from so wretched a beginning. Every morning held new promise, every month held new delights, every year held new adventures. Every supposed ending was only a new beginning, hopeful and bright and shining.

And there was no true end in sight. Nothing to dread, nothing to fear, nothing to regret.

"Now, my love, look weak and swooning," Derek whispered in her ear. "You have just been rescued, remember."

"Yes, I have, darling," she sighed, taking on the appropriate air, but putting real emotion behind her words. "Yes, I have."

Coming Soon

Secrets of
a Spinster

*"Never underestimate
a wallflower."*

by

Rebecca Connolly

CPSIA information can be obtained at www.ICGtesting.com
Printed in the USA
BVOW02s1211290616

453897BV00011B/94/P